JUBILEE

THE HEIST TO ERASE DEBT

joseph preacher

Possible with the love and support of Megumi

1

ROMAN Hawker glanced furtively down Broadway, scanning from left to right. The air was crisp, biting at his exposed cheeks, and his breath came out in dense blasts of vapor that slowly expanded and disappeared into the night. Disappearing without a trace, the same way he and his friends would need to.

If they didn't, NYPD squad cars would appear from every angle. Their sirens would come blaring, lights blinding, and tires screaming down the New York City streets at him. They would be coming for him, chasing him down. He and his friends would finally be caught and there would be no hiding their secrets any longer.

But for the moment, Roman remained confident that they would escape. His white earbuds reported only silence, which meant that everything was going according to his plan. He was nonetheless wary. It was his responsibility to be cautious, and he had to consider every possibility. If he had miscalculated any small detail, he would surely get caught. So would his closest friends. He looked across the street to see that Bryce was still inside the bank vestibule, finishing up.

The steady flow of rush hour commuters on foot was starting to diminish. Cars and taxis buzzed by constantly, but the traffic allowed just enough room to bike around. Hope and Burton would be seeing the same conditions over on the Upper East Side of Manhattan on Lexington.

He shook away a sudden chill. It was cold, even for New York in February. But the temperature justified the hoodies, thicker jackets, winter hats, and scarves over their faces. All the extra layering helped cover any major features that could identify them. There were thousands of surveillance cameras that canvassed Manhattan. It was impossible to avoid all of them, but any trace of their faces, heavily covered, on the footage would be useless to identify them.

Bryce exited the vestibule and made a sharp turn uptown. He touched his hand to the top of his head indicating that all was well and that he was ready for the next stop. His messenger bag was starting to look filled to its capacity. Bryce stopped at his bike, which was chained to a parking sign post.

He clicked a small pendant that was hanging from his neck and the lock on the bike snapped open. It was a nice little gadget Reggie had put together. He jumped on the bike and headed to the next waypoint. Roman kept to his side of the avenue and rode his own bike in parallel with Bryce.

"How many more we got?" Bryce asked into his earbud's in-line microphone.

"Just two more for us," Roman replied just before a muffled female voice came over the police scanner. There was an alert for a rabid dog that was loose on 11th Street and 8th Avenue. They were far enough uptown that they didn't risk running into any uniforms looking for the dog.

Good thing, because right now, a bump into any cop would be incredibly risky. The crew didn't fit any typical criminal profiles, but strapped to their backs were over-sized sling bags. Any uniformed officer would consider stopping them for a quick peek inside. Stop and frisk was no longer in full effect, but New York City's Finest maintained a perpetual high alert for anything suspicious.

"We're on 89th," Burton's voice came in.

The five of them were communicating over a conference call system Reggie had set up on an anonymous server. With the right tech, any governmental agency could easily figure out how they communicated. Lucky for them, they had Reggie. He made sure there was nothing that could be traced to them. The credit card and identity that set up the server space were both counterfeit. The same alias had signed up for a prepaid SIM card, and the burner phones had been purchased using cash from a bodega in Queens.

The next stop would be their eleventh. This part of the score was going quickly, considering they started only three hours ago.

"I gotta admit, this is a good workout," Bryce said as he slowed his approach to 96th Street. "Let's hurry this up. We need to have enough time for a drink afterwards. It's a school night for me."

"No one told you to have a nine to five," Roman said.

"Sue me for wanting to be an honest contributor to society."

"I think I could use a few drinks," Hope's voice came in. "We're on our second to last."

"How does the grid look?" Roman asked, implying this question to Reggie. He was monitoring all the governmental network traffic for any spikes in activity. If any occurred, he would be able to dig deeper and see if it was related to what they were doing.

"Everything lekker, baas," Reggie responded. His Afrikaan--erisms came out when he was tired.

"What did you say?" Burton was partially joking, mostly annoyed.

"Speak English, man!"

"Ag, don't get your broekies in a knot."

Things were going smoothly, but just about fifty hours of unabated stress were starting to take their toll. The adrenaline had ebbed, but Roman could still feel the high. He lived for moments like this, when the risks were immeasurable and the pressure was on. It was like a drug. In between jobs, the withdrawals would come, and he'd be back like an addict, plotting their next hit.

Bryce stood next to his bike as it leaned against a thin tree coming out of a small dirt section of the sidewalk. Roman dismounted his bike and locked it on his side of the street on some scaffolding. It looked like it had been there for years. Two graffiti-filled security gates protected a nail salon on one side and a barber shop on the other. Between them was a secured glass vestibule that had three bank ATM machines inside. It was well-lit and looked like it would be a safe place to pull out some money.

Roman looked to his left and right. All was quiet. There was only a homeless person, rolled up in layers of besmirched sleeping bags. He was of no concern, dozing under the far end of some scaffolding. Roman walked up to the glass door and pulled out a white plastic card with a magnetic strip. He pushed it into the slotted scanner next to the door. A small red light turned green and then a magnetic door lock released with an audible thump.

With a deep breath, he walked in. The door thudded as the magnetic lock reengaged. Without any hesitation, he walked over to the farthest ATM on the left.

He searched on the left hand side of the bezel for a metal engraved label. "I am at 0-9-8-6-5-3-7," he read as clearly as he could.

"Madder," Reggie replied excitedly.

Thirty seconds later, the ATM's screen flashed and then went to a black screen with white text. It indicated that it was entering maintenance mode and asked to enter a passcode with a blinking cursor. Roman readied his gloved hand over the machine's keypad.

"Passcode is 9-5-0-6," Reggie said as Roman typed.

He pressed enter and the screen began scrolling text. The machine relayed that it was running its maintenance protocols.

Reggie's voice spoke slowly, multitasking as he always did. "Be ready. Feed test will begin in 5-4..."

Roman held both his hands in an open claw position over the cash dispenser door.

"...2-1." The dispenser door slid open and sounds started coming from the machine's inner mechanisms. After only a few seconds, money dispensed out in neat stacks. They came through the teeth and rollers and then into Roman's ready hands. He let the green bills fall freely, adjusting his thumbs as the stack in his hands grew.

The machine stopped when the stack was nearly six inches thick. With a quick calculation, Roman knew he held close to twenty thousand dollars in twenty dollar bills. He could feel the crispness of the cash, warm from the dispenser, between his fingers. The first few times he had done this, it was exciting and he had held his breath. At this point, it was tedious to wait.

As soon as he was positive the machine was done, Roman held the bills tightly and forced them through a hidden slit on the side of his bag.

He then went to the next machine. He paused as he heard Hope on the line, doing the same procedure with Reggie. After she was done, he read his new machine's number out to Reggie and continued the process. The second machine went quickly, and then the third. As soon as he stuffed the last stack of cash into his bag, he turned and exited the vestibule.

Bryce was already on his bike across the street. Roman tapped the top of his head and went for his bike. He unlocked it with the pendant and mounted the seat.

"Last stop," he said out loud to everyone on the line.

They both rode into the uptown night to finish the job.

2

REGGIE Dymond wanted to take a break and stretch his entire body down to his fingers, but this wasn't the time to do so. There was only one last stop and he had to stay focused.

He had multiple virtual desktops going on his laptop. Each contained its own predetermined task. He swiped through to each one every few minutes to make sure everything was going as planned.

He was sitting in the back of a Starbucks near Union Square. It had taken him an hour of playing musical chairs to get to the perfect table. It was a small round table that was in the back corner by the barista station. With his back to the wall, he was safe from prying eyes. It was a bonus that the wall power outlet was within three meters.

He preferred being in his own room, away from the madness of the general public. But while they were on the job, the safest place to operate was away from home. This was one of the busiest Starbucks locations in the city. It was always filled with students, tourists, and casual New Yorkers. A third of them were, like him, busy with laptops, working on reports, presentations or the like. He didn't look out of place here, with his baseball cap hiding his eyes as he focused completely on his screen.

He knew not to trust the free wi-fi, so he used his own high-speed cellular hotspot. It was secured with encryption from any casual or pointed sniffing attacks. Reggie wasn't naive enough to think that he would always be the only hacker in the building.

"Ready," Hope's voice came through his bulky over-ear headphones.

He swiped to the virtual desktop that contained the remote window. He had infiltrated the ATSI, Automated Teller Solutions Inc., servers. The remote desktop window connected him directly to their servers as if he was physically next to them.

"4-6-1-8-2-8," she said.

He wasted no time and began running the scripts set-up to initiate the maintenance program. He plugged in the serial number for the specific machine that Hope was standing in front of.

For three months, Reggie had impersonated a remote contractor based in India. He went under a vague Indian identity that was completely verifiable. Not that ATSI cared to validate it. They paid him next to nothing for the amount of work they contracted him to do, but the job had allowed him enough time to access their entire system.

Of course, ATSI had tried their best to sandbox him in an environment that should have kept him in a limited area of their network. They had most likely spent very little for that system as well.

After his project had wrapped, they had changed his credentials, believing they'd locked him out. They had yet to find the multiple backdoors he'd made for himself. These weaknesses gave him more access to their network than even their Chief Technology Officer could wish for.

When the correct line of code came up, he read in a hushed voice, "Passcode is 2-0-6-7." This code's purpose was to verify that an authorized person was physically in front of the machine.

He could see the system working. Most modern ATMs are monitored remotely through software like the one provided by ATSI. The company also offered remote software maintenance and constant updates whenever needed. This also included checking the physical mechanisms within the ATMs, which was exactly what they were doing.

The text scrolled by quickly as the system readied the dispenser's feed test. It read that there were five hundred and seventy-seven bills in the machine. Eleven thousand, five hundred and forty dollars. The module then asked him to confirm, Y or N. Reggie typed Y.

It then read that it was ready for dispensing.

He read out to Hope, "Be ready. Feed test will begin in 5-4..."

He envisioned her setting up her hands over the dispenser as they had practiced a hundred times.

"...2-1," he said. Pipe symbols repeated on the screen to indicate it was currently dispensing the bills.

He took the moment to look around the coffee shop to see if anyone was watching him. Everyone was focused on whatever they were doing, not noticing him at all. He did his best to keep from getting too excited.

The others were not yet aware of the amount of money they had drawn in the last few days. They had been working at a breakneck pace over the last fifty hours to hit as many machines as possible. They had targeted machines in Washington, D.C., yesterday,

Sunday morning, just after they were refilled from Saturday's shopping withdrawals. They finished Boston late last night, and were finishing up closer to home now. The authorities would already be investigating Washington and Boston. With any luck, it would be days before they made the connection between all three cities.

While the rest of the crew could not yet know how much the take was, Reggie had recorded the exact numbers. He swiped over to the desktop where he kept a spreadsheet to track the locations, serial numbers, and notes of all the machines they had hit. He plugged in the new amount for Hope's latest withdrawal. The number in the total box made him smile. He could not wait to tell the others.

"I'm done," said Hope.

The thick bordered cell read, "Three million, two hundred, forty-five thousand, three hundred and sixty dollars."

Roman's voice came in, "Let's all head home."

3

IT took an hour to weave through the city streets in a way that avoided the known surveillance cameras. They remained in separated pairs until they arrived at an older area in Alphabet City. They were sure that no presence of big brother existed for at least a few city blocks. Even after a few decades of gentrification, there were still neglected stretches. Areas that kept them hidden and anonymous. Roman and Bryce slowed to a crawl when they arrived at the alleyway meeting spot.

Burton Warner and his younger sister, Hope Warner, were already halfway done changing when Bryce and Roman arrived. Without a word in the quiet chilly night, Roman and Bryce dismounted their bikes. They began by changing out of their thick jackets and hoodies into NorthFace fleeces. They stripped their extra baggy jeans, exposing more stylish, better fitting jeans beneath. Scarves stripped, and their winter beanies were replaced with baseball caps of different teams.

The inner liners that held the cash were removed from the messenger bags and transferred to different styles of bags. Roman had a gym bag. Bryce a regular backpack. Hope carried a flower print overnight bag. And Burton had an old military field pack.

All of the removed clothing and gear went into large black trash bags. They added their trash bags to the large pile already gathered on the sidewalk. They leaned all four of their bikes, unchained, against a nearby sign post. Anyone rummaging through the trash this morning was going to find some nice prizes. Leaving anything on the streets guaranteed that it would disappear into the city forever.

They each took different paths through the neighborhood, building distance between each other. It took a lot of discipline for them not to show their excitement in public. There would be plenty of time to celebrate together later that night. Hope jumped into a cab as soon as one crossed her path. She would arrive at the apartment well before the rest. Chivalry still existed in this crew. Burton would grab the L train on 14th Street. Bryce would grab the M15 bus downtown. Roman would enter the subway on Houston and take the F train.

Roman was the last to arrive at the apartment. The route he chose was the shortest but had the most traffic in the evenings. Walking would have been faster.

The apartment was the top floor of a ten floor building. Built in the 1920s, it had been renovated countless times since. It was on the edge of what is considered the Financial District, on an adjacent block to the New York Federal Reserve. The penthouse apartment even had a great view of the Fed from its large bay windows. The safest place to be was where the authorities would least expect.

On paper, Bryce owned the apartment. His day job salary justified its price tag, but Reggie and Roman contributed to the mortgage. Roman accepted it for being a central location with multiple routes in and out of the city. Bryce especially enjoyed the short walk to work. Reggie couldn't care less where they lived. Even though Burton and Hope lived uptown, it was spacious enough for them to stay over often, as they did.

The curtains were already closed. The others stood around the dining room table. It's dark wood was piled high with the weekend's take. Though their eyes were tired, each one of them beamed. Roman pitched his bag to Bryce, who enjoyed what he did next more than anyone. With the excitement of a child, Bryce held the bag over the table. He poured the green bills, adding to the already large green bank. He tossed it up like it was confetti at a championship parade.

"What was the total, Reggie?" Roman asked as he grabbed the glass of scotch Hope held out for him. He accepted the tumbler, briefly registering her fingertips as they touched. It was only a small moment that he was sure she didn't notice.

Reggie took a deep breath and recited the amount one digit at a time.

"Three million. Two hundred. Forty-five thousand. Three hundred. And sixty dollars."

They all looked at each other, speechless for a moment. It had been three months of intense planning and execution. But the result was more than worth it.

It wasn't their largest take, but any job they could walk away from without any complications was enough to be satisfied about. They could rest easy and take a hiatus for a while before Roman thought through another job for them. He was proud of his small group of friends. They trusted him more than he even trusted himself.

"So does this mean we can take a break, boss?" Burton asked, throwing a light jab at Roman's side.

"Let's take a month before we start another. Good job everyone," he said as he held up his glass. They raised their own next to his.

Joseph Preacher

The only thing better than a job well done was getting away with it.

4

THE crisis action team room was buzzing with activity by the time Tim Steep arrived at the far section of the SIOC. The Strategic Information and Operations Center had been set up as soon as the details of the heist started flowing in.

His team was excited to be back in the SIOC. It was the FBI's global watch and communications hub. Located in the J. Edgar Hoover Building in Washington, D. C., it was their grand stadium. Proving grounds to display their proficiency.

Outside observers would think his Cyber Action Team was a strange bunch. Three quarters of his twenty man and woman team were analysts, all wearing jeans and t-shirts of bands and comic book characters. Over the years, he had become accustomed to their casual attire.

The FBI needed to recruit top talent. Talent that could keep up with the pace of technology. They were more attracted to the Silicon Valley culture than the conservative suit culture of old time Feds. The policies around attire needed to relax. For his team at least, it did. Due to their astonishing work ethic and drive to excel, he didn't much care.

The remaining quarter of the team were his special agents and support personnel. They kept to the conservative business attire. They were also tech-savvy, but their skill sets focused on case work and investigation in the field.

The workstations were set up on a tiered flooring. All faced a wall completely covered in screens that came to life as each of his team members logged in. As the ASAC, Assistant Special Agent in Charge, Tim Steep's temporary office was the glass box in the back of the room. The team room was only a small part of the forty thousand square feet that made up the entire SIOC.

Steep's cyber action team was about to prove their worth and would be the center focus of the complex. Every level of the leadership and representatives from other agencies would be watching their every move. Each group was compartmentalized into different rooms with different levels of access. Some would provide support. Most would be getting in the way.

He looked at his watch. It was already 21:30 and he dreaded calling Jill to tell her he wasn't coming home tonight. She was already upset with him about missing dinner. From the details he had seen coming in, he would be missing many more dinners.

The local D.C. authorities reported that ATMs across the city were completely emptied out. By 16:00, it was determined that this was a bigger job than just a few machines. There was no evidence of physical tampering and customer accounts were not affected. Not a single alert was triggered. Most of the bank locations didn't even realize they were thefts, not until their service men made the connection that it was happening all over the city.

"Padilla, what's the final count of how many machines were hit?" Steep asked his junior analyst.

Padilla nervously searched some documents on his screen. "Looks like they confirmed twenty, but not sure if that was all of them."

"Well, let's figure out where these twenty are. There must be some kind of pattern. I want it placed on the main map."

"Right away," replied Padilla, as he began getting the task done.

"This was a sophisticated team, but there must be some evidence we can get from these locations." He looked around the room, still not accustomed to where everyone was. "Summers. I want you and Pickles to look through every surveillance footage we can get our hands on. Anywhere near these ATMs," he said to his lead agent. "We need exact times, how many suspects, vehicles, anything. Get with CyWatch and see if they can provide you with some resources from the video surveillance center."

Steep walked down the tiers until he was at the lowest level. His most skilled analyst had the prime work station in front of the wall of screens. Ivan Blazevic already had his space arranged like he preferred. A massaging seat cushion that was always running. An upside-down milk crate that he used as an ottoman. His keyboard on his lap as he leaned back completely. His trackball sat on a rolling file cabinet that he placed at his right hand's resting position. Ivan was six foot four and looked more like a Croatian basketball player than a computer genius who sat in this position at least ten hours a day, six days a week. He was the best information engineer and hacker that Tim Steep had ever met or heard of.

"Ivan, do you have anything for me yet?" asked Steep. He was careful not to intrude on Ivan's personal space. Instead of looking over Ivan's shoulder, Steep looked in front of the station. Along the wall, four sections of screens represented Ivan's monitors. There were many windows already open, some that Tim understood, others that he didn't.

"With this many machines affected, I am thinking that it must be the software that maintains them," Ivan said. "I will need access to the company..." he paused to look through his notes on the screen,"... ATSI. Search their systems for vulnerability."

Steep looked at the analyst that sat behind Ivan on the next tier. "Robbie, find the home address for the CEO of ATSI. Send a street agent that's nearby to deliver the abstract. The agent will need to encourage him to give us full access of their systems and their lead engineer. We need this ASAP."

Just as he was about to turn back to Ivan, an analyst from the ADIC office ran down the steps toward him. Nearly out of breath, the young woman handed him a brown file folder. "The same thing happened in Boston." She leaned on the table next to her. "They found fifteen ATMs emptied so far. The ADIC just transferred it from the Boston office to us."

Tim took the folder. He couldn't reject a transfer made by the Assistant Director in Charge, his boss's boss.

He looked over the documents. They abstracted all the details and provided reference numbers. He would need these to transfer all the case work to his team.

He looked up at the large map displayed on the video wall. "So far."

5

THEY were the only people in the bar - just the way Roman liked it.

The crew hung around the two tables in the small billiard space. Bryce and Roman played on the table closest to the bar. Burton and Hope faced off on the other. Reggie sat in an old plush arm chair that didn't seem to fit the motif of the bar, tapping away on his smartphone.

This was their favorite spot. O'Neill's considered itself a "classic" Irish pub - although, with its modernized menu and extensive list of craft cocktails, its name was probably the most Irish thing about it. The dark, hardwood interior of the place gave O'Neill's a cozy feeling, and the ancient bar counter was one of the oldest in the area. It was a restaurant for most of the evening, but stayed open for as long as anyone wanted to drink.

O'Neill's was only a few blocks from the apartment, so the crew would come here at least once a week. In the later parts of the evening, they would often have the place to themselves. The music played low, and they could relax and be themselves here. Jimmy, the owner and bartender, was in his fifties and enjoyed their company as much as they enjoyed his heavy pours. What Roman appreciated the most was that the man knew when they needed their privacy. They had many problem solving sessions and celebrations at this bar, and Jimmy always knew when to walk away.

Roman slid his cue stick along the bridge of his hand, aiming to put the solid orange five into the corner pocket. Just above the spot his eyes were trained for aiming, he could see Hope. She was leaning over her own cue stick, readying for a shot.

Roman could feel himself holding his breath. He tried his best to concentrate, his mind straining not to look over the ball at her slender shape. Her long brown hair rested on her shoulders. Her profile was further defined by the billiard table lights' glow.

He lost himself in thought and only felt the strike of the cue's tip as it contacted with the cue ball. The sound of the orange five ball sinking easily into a pocket jolted him out of his momentary daze.

When he realized where he was, he looked around the space. Had anyone else noticed his distraction? Burton was on the other side of his sister's table, still waiting for her to take a shot.

Roman respected Burton as his own older brother. Growing up, that's what he had been, for all of them. Always protecting them from outside problems, no matter what they were. Roman wasn't even really sure why. Without Burton being there, he couldn't imagine how different his life might look.

He glanced up at Bryce, and the expression on his face spoke volumes. The knowing look on his other childhood friend's face indicated that there was no confusion about what was going on. If Burton was his big brother, Bryce was like a conjoined twin. Roman couldn't hide anything from him.

Roman stepped back from the table. "I think I'm about done. I can't even finish this game," he said, hoping to lead Bryce's thought away.

"Giving up so soon? That's not like you at all," Bryce said, smiling and reading Roman's mind.

Roman hated when he did that.

"Alright, I'll let you go this time," Bryce teased, letting Roman out of his mental headlock. "Let's have one more, and we'll call it a night." He turned and took two steps to reach their spot at the bar. Most of the stools were already placed upside down on top of the tables, with the exception of their section by the pool tables. Jimmy had started his closing, but didn't look like he was in any hurry to push his favorite people out the door. "Jimmy, do you mind if we have one more?"

Jimmy paused doing his inventory and walked over with a big smile and a bottle in his hand. "You're welcome to as many as you like. I still got a few more things to take care of."

"Not for me," Hope said, coming up to the bar. "I think Burton and I are going to head out."

"Yeah, this was fun, but I have a day job, too." Burton gave Roman a brotherly embrace with clasped fists. "Poker next week?"

Roman nodded suddenly thinking of Burton's thick arm around his neck. His bicep and forearm squeezing out Roman's thoughts of his sister. "Yeah, definitely. Get home safe."

Hope came up to Roman last, her deep gray hazel eyes mesmerizing him. She embraced him, and he held her close, conscious of how tight and long he held.

"You boys don't stay out too late. I don't want to hear you've wandered over to the strip club or something like that." Hope jabbed him playfully in the ribs.

Roman held his hands in the air. "Who, us? Never. We'll go

straight home. We're good boys." He grinned, thinking ironically of their activities of the day.

Hope gave Reggie a hug as he remained seated and the brother and sister left with a wave.

Jimmy placed a fourth round of Dewars on the rocks in front of them and stepped away. Or was it their fifth? It didn't matter.

Roman lifted his glass with a smile, "Here's to what we will think up next."

"To the take being even greater!" Bryce clinked his glass against Roman's.

Roman looked at his glass of blended whisky, a perfect amber tone swirling around a single large ice cube. He lowered himself on the stool, unexpectedly somber. "I really want to do something greater." His eyes focused on the cube as his mind wandered.

"I wouldn't say what we just did was insignificant." Bryce looked back at Reggie. He had passed out and was now curled up in a ball on the armchair.

"That's not what I mean. Yes, it was a small thrill, but in the end, what does it matter? We gained some extra cash. There has to be a way for it to mean more."

Bryce took a sip from his glass and looked past the windows of the front of the bar. Roman could see that for once, his friend wasn't following his train of thought. "You want to start doing art or something?" he asked, his eyes wondered.

Roman shook his head. "No, nothing like that. I don't know what I want to do next, but I wish we could do something that..." He paused trying to find the correct word. "That matters."

"There has to be something we can do that matters more than money. We've been doing this a long time. We have more money squirreled away than we could spend in ten lifetimes. But what's the point? What have we done to make the world a better place?"

"I see what you're saying, but what do you want to do? Volunteer for the peace corps? Run a marathon? Become some kind of Hacktivist?"

"I'm not exactly sure myself. Maybe I'm just drunk," he said, lifting his glass to take another sip. He really wasn't sure what he was saying. The more money that built in his reserves, the less significant he felt about his purpose in life. Whether or not even he had a purpose in life. He never expected that his role of being a career criminal could be a vital thing in society. Shouldn't he feel like he was living up to his potential?

Another sip. He wasn't sure if Bryce was lost in thought or just had nothing to say.

Roman looked at his watch. "We should get out of here. You got work in a few hours."

Bryce signaled Jimmy to close their tab. "Way to ruin a great night." Though he didn't show even a hint of a smile, Roman knew that Bryce was teasing him.

They both went to the armchair and helped Reggie to his feet. Jimmy held the door and locked it after them. The three of them stumbled through the quiet narrow streets that defined downtown Manhattan. It was a short and clumsy walk back to the apartment, with a brief dry heave by Reggie over a service grate.

Roman was ready for bed when they exited the elevator on their floor, but the night was about to take another turn.

All three froze at the sight of two police officers dressed in their familiar navy blue uniforms. Their hands perched on their utility belts, carrying their firearms and handcuffs.

Roman didn't want to believe what he was seeing. There was no way they could have been caught. Especially not this soon. He looked at Bryce and the two shared a brief, wordless discussion on whether they should simply turn and run right there.

But there was no way they were going to escape this one. Not with Reggie in his condition. They were good at improvising out of tough situations, but there was no option here other than to steady themselves and say nothing.

The two officers swaggered their way closer and one of them looked cautiously at the three of them. "Is one of you Roman Hawker?" asked the one that stepped forward.

There was no way this was possible. Roman considered lying, but thought better of it. "Yes, that's me. How can I help you, Officers?" He willed his expression to remain steady. He suddenly felt sober and warm.

Roman's fear of getting caught created nightmares that were more vivid than reality. Scenes where SWAT teams would bust through the doors and windows, grabbing at them through smoke and chaos. Moments where they were just finishing a job, then bottlenecked into a barricade of squad cars. Never had he imagined that it would come down to two Officers waiting at his doorstep. He looked around the hallway helplessly, wishing he could see through the walls.

The officer that was doing the talking looked at each of them in the face, pausing longer at Reggie. It looked as if he was considering if he should acknowledge the intoxicated state they were in. "Is he okay?" he asked, pointing to Reggie.

"Just coming back from a bachelor party." It was the first thing Roman could come up with.

"On a Monday night?" The Officer didn't look like he bought it.

"It was a weekend thing." Roman trailed off. The less he said the better.

The other Officer came up closer behind his partner, shifting his belt slightly. Roman didn't say a word. They all stood there looking at each other in the dim hallway. Roman could picture the large bags of cash sitting in the living room just behind their front door. At least it wasn't still piled on the table. Bryce didn't say a word, frozen and tightening his hold on Reggie. He would wait to take his cue from Roman.

"There has been an incident. The Tarrytown PD has asked us to notify you." He cleared his throat. "I regret to inform you that your father, Jacob Hawker, was found yesterday at his home, deceased. Cause of death has been determined by the medical examiner to be self-inflicted. You will need to contact..."

The officer was still talking but nothing else registered in Roman's mind. His hearing blurred as the pressure increased from his temples to his eardrums. His knees went limp and he dropped to the ground to his hands and knees. He felt his friend's hands holding him up by his shoulders. He could feel his tears build up in his eyes. His eyes unfocused, all he could see was black.

6

IT was just past midnight. Instead of sleeping, Steep was well into his fourth coffee. He looked out into the team room from his office. Most of the team had already worked a full day before the ATM case had come in, and it was starting to show in their eyes and body language. He made a note in the back of his mind to start sending them home in shifts to get some rest.

Most of his special agents were combing through hours of surveillance footage. The FBI had the best facial recognition software and algorithms that existed. All of it had proved useless in this instance. They still needed to review hour after hour of video with their own eyes. It was painstaking work. They now had video footage from every camera near the machines hit in D.C. and Boston. In the last hour, there had been more reports, indicating that New York might have just been hit. The unsubs were going from city to city, and there was no way to chase them.

The agents going through the video footage were each viewing multiple videos at a time in hopes of finding similarities in face, body, or clothing. So far, they had come up with nothing.

His analysts were also working to their limits combing through ATSI's entire network. The street agents that visited the CEO in upstate New York had been very convincing. The CEO had signed the approval to give the FBI full access to his network and staff for the investigation. It was rare for a company to allow authorities to come in and do their jobs, but the guy was scared. There was going to be a media frenzy around this. The banks and the insurance companies would also be unhappy. Cooperating fully with the investigation was his best option.

Steep threw his empty cup in the already full trash can and left his glass box. He took a second to compose himself, stretching his back slightly. He descended down the steps to see Ivan, who was sitting in the same position he had been in for the last twelve hours. The only things moving were his hands above the keyboard and quick movements of his eyes.

Steep could see the conversations spinning on multiple chat windows. He was working with the other analysts in the room and with FBI's many remote contractors. In this day and age, picking up the phone was a waste of time.

"Any luck so far?" Steep asked as he stopped behind the invisible barrier.

Ivan didn't look up or pause his rapid typing. "We have found possible back doors, but it is hard to tell. I guess it was an inside job. They knew exactly what they were doing and how to do it. Doesn't look like they were searching any directories or sniffing the network. No sign of password cracking or viruses. They were familiar with the infrastructure."

"No TTPs?" Steep asked.

TTPs were tools, techniques, and procedures that made up a hacker's signature. Some hackers enjoyed the thrill of leaving their mark wherever they went. It was similar to tagging graffiti on private property. Some would even leave jokes for whomever would find their code, which Steep knew from the particularly humorous ones that had been shared amongst the entire division. TTPs made it deftly easy to track them down and trace their hacker's movements. It was the equivalent of leaving a fingerprint in the code. The FBI, along with the other agencies, maintained a database of known hackers and their TTPs.

"Nothing. This guy- or these guys - are very professional. Very precise. It was as if they weren't even there. The logs look like normal activity, but nothing showing when or how they empty the machines."

Ivan paused, realizing what he had said. His typing speed notched up as the chat windows filled with instruction.

Steep had worked with Ivan long enough to know not to interrupt his flow.

Ivan had been only nineteen when he had hacked into the FBI networks. From inside the network, he'd written a memo to Steep that he wanted to be on the Cyber Action Team. He had included a five page document of the steps he'd taken to breach the FBI networks. He had emphasized his intention to disclose this immediately for no monetary reward, and spoke of his love for America. Ivan had come from a poor family in Croatia and had escaped during its war for Independence in the early 90s. All he had wanted in life was a green card and to serve America the only way he knew how.

After getting over the shock and his initial inclination to arrest Ivan, Steep decided that he was the very thing the FBI needed. Back then, the FBI was just starting to understand the new world they were in. They needed someone that could maneuver in it. He had taken the kid under his wing and it had proven to pay off a hundred times over the years.

Ivan's voice rose with excitement. "I have found out how they made the machines empty! There is a maintenance process that only technicians can initiate. The logs for the machines show that the process ran many times on Sunday. And today."

"Does it give us the times?" Steep asked, leaning closer to the wall of screens.

"Yes! I have the exact times the process ran. I can also search for all the machines that it was run on."

"Make me a list of every machine you can find that ran this between Friday to now. We'll need times and locations. Get that list to the team."

Steep turned sharply and looked up at the group that was reviewing the video. He spoke loudly as he walked up the steps to them. "Ivan is going to get you a list of exact times and locations. Find them in the videos. This should get us closer to figuring out who they are."

He considered letting a few go home to rest, seeing some of their eyes glaze over. If they could track the crew's movements, they could possibly find their next location. Time was of the essence. He decided to reconsider in a few hours.

7

BURTON took a sip of his coffee. It was generic gas station grade, but with enough sugar, it was satisfactory. He slotted it into the cup holder that he had bolted into the tow truck's dash. It was an older tow truck that was well maintained. Unfortunately, it was manufactured in a time when cup holders were not designed as a standard option.

"So you know what to do this time?" Burton asked his assistant, Greg Gonzales.

"Yeah, definitely," Greg said, staring across the street at the closed garage door.

"You got this." Burton liked the kid. Greg was just a boot Corporal when Burton had gotten out of the Corps. But even then, he could be trusted with anything. Now that Greg was trying to make it on the outside and going to school, Burton gave him a gig whenever possible.

Greg had followed Ash around town, watching his movements and looking for their opportunity, while Burton was busy preparing for the ATM job. He had called this morning to tell him the time was now. Even with only four hours of sleep and a major hangover, Burton knew that this could be their only chance.

"I got your back, boss," Greg said, nodding slowly as he looked up and down the street. It was a well-groomed neighborhood in Orange, New Jersey, but one with a long list of violent incidents. This was where drug dealers and mid-level gangsters lived. Far enough away from their territories to feel safe from their business; except their business usually followed them.

Burton stepped out of the truck and headed to the target house. If everything went right, they would be out of there in ten minutes. He brushed his hand across his lower back to do a quick check that his jacket was still covering his Beretta M9 pistol. He walked at a natural pace up the driveway and bee-lined to the right of the garage. He reached the edge of the building, where he knew the view from the street was slightly obstructed. He shuffled faster along the exterior wall and headed to the back.

He came up to an eight foot high wooden fence. The fence door latch was locked with a padlock on the other side. He reached into his jacket, and pulled out the crowbar from its carrier. With steady motions, he pried the door at the two hinges. Burton prayed that the cracking noise of the hinges coming off the fence couldn't be heard from inside the house. He wouldn't wait for a confirmation. He pulled the door back and crouched into the backyard. His breath started to hasten as his adrenaline began to pump. He pulled his gun from his belt holster and released the safety. He held it with both hands, aiming and moving as his eyes watched ahead of him.

He paused to listen for any dogs. He hated when there were dogs. If there were, he would have to run and try another day. There was no way he could take one down. He made a mental note that he needed to figure out a better solution for that situation.

There was no barking, so he continued forward to the back of the house where he should have been able to get into the garage.

Burton usually staked a house out for at least a day or two to get a feel of the layout. He only had an hour this time. He had been looking for this skip trace for a week now. It was for a hundred thousand dollar Porsche that the borrower, John Ash, no longer felt like paying for. Instead, Ash had decided to hide it in the garage of a friend who also happened to be a drug dealer. There was good chance there were guns and other weapons in the house, therefore he would have to repossess this one in a more aggressive way. Breaking and entering to repossess a vehicle wasn't exactly legal, but Burton was pretty sure that Ash wouldn't report it to the police. As long as Burton did it without getting caught, it would be a clean job.

Typically, he would be respectful as a repossession agent. He would approach the borrower first. Explain that he was there to take their vehicle back because they were not paying their bills. That they were welcome to take their belongings out before he took possession of the car. Seven out of ten times, the borrower knew it was coming and the transfer was a breeze.

The other three times were challenging, at best. He'd seen everything, from attractive women trying to seduce him, to large, angry men trying to kick his ass.

John Ash was in the narrow spectrum of unpredictable violence. Burton had approached him at his own residence the previous week for the first time. He had walked up to the front door, paperwork in hand, and the door had burst open. A shotgun muzzle had come out to greet Burton, aimed at his face. He'd thrown his hands up and shown his palms. He could tell John was either taking meth or was on his eighth day of a coke binge. Maybe both.

Without saying a word, Burton had backed up and walked away. Thankfully, Ash had gone back in the house and closed the door. He most likely had forgotten the entire incident.

After realizing the Porsche was no longer at the house, Burton had instructed Greg to follow Ash around. It didn't take long, but after following him for a week around town, Ash had led him to this house. Ash and his drug dealer friend had even opened the garage door and had a few beers as they sat in the Porsche. As if just sitting in it was enough to make them feel like big shots.

Burton's situational awareness kicked into high gear. It had kept him alive as a Marine. It would at least keep himself from stepping into a shitstorm now.

He trailed along a brick wall that formed the back of the garage. Crap. There wasn't a door. The entrance to the garage must have been inside the house. The only opening was a long horizontal window, five feet above the ground. Breaking a window would definitely get some attention from whomever was inside.

Another option would be to sneak inside the house through the back door. He would then have to find the door leading to the garage. Burton had done that before, with mixed results. He looked at the back door that was further along the wall and considered it.

He went for the window option. Instead of breaking the glass, he levered his crowbar next to the latch. The window frame popped open with minimal effort. The crowbar: never leave home without it. With his gun in hand, finger off the trigger, he held the window open as he hopped up and pigeon-winged the window. He lifted the rest of his body until it was parallel to the ground and slipped into the narrow opening.

As soon as Burton touched ground, he stayed in a crouched position. He listened for any reactions to the sounds he had made. He tuned his ear to anything like running or the opening of doors within the house. The garage was unkempt and had what smelled like bags of old garbage all over the place.

He looked all along the walls for the button that would open the garage door. His eyes took half a minute to adjust to the lighting. He could see the motor and chain mechanism for the garage door on the ceiling. There was wiring that led to a push button by the door. There were two parking slots; in the one closest to the door sat a current model Hummer in yellow, the kind that wannabe gangsters and soccer moms loved equally. In the other garage space was the black Porsche. It looked like it hadn't been washed in a few months, but other than that, it was in excellent condition.

The loan company cared very little about the condition the car came back in. In repossessions, the goal was to take the asset away from the borrower. It would get auctioned and written off on the accounting books as a loss. It was nothing more than a punishment. A person knew that if he did not pay his debts, this would be the result.

Burton didn't like being the one to take things away from people when they were down on their luck. He'd fallen into this kind of work after doing a favor for an acquaintance a few years ago, and it had become a time-filler between jobs with Roman. Like it or not, it was something he was good at.

Sometimes he felt bad for the people he took the cars from. Most times it seemed like they were living beyond their means. It wasn't his job to fix society.

Burton, with his gun still at the ready, came up next to the Porsche's driver's side door. He reached into his jacket for the lender's copy of the remote key. He unlocked the door with a push of a button. A noise from behind the door to the house made him freeze. He cocked his head to get a better read of what it was. It sounded like voices. The voices were getting louder and clearer as they approached the garage door.

"Sous vide, man. We gotta do that sous vide, man!" The voice was monotone in an airy way, indicating the person was high.

"What the hell is... sous vide?" said another voice. This voice was of John Ash. Burton recognized it immediately as the voice behind the shotgun from their first encounter.

"It's, like, the best way to cook. You throw a steak in a bag. A plastic bag. And then put it in this warm water bath for like ten to twenty hours. And it comes out perfect. Perfect!"

"What? That's forever. Why would you wait so long? Just throw it on a grill."

"You've never had steak like this though. Never."

"Have you done it before?"

"No, but it was on the Food Network. It's gotta be the shit."

The voices were getting closer with every word and Burton had seconds to react. He didn't have time to run to the garage door switch and then run back to the Porsche.

He reached down and felt at the garbage next to his feet. With his fingertips, he could feel the foil of an empty bag of chips, an empty carton of milk, then a water bottle. He picked up the water bottle and, judging by its weight, it was three quarters full. He would have only one chance. Without enough time to aim, he pitched the bottle like a throwing knife at the garage switch by the door.

He was already at the driver's side door of the Porsche before the bottle made contact. The sound of the garage door motor clicked on and the rising door started letting light into the garage. He slipped into the driver's seat and eased the door closed so it wouldn't slam.

Two figures appeared at the door leading from the house. The voices were muffled, but there was no tone of alarm. They may have been too high to consider why the garage door was opening on its own. The Porsche had a dark tint, so Burton was confident he was well hidden, as long as they didn't decide to get in the car. He held his fingers on the ignition switch without turning it as the two men walked to the front of the garage. They were talking with an intensity. Burton heard the words "Sous vide" again. They were definitely high. The door continued to rise as they stood there.

It was as if they were waiting for it, like he was.

Just as the door reached to halfway open, he could see Gonzales slowly backing up the flatbed hauler up the driveway, with the flatbed positioned at an angle like a ramp. He was following the plan exactly on cue. The only problem was that there wouldn't be time to throw the car onto the bed. These unstable individuals were only a few feet away. The degenerates could not yet see out the garage as the door was still blocking their view outside. Burton chanced it, and turned on the hazard lights.

The blinking red lights lit up the inside of the garage. He could see their reactions. They were trying to comprehend where the blinking lights were coming from. He had to risk it. If Gonzales kept coming up the driveway, it would block Burton's exit.

Burton could see from his peripheral that Ash was walking towards the Porsche now. The voices became louder and angrier. There was no going back now.

Burton turned the ignition and the Porsche revved to life. The garage door was completely open now. Ash was looking at him directly through the windshield and he knew what was going on.

It looked like Gonzales had taken the hint and had stopped backing up the hauler. He was sitting on the front edge of the driveway halfway onto the street. The flatbed was slowly moving from the ramp position to the driving position.

From the corner of his eye, Burton could tell that Ash's buddy was up to no good. His friend ran to the Hummer's back hatch and was digging for something. Burton could only assume it was something that would be used to stop him.

Ash was banging on the windshield now, yelling at the top of his lungs. "Who the fuck are you? Get out of my fucking car!"

He jerked at the passenger door just as Burton shifted to drive and slammed his foot down on the throttle.

The Porsche's tires squealed as the car propelled forward and out of the garage. It took his lightning reflexes to swerve the wheel to avoid the back of the tow truck. He made it around and prayed there were no cars on the street coming his direction. The back window shattered into pieces as he turned onto the street and he didn't have to look in the rear view to know that it was from a shotgun blast from Ash's friend. He took a quick look in the mirror to make sure Gonzalez had pulled away. It was reassuring to see that the truck was right behind him.

Burton preferred an uneventful repossession, but he'd take just getting away safe and sound. Only when he sped onto the highway and was sure that the two losers weren't following them did he relax. It was a good thing that Billy didn't care what condition the car came in as. It only mattered that the car came in.

8

HOW many hours? Maybe a total of eight or nine? Steep struggled to recall how much sleep he'd managed to catch in the last three days. He made sure that his agents and analysts were all taking the proper shifts to refresh while he remained in the SIOC, only leaving to take showers in the locker room by the gym. He ate his meals at his desk as he continued to scour the information that his team was gathering. Every new detail proved to be a dead end. Nothing led them closer to the identities of the ATM robbers.

His eyes were fighting the urge to close when he heard a knock on the door of his glass box. He looked over to see the aide of the Assistant Director on the other side, looking at him nervously. He waved his hand to invite her in.

She held the door open but remained where she stood, intending not to be there for very long. "The AD wants you in his office... Now," she said, her lips stretched thinner than usual. Steep read her tone loud and clear. He should be ready for some hard interrogation.

"Thank you, Susan. I'll be right there." He stood up as she turned and walked away, taking a brief moment to examine himself in the reflection of the closing glass door. He looked too disheveled to walk into the office of his boss's boss. Steep attempted to straighten out his hair, thankful that he had taken a shower that morning. He didn't have time to shave. He slipped on his suit jacket and adjusted his tie. Grabbing the case folders from the corner of his desk, he left the glass box without a second look.

The walk to the Assistant Director's office was always the longest. It must have been made purposely complicated, having no direct access from any of the main corridors. He felt like a mouse in a maze. But the walk did provide him with time to think through how he was going to present the details of the case. He would have to be ready to answer any question that came at him, and there were too many answers he didn't have.

He reached a glass door and was immediately buzzed in by the armed guard that sat at a small desk behind it.

"They're waiting for you. Go ahead and go on in." The guard nodded to the dark wooden door behind the reception desk. This was the Assistant Director's office. It was one of only a few offices in headquarters that acted as a vault to discuss secret details on cases. All electronic devices not installed in the room became useless as you passed over the threshold.

Steep nodded and took a few deep breaths as he reached for the door. He caught his breath as he realized who else occupied the room.

The office was well-appointed, with mahogany furniture that must have been there from the very first years of the Bureau. The room was dark, despite the few floor lamps. The only area that was well lit was the center of the room, where a six seat conference table dominated.

In the power seat facing the door was the head of the Bureau, his eyes meeting Steep's as soon as he walked through the door. Thomas

Covey. On Covey's left was Steep's boss and Special Agent-in-Charge, Adam Pistone. Sitting on the Director's right was Pistone's boss, Assistant Director, Clarence Adams.

Only one of the men could Steep not instantly identify. There was an older gentleman behind them, perched on the edge of the AD's desk. His features were unclear, as he sat in the shadows of the unlit part of the office. He was stocky with a protruding midsection. He must have been in his late fifties, early sixties and showed his age. Dark, conservative suit. A sharp gray haircut. Steep felt he recognized him, but with his focus on the Director, he couldn't place the name.

"Good morning, Tim. Have a seat." The Director gestured to the seat directly across the conference table in front of him.

Steep quickly glanced at his boss, then the AD, and sensed they were feeling as uneasy as he was. He took his seat and laid his case files in front of him. There were two bottles of water and a glass ready for him.

"How is the case going?" asked the Director. The words were casual enough, but his voice boomed with a force that nearly knocked Steep out of his seat. Covey wanted answers.

Steep took a sip of water, calming himself. He knew to ignore the pressure to rush; in nearly fifteen years of service, he'd learned that the best thing to do in a situation like this was to keep calm and control the timing.

"So far, we have the entire timeline and related surveillance footage along the criminals' path." He spoke in an even tone as he flipped through his files. Steep laid out photo prints of the best shots of the suspects his analysts had been able to get from security camera footage. "There are at least four, maybe five, unidentified suspects, all skilled and precise. This was a well-choreographed heist that spanned three cities: D.C., Boston, and New York. There could have been three crews, one in each city. But from the spread of when one city finished and the other began, I think it's one crew."

"Are you saying we still don't have any potential suspects?" the Director interrupted, fingering the photos. "Did we at least get one of their faces?"

"None so far."

"Why these cities? Not Baltimore, Philadelphia?" The Director had his own idea of timing.

"We were able to determine that the perpetrators infiltrated the ATMs' back end software company, ATSI. Automated Teller Solutions, Inc. They chose these cities because of the concentration of machines that use ATSI software." Steep paused again, trying his best to maintain control of his voice, without betraying his intimidation. "They used a maintenance process that tested the feed mechanism in these machines. Using the timestamps of that process, we gathered all the surveillance footage from around these machines, even the cameras along their routes from machine to machine."

Over the years, D.C. and every other major metropolitan area had added more and more cameras to their surveillance portfolio. There were traffic cams and speed cams. Cameras that covered every public space where a crime could ever happen. There were federal and local limitations on actively monitoring these cameras. But it was the simplest evidence for everything, from murder investigations to petty larceny. It was now the first thing that any investigator looked for at any crime scene.

The Director didn't interrupt, but his dark eyes pierced through Steep like a laser.

Steep did the only thing he could, and continued. "In D.C. and Boston, they used Honda CBR racing motorcycles, wearing full racing suits and keeping their helmets on. In New York, they used bicycles and kept their faces covered in hats and scarves. They knew exactly where there were cameras and they never appeared in the same frame. Each city took three to four hours and there's no sign of them traveling in between. After New York, they disappeared."

The Director leaned back in the leather conference chair and looked back at the unknown man. He was still perched on the AD's desk, his arms folded over his chest. The man simply nodded twice.

The Director turned back to Steep, "It's been three days since the case opened. Do you think they'll hit another city?"

"Unlikely. They must have realized we would figure out how they did it by now. The process has been disabled nationwide. The three cities were their score."

The Director leaned forward leaning on his elbows. "What are the chances of us finding out who they are and catching them?"

"Right now? Slim." Steep hated to admit. "There's no feasible way of identifying them. We can keep looking."

The Director looked through Steep, not saying a word. Almost not breathing. Maybe he should have said that there was a high chance of finding them. Buy himself more time. He kicked himself for having integrity. The minutes stretched to feel like hours. Pistone and Adams traded looks, but didn't show any signs of saving him.

"I think for now, let's make this case ongoing. Keep it under restricted clearance. We don't want the media to get a hold of it. Release the crisis action team room. ASAP." The Director was directing his statements to not only Steep, but to his bosses as well.

Steep kept his composure, but his mind was reeling. Was the Director burying his case?

"Send out any standing alerts you think best, but it looks like we'll have to wait until this crew pops up again. I hope I am being clear enough. Nothing to the media."

Steep and his bosses nodded. This wasn't a discussion. Covey had given his orders.

"Thank you, Tim. You did a fine job. We'll get them next time," said the Director, with a hint of a forced smile and a slight nod to the door. That was his cue to leave the room.

"Sure thing," replied Steep, dumbfounded as he gathered his files.

He took another quick look at the older gentleman as he stood up from the conference table. He recorded what he could to memory.

He would find out who it was later.

Without another word, he left the room.

9

THE house was no longer a home.

The memories that filled it would soon be stripped away. Roman had never given it any thought before. He had come only a handful of times since he had left home for college. He kept a barrier between his life and his parents.

It wasn't that he didn't love his parents. Recollections of his upbringing in this, his childhood home, were all filled with affection and stability. In fact, it was because of his love for his parents that Roman had made the calculated, conscious decision to stay away.

If they were ever pulled into the current state of his double life, it would have broken their hearts. They would blame themselves for the way they raised him. And, as Roman was well aware, they had raised him well enough to not be at fault.

After his mother had died two years ago, he had come to visit even less. He had wanted to be there for his father, but the deep silences and unspoken thoughts were unbearable. His mother had been the communicator between the two of them. Without her, the distance between his father and him grew impossible to broach. Or at least, that's how it had seemed.

Regret filled Roman's chest at the thought that he should have tried harder.

Soon, there would be no house to come back to. He held the foreclosure eviction notice in his hand as he walked through the foyer. The notice was dated the day his father gave up on his own life.

Bryce stood by him in the living room, the space that hadn't changed since they were best friends in elementary school.

"How long do we have?" Bryce asked, patting the old couch that sectioned the space. It was the same couch from when they were kids. Roman remembered all those nights his best friend had slept on it, nights he had come over to get away from his father.

"The lawyer said we only have a few hours. The county sheriff will come by at five to make sure we've vacated the premises," Roman replied without any visible emotion.

"What are you going to keep?"

In a whisper, Roman replied, "Nothing."

There was nothing in this house that he needed.

When he had left for college at age eighteen, he had left everything that wouldn't have made sense in a dorm room. The intention was that he would come back for it all one day, when he was done with college and was settled somewhere in a career. Graduation never came, and his career didn't allow for settling down anywhere permanently.

He looked at the framed pictures on the walls. All of them had been meticulously set throughout the house by his mother. So much care had been taken in placing them. He didn't even recognize the young boy that grew up in these pictures. These were his mother's memories of him. They weren't unpleasant. He just wasn't sure if he cared to keep a record of it. Maybe they were something that kept his father going as long as he had after she'd passed away. Or maybe they were reminders of what he had lost. Maybe they'd pushed him over the edge.

These pictures and little keepsakes of his parents filled the house. Parents he no longer had. The thought of collecting it all was unbearable. Gathering it and moving it to another place where he would never see it again was tragic. The bank not giving him a choice, taking it all away, was almost a blessing.

He didn't even recall what was left in his old room. He hadn't stepped upstairs since his mother died. He closed his eyes, trying to remember what the room looked like. It was a memory of someone he no longer was.

"What's all this?" Bryce asked, lifting the tops of a group of file boxes. They were stacked four high and three across against the back wall of the living room. Next to them was his father's small side desk, piled high with stacks of ripped open envelopes.

"I don't know. That wasn't there the last time I was around."

Roman walked over and started picking through the top layer of boxes. It looked like bills and notices from banks, hospitals, and insurance companies.

Just as he started looking through them, he heard Hope and Burton at the front door.

"Wow, this place hasn't changed at all," said Burton as he came into the living room. "What can we do to help?"

But Roman barely heard him. As he went through the piles of paperwork, his mind focused and his friends' conversations faded in the background.

There were hundreds of notices, dating back to when his mother first started to go to the hospital weekly. They started out being paid in full, and gradually increased to more and more being due. Insurance companies not accepting all expenses. Late payment notices from hospitals.

The notices became more aggressive and the number of companies demanding for money increased. Roman examined the bank statements, filed in neat cohesion alongside the meticulously ordered bills. His father had emptied his savings, then his retirement accounts, taking every tax penalty that existed. He had refinanced the house in the final weeks of his wife's life. That was the last time the medical bills were shown to be paid in full.

The notices became more varied after that. There were condolences from Roman's father's employer that quickly turned to letters of reprimand. His father had lost his accounting job of twenty faithful years only a few years before retirement. There was no sign of a severance package.

The overdue medical bills continued, in addition to mortgage notices. The credit card bills grew. They were followed by debt consolidators promising an easy way out. They were waiting to pick at his father's bones like the vultures they were. It continued as the bank began the foreclosure process.

The paper trail ended with one final ripped envelope. It was the final notice from the bank that the house was up for auction, and all contents would be taken at a certain date.

The date his father had decided it was over.

Roman went through the paperwork for what felt like hours until he couldn't take it any longer. His anger and frustration increased with every past due notice. He could have helped his father through this. He could have taken care of all of it.

His heart tightened as he realized all the times he should have come to check on his father. All this time, his father had been alone to agonize under this mountain of debt. It must have felt like there was no end in sight. Nowhere to turn to.

Roman wanted retribution, but from whom?

Was it the hospital's fault for not healing his mother, but still charging huge sums of expenses? Was it the health insurance's fault for not being able to provide the financial security they were trusted to provide? Was it the bank's fault that they had taken his father's home away?

To Roman, they were all to blame. The system that had forced his father to keep digging a hole that he would never be able to escape from. Not on his own. Not without help or relief.

It was also Roman's fault. There was no denying that. There was no denying that he should have been there to help his father. There was no excuse for not knowing that this was happening. If Roman wasn't so selfish, so into his own chaotic life, maybe he would have done something.

He didn't know what was going on then, but he knew now. It was only mattered what he was going to do about it.

10

THE train car was close to empty. The only other person on board was a young man with headphones on, curled up and sleeping at the opposite end of the car. The Hudson train to Grand Central on a late Sunday night was a barely commuted route on the Metro-North. They sat in a section where two rows of seats faced each other. Roman looked out the window into the darkness, facing in the direction of movement. Bryce and Reggie were with him in one section. Hope and Burton sat across the aisle. Hope couldn't help but glance over at Roman every so often.

She wished she could take his pain away. He was stoic by nature, but this was a deeper quiet. He had said little since the funeral. She and the others had hovered around him throughout the week. They had done their best to take care of the house and funeral arrangements. She had packed the photos, leaving their now-empty frames stacked neatly on the floor in nearby corners. He had said he didn't want them, but she had carefully packed them into a small box when he wasn't watching. She knew the day would come when he would want them. They'd left most of the house as it was, watching the movers as they started to fill the semi-truck trailer. The bank knew exactly what they were doing.

At the funeral, Roman had remained detached. He only nodded as people came up to him to give their condolences. Hope wished she knew what to say or do. Something that would make him feel better.

"I think I am on to something. Stuxnet had three components. A worm, a link file, and a root-kit. The worm propagates itself and runs the exploit."

Reggie was incessantly talking at Roman about some nerd project he was working on. Hope wasn't sure if Roman was even listening. Reggie didn't seem to care either way. The project was a variant of Stuxnet, a highly advanced computer malware that was discovered in 2010. There was a theory that it was an American-Israeli built cyber weapon. Considering its target was Iran's nuclear program, it was probably true.

Hope only knew this because it had been all that Reggie had talked about for the last few months. He was obsessed with what it was able to do.

A simple USB flash drive was the delivery vehicle for Stuxnet. Someone accidentally or intentionally plugged it into a network near the target. It then spread to any computer it came in contact with, only affecting its targets; a specific model of a programmable logic controller. PLCs, the computers that control machinery, were everywhere, from factories and power plants to building systems. Anything that needed automation in some way. These specific PLCs controlled Iran's centrifuges. Stuxnet was a sign of how cyber warfare had evolved.

Roman didn't seem to acknowledge anything, but that didn't stop Reggie. "The link file executes all the copies of the worm, and the root-kit hides it all. There're many variants of it out there now, but none of those interest me. My version will be boss."

Reggie paused for dramatics. Hope could tell that Reggie was about to pitch an idea. Everything before had been nothing but a hard-sell tactic to lay the groundworks.

He took a deep breath and spoke slowly. "I think I'm on to something. It's a worm that propagates quick. It seeks out whatever unique piece of data you are looking for and scours the network for any existence of it. And then erases it from existence. All done at whatever specified time you'd like."

His voice pitched higher with excitement. "It's like a search and destroy. It will latch onto data transfer packets, and go from one system to another. It will even piggy back to the backup system and look for its target data there. It's unstoppable. You can even make the target a variable. So it could have millions of unique targets. All you need is a source to define the targets."

Hope wished he would just shut up. Maybe if Roman had a second of silence, he would look up at her. He would notice that she was looking at him.

She glanced at Burton. Her brother would never understand. Burton was knocked out, his chin touching his chest. He was close to snoring. He was overprotective, and would never accept an affair between her and Roman. He could barely handle her dating anyone he didn't know, let alone one of his best friends.

What was she even thinking? There were no signs that Roman would see her in any other way than as a little sister. Ever since Burton had met Roman and Bryce in high school, it was like she had three older brothers. She was only three years younger, but they still treated her like a little girl. Why would Roman ever see her as more than the skinny, freckled, awkward girl? The one he protected from bullies in school?

She wasn't sure when she had started feeling this way. She didn't even know what this feeling was, if it was real at all. It had to have been recent. She had graduated from college with her art history

53

degree. She had been able to pay for it with the help of a gymnastics scholarship, but the rest were loans that she would be paying for the rest of her life. The degree led to an office job for a museum where she did nothing that was even remotely related to art. She quit after a year.

Burton was around Roman and Bryce a lot more, so she started seeing Roman just as much. She began helping on scores. The jobs they all did together became all she wanted to do. Part of it was to be near him. There was an intensity about him that started to attract her. His intelligence and ability to solve just about any problem that came up.

Roman sat there, looking into the darkness. An occasional light from lampposts or billboards would stream across the window pane. Every once in awhile, his eyes would close and then open again, as if he was visualizing something. Thinking through some puzzle or problem. She had seen him do this many times before. What could he be trying to figure out? His father had died, but there was nothing he could solve with that. She wished she could hear his thoughts just once. To see how his mind worked. Whatever he was planning to do, she knew that she wanted to be a part of it.

Just as she realized she had been gazing at him for too long, Roman turned his head and his eyes met hers. She wanted to look away from his deep gray pools. All she could do was give an uncomfortable smile, which she could feel under her warm cheeks. He returned it with a slight raising of the corners of his lips. In a moment, his eyes widened, as if realizing where he was. Hope caught his eyes flash at Burton for a split second, then Roman quickly returned his gaze to the darkness outside the window.

Hope felt her cheeks flush. Why would she stare at him like that? She was a creep. That's what he must have been thinking. She turned her head towards her own window and closed her eyes. She bit her bottom lip, hoping that could hold back any expression that might pour out of her. She took a deep breath, held it, and then exhaled a slow steady stream through her nose. Slow and steady. She did it one more time and could feel herself begin to calm. It wasn't a big deal. It was nothing at all.

Burton began opening his eyes and turned his wrist to peek at his watch. "We should almost be there, right?" his voice nasal and groggy.

Roman turned so that he faced the rest of them. "I have an idea."

Bryce lowered his phone, not bothering to turn the screen off. He gave Burton a tap on the leg from across the aisle. Bryce's eyes widened and grinned slightly. "What is it? What's the score?"

Hope was able to compose herself enough to look at Roman again, but she couldn't hide her excitement. When Roman came up with an idea for anything, it was worth giving it your full attention. Burton even straightened in his seat and faced across the aisle.

Roman rubbed his chin as he looked over everyone. Hope knew him well enough to know that he was careful with the things he considered. He was still wondering if he should even mention anything. Just as the anticipation was getting to her, Roman leaned forward.

"How about we wipe out everyone's debt?" He scanned their eyes back and forth, as if trying to gauge their interest.

Reggie leaned in. "Do you mean all of our debts? I could do that quick."

Hope had to admit, she was thinking the same thing. She had a ton of student loans. Though they made money from their scores, she lived on credit cards until the money was cleaned. But why would Roman want to do that kind of job? It didn't seem worth it. Looking at the others' faces, they felt the same. Roman cleared his throat and started waving his hands around. Hope thought he looked like he was performing a magic show. She couldn't help think that it was rather adorable.

"Not just ours. Everyone's."

He paused to let it sink in. "I want to erase the record of debt for as many people as we can. I want to wipe everyone's slate clean, all at once."

Reggie's eyes widened as he started to make the connection. "You mean, instead of stealing money, we're going let everyone keep it?"

Roman's looked back out of the window. His eyes were focused in thought. "That's right. We need to steal everyone's debt."

11

BRYCE Kingston stood in front of his office's floor to ceiling windows. He barely registered the breathtaking view over the Hudson River. He sipped on his coffee, not enjoying the aroma as he usually did. His mind was too distracted by Roman's idea.

Was his best friend going crazy?

It was seven in the morning, and the rows of analysts and traders seated outside his door were already buzzing with activity. Each seat had an array of four or more screens, displaying the market information, transaction systems, and live news. His people felt they needed all this to make smart trades. They would never admit they were only guessing.

Inside Bryce's office, it was much more serene. His desk was clear of clutter and screens. Reggie had worked his magic, and installed for him two sixty inch flat panels on the wall. They acted as his computer monitors so that he could do his computer work from his office couch. He never enjoyed being stuck behind a desk the entire day.

Other than that, his office was spartan. The lack of decoration kept his head clear and focused. That was how he had moved up the ladder at Jacobs and Krain. They were one of the top twenty hedge funds in the business, with billions under management.

Bryce had been promoted to portfolio manager in under four years, which was unheard of. His career success had displeased many in the senior ranks. But Bryce was good with people and knew how to keep clients happy. All he had to do was make sure that everyone outside his door was making money for the company.

He had gotten a lot of help from Roman, especially in the beginning. Roman could figure out any system or problem, no matter how complicated. He saw everything in a way that Bryce could only grasp after a detailed explanation and a few drinks. Even though Roman would never get a 'real' job himself, he knew how to navigate the office culture.

That's how Bryce had been able to thrive at an office like this one as quickly as he had. Roman had helped him plan his climb up the ladder. It was the right firm with the right number of senior staff retiring at the right time. Roman planned the connections Bryce needed to make. He envisioned the hard conversations and negotiations Bryce would have to have. And it was Roman who had unearthed the breakthrough market deals that made him look like a financial genius.

If Roman had engineered a complicated climb up the corporate ladder in one of the most competitive hedge funds in the world, he must be able to figure out this next impossible score... right?

Eliminating everyone's debt. What did that even mean?

Bryce took a larger sip of coffee with his eyes closed, trying to see things as Roman would. It was impossible. Ever since they were kids, Bryce was always amazed at how Roman figured things out. They always looked for trouble. And they were always able to escape the consequences.

Their early escapades started off innocently. Stealing toys, comic books, or whatever else eleven-year-old boys wanted. The targets were always easy enough, but their plans were never straightforward. It wasn't the prize that mattered. It was the adventure of planning and executing without getting caught.

As they grew older, the stakes became higher and the threat of capture more possible. Their innocuous thefts slowly turned to federal-level crimes.

Over time, an arms race had grown in the security industry. It included everything from physical barriers, to traps in their virtual networks. It all just made what they did more exciting.

Samantha, Bryce's business analyst, came in with his next cup of coffee in one hand and file folders in the other.

She handed the coffee cup to Bryce, "It should be pretty quiet today. You only have lunch with Roman, and there's a conference call with the Beijing office, which I can dial in for you."

Bryce handed her his near empty mug and took the fresh one with a nod. "That would be great, Sam. Thanks."

Samantha placed the contents of her other hand on his desk. "These are today's reports. Once you've had time to look them over, I'll send them up the chain."

She paused for a second, standing behind Bryce as she held his empty cup in both her hands. "Is something the matter, Bryce?" Her eyebrows raised with genuine concern.

He snapped out of his trance over the Hudson and began clearing his throat. "I'm just fine, Sam. Just lost in a thought." He turned towards her, flashing his patented million-dollar smile.

Sam's expression relaxed as she turned towards the door. "Well, you should have plenty of time for thoughts today. I'll try and keep the interruptions to a minimum."

Bryce was in the middle of a thank you as the door lightly closed behind her. His smile reverted to a straight line as he turned back to the window.

He had to come to terms with Roman's idea. If Roman was the brain of all their schemes, Bryce was the heart. He kept the plan going even when Roman's cautiousness and worry began to get the best of him. Once Bryce bought into the main objective, he knew he would have to keep Roman from backing out.

Bryce wasn't too sure about this one though. The stakes were too high, and for very little benefit for the crew itself. He didn't have much consumer debt to worry about, but he was sure Reggie and Hope had some substantial student loans and credit cards. Burton and Roman lived off credit cards while their scores were at the cleaners.

Bryce didn't, though. He rarely needed the money from their illegal endeavors. His family had always been well-off, and the salary from his day job was substantial.

Bryce didn't care about the money, but he craved the excitement. Nothing came close to the thrill of carrying out Roman's plans. This one, if they succeeded, would be a landmark for hackers and thieves everywhere. Not to mention the most exciting, impossible, adrenaline-filled heist they had ever pulled off.

Bryce had to make a choice and there was no avoiding it. Roman was motivated by his father's death, but there was a bigger reason he wanted to do this. Roman wanted to do something that was much bigger than themselves. How had he phrased it? "Something that matters."

Bryce trusted Roman more than anyone else he'd ever known. As he watched the sun rise and the city wake up below, he reminded himself of this. The score would be as epic as it was seemingly impossible. But was it possible for them to do?

12

THE diner was half-empty, as usual. It was a classic New York mom-and-pop that the foodie TV shows and review sites ignored. A place where breakfast was served all day long and the food was unhealthy but comforting.

Roman sat in their usual booth. He scrolled through websites on his phone as he waited for Bryce to arrive. Roman had been using every moment he had to research the debt industry. He had an end goal, but he needed an exact target to define the plan to erase everyone's debt.

It wouldn't be enough to take down a few banks, or a single conglomerate. He would have to understand the entire system and then find a central point where a hit would make the most impact.

It would be pointless to try to take down every single company that made loans, one at a time. As soon as they hit the first company, there would be a concentrated effort to stop them. Even worse, they could be exposed. There had to be a solution to take the entire industry down at once.

When he noticed Bryce approach, he placed the phone aside and took a sip from his coffee mug. Bryce sat down across from him and ordered a black coffee from their favorite Ukrainian waitress. It felt like they had known her for decades.

He looked over at Roman. "So... what are we having?"

Bryce always asked the same question. And he always ended up getting the same thing. Steak and eggs, over easy. The steak here wasn't grade A, but it was decent. There was just something about the combination he couldn't resist.

"Haven't ordered yet, but... I'm thinking steak and eggs, over easy," Roman smirked.

Alana, the waitress, came by and set Bryce's coffee in front of him. She pulled out her little receipt pad. "What would you boys like today? Steak and eggs? Over easy?" She glanced at Bryce through her black rimmed glasses, with a thin smile.

Bryce handed her his menu. "Are we that predictable, Alana?"

Alana smiled wider. "Only a little."

"I'll have the same, of course. Thanks," Roman said. As she walked away, Roman leaned forward over the table. "So, have you thought about it anymore?"

They always jumped into the subject right away. There was no need for filler conversation between the two of them. The only subject that mattered at the moment was the idea. There had only ever been one rule in this game they played: they both had to agree on the target. It was rare that they ever disagreed, but if they did, it was safer to just walk away.

"Yes. A lot." Bryce took a small swallow of the coffee. It was a far cry from being the best coffee in the city, but the familiarity of its taste was somehow relaxing. "I don't know, Roman. Is it really doable? Is it even worth it? We're not making any money off this one."

"Since when do you care about money?"

"Never," Bryce scoffed. "But for you and the others. Is it going to be worth our time? We don't even know if it's going to work. There's always a risk, but there's usually a payoff that's worth it."

"We'll wipe out our own debts. That's as good as getting paid."

Roman knew the only debt Bryce really had was mortgages for a few properties, including the apartment. That was at least a few million in debt that would disappear.

Bryce looked puzzled. "Won't this screw up the economy? It'll be chaos. All these mortgages and loans out there. All the credit cards. Banks are going to fail, and there's no way they'll be able to recover. All corporations will fall behind them. If the banks fail, what will happen to money? People are going to lose their jobs everywhere." Though he'd spent a good amount of time and energy building his career in finance, Bryce didn't feel any loyalty toward the institution of American banking. But his mind still spun with wonder as he calculated the cost of such an operation. "We would cause a financial Armageddon," he concluded.

"At first, it will be painful." Roman slowly shook his head. He had prepared for this point and was relentlessly thinking about the big picture consequences. "But... there will always be winners, and there will always be losers. We've talked about this so many times. The game is rigged against the lower and middle classes. People like my dad." Roman swallowed hard, before continuing.

"There's no end in sight. People think they are competing in an economy, but they have little to no control. The rich and powerful are controlling it through their tight hold of politics and media, and every law rules in their favor. During every bust, they get bailed out of whatever risky bets they made, and the rest of society pays for it.

No one is going to bail out the honest, hard working men and women who only want to take care of their families. The ones that are forced to go into debt just to get an education and a chance to survive. Their wages remain flat, while the cost of living keeps increasing. Someone needs to bail them out.

"There will be losers. Investors that bet against the prime and subprime borrowers. They knew the risks, but ignored them for the potential gains. The unfortunate losers will be the pensioners. People that relied on all their fund managers. The ones that placed them in these kinds of investments that are a burden to society." Roman paused. It was the one problem he had with this idea, the only thing that gave him a moment's pause. "But there's no way to avoid those collateral effects. There's only one way we can reset the system. We're not taking the money and assets that everyone has. I just want to erase what everyone owes. Everyone. Rich or poor. How it will turn out exactly, I'm not sure. But it can't keep going the way it is. It's unsustainable. If we don't do it, who will?"

Alana had come by with their food. She placed each plate in front of them. The smell of grilled steak, eggs and toast wafted in the air. "There you go, boys. More coffee?" Without waiting for an answer, she picked up each of their mugs and poured into them from a full cistern.

"Thanks," they both said in unison.

"If you boys need anything else, just call out," she said with a smile. She stepped away towards the counter.

Roman leaned forward, his intensity rising. "During biblical times, maybe even before then, rulers would enact Jubilee. They freed slaves and prisoners, debts would be forgiven and land released from obligations. Even back then, they knew debts caused nothing but pain after a certain point."

Bryce picked up his knife, but was completely entranced. "Really?

Why would they do that?"

"Rulers did it to keep their society intact. As years went by, debts would build. Back then, debt was ultimately repaid by years of indentured servitude - slavery. As the imbalance of citizens and slaves grew, anger and discord would build into chaos."

Roman started cutting into his steak, but had no intention of stopping to eat. "So before the rioting would get out of control, about every fifty years, the rulers would call for a relief of everyone's debt. They released all the slaves so they could all go home to their families and live the rest of their lives in peace. Everyone would be happy and praise their ruler. The few rich would accept their losses, still having more than they needed to do well. They would plan for their renewal and continue their activities, putting new people into debt slavery. But with a clean slate, even they started fresh."

"This really existed?" Bryce was incredulous.

"From what I've read, Jubilee must have existed." Roman took his first bite of steak.

"So why isn't it still in practice now? There must be a good reason."

"Not sure. It may have ended before the Roman Empire fell. The banking system evolved into the system we have now, which is practiced globally. There's no way for us to completely fix the system, but we can give it a reset. Force it to change. Maybe, from there, society will figure out a better way forward."

Roman paused to let his friend take in all the information.

They didn't speak for a long while, Bryce eating his steak as he was lost in his own thoughts. Roman finished his coffee, but didn't signal for a refill.

Bryce looked up from his plate. "So we erase everyone's debt and... see what happens?"

"Pretty much."

Bryce's smile broke through. He had decided at last. "Let's see what happens."

13

BURTON walked into the parking lot of the Billy Stephens Auto Emporium of New Jersey. There were various makes and models. Everything from a 2000 model Chevy truck to the Porsche that he had picked up a few days ago, repaired and ready for sale.

Other than the cars, the parking lot most likely looked the same as it had in the 70s. Strings of brightly colored triangles were tied diagonally from every light post. White shoe polish writing covered the windshields of each car, each stating how much one could save if they "purchased today!" There were a few potential buyers strolling around, looking in the windshields. Salesmen circled like sharks, waiting for the right time to come in for the kill.

Burton walked up Billy Stephens. He was a rather round man, with a buttoned down gut that protruded completely out of his suit jacket. His arms and legs were disproportionately smaller than his midsection. They looked as if they could have belonged to a different person. Even in the cool pre-spring morning air, spots of sweat glistened on his forehead.

"Burton, m' boy. Glad you could come in on short notice," said

Billy, reaching out his pudgy hand. Burton shook it, thinking he should use some hand sanitizer when he got back to the truck.

Without waiting for a response, Billy started his request. "So I've been chasing this particular vehicle for months now. It's nothing special, but I have a client that is looking for this make, model and color."

Billy turned around and waved for Burton to follow. He walked onto the showroom floor, following a straight path to his office.

He spoke without a hint of a pause. "This should be a really easy job for you, m'boy. Really easy. One of my other guys spotted it in Elizabeth, just parked in some shopping center. He didn't have time to grab it, so you're in luck. This recovery will rate a bonus for bringing it in by this afternoon."

Burton didn't feel the need to respond. He knew that anything he said fell on deaf ears. It would be a waste of effort and breath to say anything at all. He just followed the self-centered lard into his office. It was a small closet-sized room, with a large square window facing the showroom floor. The office furniture was typical: a desk, task chair, and two guest chairs. It was surprising that a person of Billy's size and shape could even maneuver in this small space.

He rummaged through the pile of paperwork on his desk and found a manila envelope. "Here are the paperwork and keys." He held out the envelope and released it, not caring if Burton had a hold of it first. Burton caught it in time, but contemplated chunking it back at Billy.

The large man found a sticky note and scribbled on it, "Here is the address." He handed it to Burton in the same manner and gave a big grin. "Remember, if you get it here by two, I'll make it worth your while."

Burton turned and headed to his truck. Saying anything like a goodbye would also have been a waste of breath.

* * *

Burton pulled into the Elizabeth Town Shopping Center parking lot. He maneuvered the flatbed wrecker truck through the maze of cars, trying his best not to scratch them. The shopping center had open parking on three of its sides, with a five floor parking structure on its east. It would have been nice if Billy's other guy had left an exact location in the parking lot. But that would have been too easy.

What Burton did know was that he was looking for a three year old black Cadillac SUV with New Jersey plates. There was no problem with finding a black Cadillac SUV. It was the car of choice for many New Jersey suburban moms and gangster-wannabes alike. He would have to come all the way up to each one he came across to check its VIN number in the windshield. It was possible to change the license plate, but changing the VIN was rarely done.

Driving the wrecker through the tight spaces was unnerving, so he decided to park it and go on foot. The late morning sun shined bright above his head. The weather was still cool and breezy, but his internal temperature rose from his brisk pace. Within an hour, he had come across six of the same exact Cadillacs. He was starting to think this was an elaborate joke.

The walking made his mind wander to Roman's idea. Erasing people's debt?

He had always been down for whatever score Roman and Bryce were after, but this one seemed unrealistic. He wasn't a techie like Reggie, but he had a feeling that the financial world protected their data like gold. Maybe even better than gold.

After traversing the open parking lots, all he had left was the parking garage. Burton decided it might be a good idea to start with the top floor and work his way down. Just as he reached the third floor landing, he noticed a black SUV parked in the far corner of the level. Despite the garage being open air without outer walls, the space was still dark and cold. He couldn't exactly tell what make it was.

Half-thinking it was a waste of time, he decided to walk over and check it out. He could always skip it on the way back down. It was in the darkest corner of the level, and there was a black Lincoln town car in the spot on its driver's side. As he approached it more closely, he realized that it was a Cadillac. At least it wasn't a complete waste of time.

He reached into his back pocket and pulled out his Xenon flashlight. He clicked it on and pointed in the general direction of the back license plate. His heart jumped. After validating license plates over and over again, he had the number engraved in his memory. He was ten meters away. The letter and number combination were clear against the yellow New Jersey plate background.

He had finally found it.

When he was closer, he scanned the flashlight's beam across the windows to get a look inside. He caught a small movement from inside the back seat area that made him stop in his tracks. Was there someone in there? He held the light's beam through the back of the SUV's back window. The light streamed through the interior and bits of light reached the cement wall behind it.

There were more shadows moving around inside, he was sure of it. Maybe even more than one person. He inched slowly toward the back of the vehicle, staying in a low crouch. He lowered and then turned off the flashlight, slipping it into his back pocket. He then held his right hand on just the grip of his 9mm. Hopefully, he wouldn't need to use it.

Whomever was inside already knew he was there, but he had to be cautious how he approached them. There was no telling what they might do. He had been shot at too many times when he wasn't prepared.

He reached the town car and crouched behind it, leaning his left shoulder on the trunk. He peeked around its passenger side tail light. He was so close now that he could see the SUV swaying slightly from the movement inside.

He heard one of the doors open and the swaying became more pronounced. He had to peek further to get a view of the Cadillac's doors. He inched forward until he could see the driver's side back door completely open. He let out a slow breath. Standing in the doorway was a blond woman in her early forties.

She didn't seem to know he was there, but instead was focused on the backseat. "Come on, honey. Get your shoes on. We have to go get something to eat." Just as she said that, a small blond boy inched his way out of the backseat with one shoe in his hand. His right sneaker was already on, just waiting to be laced.

Burton relaxed, released the pistol grip and lowered his right hand. "Okay," he thought to himself, "This isn't going to be easy, but at least it isn't dangerous."

It was just a mom and her kid, coming to the mall.

It didn't make sense though. The tip had said that the car was already there hours ago. Had she and the kid been here this whole time?

He took another deep breath as he began to stand up straight. This was going to feel terrible, taking transportation from a kid and his mother. He was on a time crunch and had to get it done.

She must not have known he was there. As soon as he stood, she turned with a startled expression. She reached for her child still sitting in the SUV.

Burton showed his palms. "It's okay. I'm not going to hurt you or anything." He said it too late.

He could see a shadow move on his right, from the passenger side of the vehicle. He must have been so focused on her that he hadn't noticed the other door open. Stupid him for not being alert. There was no warning, and the shadow came upon him before he could fully react.

Just as he stepped back and swung his firing hand to his lower back, the sound and blur of a swinging bat came down on him.

Instinct made him crouch and raise his forearms to lessen the blow of the wooden bat. The man behind it was in his early fifties, unshaven, and had an expression of fear more than rage.

He must have not been very strong. The brunt force of the bat wasn't as hard as Burton had expected. The man swung in empty air in front of Burton's face, which he thought would have hurt more if it connected.

The man backed up with the same nervous expression. He was yelling, "Get away! We don't have anything for you!" He shook his bat in the air, threatening it with ferocity.

Burton was still crouched, with both forearms guarding his head. He backed up. The shuffling of his shoes against the cement echoed through the cold garage.

"I'm not here to hurt anyone!" Burton had to be careful what he was going to say. This man was just protecting his family and was in obvious fear for them. "I'm just here from Billy Stephens Auto. I'm just here to repossess the vehicle, sir. I'm very sorry, but it's just my job."

Burton could see this registering on the man's face. In slow motion, the man's scowl became a saddened frown of defeat. His brow curled upwards and his eyes shone with a warning of the tears to come. His bat dropped to his side. Just like that, the man had given up.

The blond woman came up to her husband and placed a hand on his shoulder. "Please, don't do this. It's the last thing we have."

Burton lowered his arms and straightened up. He was always prepared for some resistance to him doing his job. "I'm sorry, ma'am. It's just what I have to do. I can give you a little time to gather your things." He took a second to think about what he was going to offer next. "I'll… I'll even drop you guys off at your home." It was the only concession he could think of. They were obviously hard on their luck, and any length of civility was the least he could do.

The bat hit the floor and the man was now the one that crouched down. His face fell to his hands and Burton could hear the sobs echo in the lifelessness of the garage.

His wife was also tearing, but managed for the moment to hold on to her composure. "You just don't understand. The car is our home. We've been living out of it for weeks now. We have nowhere to go."

Burton didn't know what to do in a situation like this. Could he believe what she was saying? People were inclined to say whatever they could to keep from getting their cars taken. The little boy had come out of the SUV and was now standing next to his mom, his shoe still in his hand. Burton guessed from his height that he must have been about four. He looked at his mother and latched onto the back of her shirt, holding it with his little hand.

"Tom lost his job a year ago, and it's been impossible for him to find another. We sold everything we could, and were evicted months ago. We've been staying with friends when possible, but now… our options have dried up. There's nowhere we can go. Our family is all the way in Nebraska. We just have to get there. And all we have left is this car." There was no reason for Burton not to believe what she was saying.

The man composed himself and stood up from his defeated pose. "I'm… sorry I hit you. I'm just… we're at the end. If there's any way you could find it in your heart..." The man gulped.

Burton could tell that, even now, it was hard for the man to admit how desperate he was for help. It didn't come naturally to him to beg. "Do you think you could just… not have found us? I've been working in the mall for a few days to save enough money for gas. We'll never be able to pay for the car, but we've already lost everything. It's our only way back to where we can start over."

Burton thought it over. How could someone with a family get themselves into this kind of situation? Was there any excuse for it?

The man must have felt the question, "It is my fault. We didn't have much saved. All our money was in our house. I was a mailroom supervisor at Hester. I'd worked for them for nearly twenty two years. We were able to finally pay for our home, buy a nice car. Then the company started making layoffs. We survived on credit cards for a little while. We tried every option possible. We couldn't qualify for any of the relief programs that were supposed to help people like us. The mortgage rate increased to the point where we could barely afford it monthly. Our credit is in shambles. We were forced into foreclosure and were evicted. We lost everything in an instant. I've been looking for a job, but no one is hiring someone of my age," he shook his head slowly.

Could Burton really take the last thing this unfortunate family had? Most times, the car was the first thing taken. A family could still get by if they had a cheap apartment, were living with family, or even crashing at a friend's. He had heard stories from the other repo guys that more and more people were living out of their cars. This was the first time he had come across it himself.

The man wrapped his arms around his wife and son. "There's really nothing I can say, but please. Please, just give us this break. We'll never be able to pay off the car unless we get out of here and get to our family. We should have gone sooner, but we just kept trying to make it work."

Burton looked in the back of the vehicle. He noticed the luggage and random household items that filled the back of the SUV. They weren't lying. They were well-kept, but it looked like it had been a while since they had a good bath or good night's sleep. The car was all they had. How could he take that away from them?

14

ROMAN looked at his two cards and replaced them face down on the table. The apartment was intentionally kept dark. An overhead lamp gave off only a slight glow. He was in position next to Bryce, being the dealer on his left. Burton and Hope were sitting across the table.

Roman had the largest stack of poker chips in front of him. Bryce was a close second. Hope and Burton were about even. Reggie was on the couch in the living area, focused on his laptop.

Roman had an ace and a ten of hearts in his hand. The community cards were already showing a flush with a king of spades, a jack of hearts, and an eight of clubs. He held his poker face by thinking of the plan.

They had been playing for a few hours. This was always a part of their planning ritual. Roman laid out the basic idea. He also gave them a rough framework of how they could do it. The first iteration of their plans still had a lot of holes and was barely feasible, but provided a good enough foundation to build on.

After his initial plan was shared, they spent the next few hours contemplating. They were silent as they played many hands of no limit Texas Hold'em.

From time to time, Roman would catch himself studying Hope. Playing poker made it acceptable, but he couldn't help doing more than just looking for tells. She was wearing a simple black t-shirt with a plunging v-neck. Simple, yet she still radiated a sophistication that made his heartbeat hasten. When she had what she thought was a good hand, her left eyebrow peaked a millimeter and she bit her bottom lip.

Every time he caught himself, he shook the thoughts away. They had known each other since they were just kids, and Roman had always seen her as Burton's little sister. The one they protected from boys that weren't good enough for her. But for the last few years, he hadn't been able to help seeing her as the beautiful woman she had become. So different from the tomboy she'd been while growing up.

Thinking about her led to thoughts of why he never kept long relationships. All the relationships in his past were shallow, ending as quickly as they began. He would lose interest. Or he felt they couldn't be trusted with his secret life. Or they wanted more from him than he wanted to give. He had come to the conclusion long ago that he wasn't ready. He was still too young and too into himself. He couldn't risk being that way with her.

"So are you going to place your bet, or are we going to just sit here?" Burton interrupted his thoughts.

Roman shook the thoughts aside. "I will raise fifteen hundred." He stacked the chips next to the pot. It was three times Burton's bet and Hope's call.

Bryce instantly called, matching Roman's stack next to the pot.

Burton gave a firm look, and placed his chips in front of him with some hesitation. "Alright, Romie. I get the end game, but I'm just not following how we're going to do it."

It was now Hope's turn. She took a good peek at her pocket cards. Roman watched as her left brow peaked and her gray hazel eyes glistened. Her eyes met his and he couldn't get himself to look away. Her lips became a smile, and without breaking eye contact, she pushed her chips forward to call his bet.

Again, Burton broke the trance. "So the only way this will work is to erase all signs of the debt, or loans or whatever, right? Say Joe Schmo has five credit cards, all maxed out. Him, times hundreds of millions of people. How the hell are we going to get into each and every account?"

Roman waved his hand to end the round of betting and Bryce dealt the turn from his deck. A queen of hearts. He easily had a flush, but there was a possible full house out there.

Roman played the odds in his head. "Everyone's data follows the same path. Joe Schmo gets a credit card. That credit card company will send all his information - name, social security number, everything - either directly or through some data processor to a credit bureau. They will then add that information to a profile they already have on him. Every piece of data that has ever existed anywhere on Joe will end up this way. Every debt he ever had, every late payment, every address, his employment history. All of it."

Burton laid his pocket cards back down. Without a word, he slowly counted and stacked thirty two hundred dollars worth of chips next to the pot.

Hope watched as her brother took his time. "How many companies are there?"

"There's close to a hundred organizations worldwide that handle consumer credit information. They all work together, selling each other data."

"So we'll hit these companies? All of them?" asked Hope.

"That's the thing. We'll only need to get into three. Experfax, Equirian, and UnionTrans. The three largest worldwide. They either own, partner, or sell to every other company related to credit out there. The drive to collect data on every living soul has virtually networked the entire industry. They are the common links to just about everyone's data in the developed world.

"Reggie's theory is that if we can get into these three, his virus will spread to every organization that sends or receives data with them."

Hope called Burton's bet. "But these agencies only collect information. Even if we wipe everyone's credit report clean, the banks and other lenders will still have their own data, right?"

Reggie looked up from his laptop and leaned towards them. "The bugger won't stop with the reporting companies. They will act as patients zeros. Or patients zero, one, two. Anyway, the virus will spread to any system that is even remotely connected to these three. That means their partners, vendors, and anything that sends them data. Even their backup systems. I'm still figuring out how to infect every system, but it should work."

"So we don't even know if it's going to work?" asked Burton.

Reggie rubbed his temples. "Ag, man. It will work."

"But not yet."

Roman stacked his call. "He's never let us down before."

Burton nodded, but still looked troubled. "So how hard is it to get into these three?"

Bryce called to match the table's bet and dealt the river card to the community cards. It was a king of hearts. A royal flush for Roman. He held his smile inside.

Roman shook his head. "Very hard. Each have multiple data centers all over the world. Each are redundant and are protected from virtual and natural disasters. Their data is more valuable than gold and they protect it better than anyone. We have to find each of their weak points, and they're not going to have very many."

Burton pushed his pocket cards towards the center of the table to fold. "So what do we do when we get past these hypothetical weak points?"

Reggie stretched his arms out. "We implant the bugger. Once it's implanted, it will spread to every system it comes in contact with, bypassing any barriers because it's a trusted connection. It will keep spreading, but remain hidden until a certain time. Then it'll initiate all its commands at once."

Burton didn't seem convinced. "Sounds easy."

Hope looked deeply at Roman now. He could feel the heat of her eyes. It was as if she was seeing inside him. No one ever made him feel that same way. He could feel his cheeks getting warm.

Roman shook the thoughts aside, hoping that his head wasn't also physically moving. "It's not. But we'll have time to make it possible. There's no deadline, but the sooner the better. Technology moves fast. Once Reggie has figured out his thing, we'll have only a small unknown window of time before it's outdated."

"Are you sure?" asked Burton. "The last one took three months, and compared to this, it was cake."

"We had a looser timeline for that one. We'll have to focus on this one full-time if we're going to make it work. I can fund the planning to keep us afloat."

"We will all chip in to back this job." Hope firmed her lips, showing that it was a fight he shouldn't start.

"I agree. We all want to do this together." Burton paused, as if trying to picture buildings in front of him. "So we get into these three, implant the virus, and then what?"

"We let the world figure out a better system. There will be chaos when they can't decide what money is worth. The existing banks and the system they are built on will crumble, but another system will take their place. One that will hopefully be more fair."

"Is that even possible?" asked Burton.

Bryce gently folded, adding his cards to Burton's. He hadn't said a word in a long time. "We have to believe that given a choice, people will figure out a way to make things better, not worse. Right now, they have no choice. People deserve a choice."

The game was now a showdown between Roman and Hope. Hope laid down her king of diamonds and jack of spades. She did indeed have a full house.

Roman showed his royal flush. "We're about to give it to them."

15

STEEP sealed the cover of the plastic moving box with the evidence security tape, and signed and dated the label that made the seal official. It was the last box, and he placed it on the other two already stacked on their rollers. In total, his team had filled a dozen boxes.

He could only imagine how much more evidence they would have if they had been allowed to keep looking.

The evidence guys would archive everything in an off-site warehouse where cases went to die. Cases that were considered ongoing, but were really no longer being investigated. Steep could only guess why his case was joining them.

He looked out onto the crisis action team room, empty and dark. His entire team was back in their regular spaces.

Even if he had more time, Steep knew that finding these thieves was a long shot. But it vexed him to think he had been stonewalled. Cut off from even the possibility of finding these guys. He had tried his best to convince Pistone to let him keep working on the case, but after the first two tries, he knew it was impossible. His boss was getting an even stronger message on the other end.

What bothered Steep more was who had made the call to close the case. It was obvious that the old man from the meeting was the main factor. Senator Rich Manning of Maryland was a Democrat who had more corporate ties than the most conservative of Republicans.

A few online searches had revealed what kind of influence the man had. Manning was a self-proclaimed liberal, but voted for bank bailouts and corporate interests ninety percent of the time. He had record campaign fundings through super PACs and corporate relationships that were beyond questionable. He was as influential as he was influenced.

The more Steep learned, the more it bothered him. How could any one person so easily control the decisions of the Director of the FBI?

But even though he didn't like the idea, there was nothing more he could do. Steep had been around long enough to know that going after anyone with that much power never ended well for the accuser.

What he really wanted to understand was why Senator Manning would even care about a case like this. It was only a few million dollars. A substantial sum, but small compared to other high profile cases. He couldn't see it meaning much to the banks. It was probably pennies in their eyes.

The only reason he could think of was that they didn't want the media to catch it as a story. The case had been blacked out from reporters. Now that it had been placed under ongoing status, it would remain classified for good. If that was what the Senator wanted, it was exactly what he got.

The evidence collection guy, Mike, knocked on the open glass door. "Hiya, Tim. All good to go?"

Steep gave him a thumbs up. "I'm all done. Thanks, Mike. Let me know if I need to sign anything else. Take it away."

Mike and a few of his admins started with the stacks down in the team room. Steep slipped his sport coat on. He felt in this breast pocket to make sure the high capacity USB flash drive was there. It was filled with anything he could digitize about the case. He was breaking every rule in the book, but there was no way he was going to let this go. He would give it to Ivan to keep digging; maybe there was something they'd missed.

Steep didn't look back as the glass door slowly closed behind him.

16

THE mid-June sun in Texas was brutal. Its bright rays made walking over concrete feel like being in an oven. Roman was relieved to be back at the townhouse, with the air conditioning on full blast. He could feel the air pressure change as he walked through the front door. He walked the grocery bags directly to the kitchen to restock the fridge and replace the empty boxes of cereal. Reggie seemed to be able to go through several boxes daily.

They were renting a three bedroom townhouse in McKinney, Texas, just outside of Dallas. It had been an easy find on Craigslist. The owner didn't ask many questions and only required a first and last month's rent. They told the owner they were in town for a short-term business project, but he didn't seem to care. He was just glad there were tenants that could afford his high rent so that he could afford his absurd mortgage.

It was the perfect location. Close to the airport and even closer to their first target, Experfax. It was also an easy flight to the other cities they had in their plan. This had become their home away from home for the last four months, and would remain so until they accomplished what they had set out to do.

After Roman finished putting away the groceries, he filled a big bowl with Cheerios and milk. He walked it into the living room that was acting as their workroom. Instead of couches and a coffee table, there were folding tables and chairs they'd bought from Walmart. Instead of a TV, there were white boards filled with lists, steps, and schedules. An organized mess of floor plans and paperwork and small electronics filled the tables. Reggie was sitting in his gaming chair, staring at his array of monitors. He slept, ate and worked in the same chair around the clock.

"How is it going, Reggie?" Roman handed his friend the bowl of cereal. "Did you eat anything yet?"

"Not yet. Escaped my mind." Without turning his attention from the monitors, he accepted the bowl and began eating.

Roman scanned the screens, full of windowed boxes of color coded text. "What are you working on?"

Reggie wasted no time chewing and speaking separately. "The testing is broke, that's all." He said a few more words that Roman couldn't understand. Reggie was in troubleshooting mode, and there was no point in trying to have a conversation with him.

Roman turned to the fold-out tables on the other side of the room. He had to work through his own set of problems. Roman unrolled a few sets of large format paper. They were architectural and security plans for the UnionTrans data center, located in Chicago. It would be the last stage of the entire heist. At the moment, it felt so far away and unreachable.

As he looked over the intricate details of the center, his mind went through the specs. It was two hundred and fifty thousand square feet, covered with sixteen inch thick concrete walls that were kevlar lined and hurricane proof. The electricity, water, voice, and data were all redundant, and sourced from different areas of the city. It was just as modern and fortified as Experfax's data centers in McKinney.

He looked up at the white boards that sat behind the tables and framed the perimeter. There were hundreds of notes written in a rainbow of colors. There were short bulleted steps of the plan, notes with calculations, and pass codes with arrows going from one item to another. The master plan.

There were a lot of plan Bs: contingencies after contingencies that Roman had come up with. Every time Roman dived into a step, he came up with potential problems that could get them caught or found out. He had to be sure everyone had a way out. A way to escape. If they were caught, it would be no one's fault but his own.

There were three targets. First one would be Experfax here in McKinney, then Equirian in Atlanta, Georgia, and finally UnionTrans in Chicago, Illinois. They all had to be injected with Reggie's virus in the span of four days. From Reggie's calculations, they could get away with injecting the virus into only one of them. The virus would keep spreading from one system to another until it infected at least seventy percent of the debt records they needed to wipe. That would take a few weeks.

Roman thought that was too much of a compromise. Seventy percent left too many people in the cold.

With the same records in the other two companies, they would eventually figure out a way to restore most of the lost data some how. The slower the malware took to spread, the more likely that white hat hackers would be able to shut it down. Roman wanted more of a guarantee that at least ninety nine percent of every existing debt record would be erased.

No one should feel like his father did when he took his own life. Roman would not accept anything less.

So it would take them injecting the virus into all three for them to succeed. The virus would spread in a matter of days, and the entire digital debt complex would crumble. It would happen so quickly that their cyber security people would have no time to recover. No time to discover the exploits. No time to stop the Jubilee.

17

SENATOR Rich Manning stepped out of the government SUV. His two-man Secret Service detail remained in the vehicle as they were ordered. He would have to walk the rest of the way on his own. He walked through the dark and damp underground parking garage; the scraping and tapping of his shoes against the bare pavement echoed in his ears.

Part of him hated meetings like these. A man of his standing should not be summoned on a whim. Another part of him relished it. It was covert and pulled on his sense of adventure. And there was a power he enjoyed in being a part of something secret and sinister.

This bottommost section of the garage only had two other parked cars. One of them was his contact's, backed into a dimly lit corner. He walked up to the black BMW sedan and peeked through the passenger side window. Sitting in the driver's side was Chester Smith, the managing partner at TRM.

The meaning of the acronym wasn't advertised. Only a select few knew it was Threat Risk Management. 'Risk management' was an all-encompassing term. It covered everything from cyber security, intelligence gathering, to covert raids. TRM was able to carry out agendas the FBI and CIA only wished they could. Nothing TRM did was legal or sanctioned by any government. But most of their clients were part of every power structure that could protect them. They only worked directly with top leaders of corporations and government offices, like Manning. It made them untouchable. Manning didn't even know if they had a real office, other than the barren building in Virginia.

Chester motioned the Senator to come into the car. Manning held back his contempt as he opened the door and slid his large frame into the passenger seat. The black supple leather still had the new car smell.

"Senator," was the only greeting that Chester gave. He didn't even turn to look at Manning, as if he was higher on the food chain.

"Chesty," was Manning's usual response. He hoped that it would take the man down notch. But it didn't seem that it did. "What is the big emergency? I do not want to be called upon..."

"Do you remember the case you handed to us back in February?" Chester cut him off. The bastard. "The one where they emptied ATMs in Washington, Boston, and Manhattan?"

Manning considered punching him in the temple. Instead, he took a deep breath. TRM was one relationship he could not risk. Mid-term elections were coming up fast. And his off-shore retirement accounts needed to maintain the periodic deposits.

He took another moment to recall from his memory. "Do you mean the one from the FBI? I recall... vaguely. What about it?"

"It looks like they are planning another attack."

"So you found them? That's good news, right?"

Chester took a glance at Manning, but returned his gaze back out to the garage. "Not exactly. We created a profile of the hacker back in February. The profile is in our monitoring system and we just received an alert that there are traces of activity reappearing. Activity that could be related to the same hacker."

Impressive, thought Manning. He gave himself some credit for connecting himself to TRM. He didn't believe half the things he said in public, but it opened so many doors that would have remained closed. Now he was a powerful senator with more money and influence than he ever imagined. It was about making the right choices. TRM was a right choice, no matter how immoral it may seem to those that didn't know how to play the game.

Manning held his excitement, watching his reaction. "I thought it was impossible to find them. Covey said there was no trace of these fellows that they could use for the case."

"We have our ways," Chester said shortly. It didn't seem like he would say anything further.

That was not acceptable to Manning. "Care to elaborate?"

Chester scanned the garage with his eyes. His crew cut hair was completely gray, but he looked much younger than he should be. He looked like he still ran a marathon a week.

After a longer silence that Manning appreciated, Chester gave a short sigh. "We did a post-mortem of the files you gave us, as well as the ATSI system. We went back into their logs as far back as they'd started keeping them. With our forensic system, we came up with a few options of who could have created the back doors into their system. They used remote contractors. Some were questionable on their authenticity. There was one in particular that gave us a full dead end. He was completely anonymous, behind forged credentials."

Chester paused, as if wondering if he cared to continue. "We created a profile and inserted it into our monitoring system."

Manning had a sense of recall. He'd heard about this monitoring system. "It sucks in all the information from the Internet and spits out terrorists, right? One of my staffers sent me a news article about some speculation that we were funding it. I had a feeling it was your outfit."

"It flags potential threats. It perpetually monitors all web traffic going through every ISP. It alerts us when there's a match to any of the profiles in the monitoring system."

"What is the name of this system?"

"The Monitor," Chester replied, as if annoyed at even starting the conversation.

Manning could not care less about Chester's attitude. This could be his only opportunity to learn as much about this system as he could. It was like finding a speck of gold in the sand. "So you're monitoring all web traffic? Private data too? Who are these profiles on?" As he asked the questions, a brief fear that he was one of those profiles emerged.

"Suspected and known terrorists. Black hat and white hat hackers that we are aware of. Organized crime members. Anyone of interest."

"Political figures?"

"I can't go into any further detail, Senator."

That wasn't the answer Manning wanted. "Sounds like this should be under NSA."

"We have fewer limitations. That is why our clients come to us." Chester seemed much more agitated now. "Back to the issue at hand. We are seeing activity we believe is related to the same hacker that worked on the ATM job. We're not sure of the target, but there are searches on the dark web that are coming from some IP addresses we have in this hacker's profile. It's most likely a proxy or VPN, so we don't know the true IP or location. But it could mean he and his group are about to do something."

Manning didn't understand some of the terms Chester had just used. He didn't want to seem naive, so chose his words carefully. "What does this all mean? What do you need from me?"

"This crew of thieves may be related to other similar heists in the past, and they will only get better and more bold. Some of our clients, who I know are some of your donors, will want them stopped. When they reappear, we will have to take immediate action to take them out. We may need to use your influence with the FBI to do so. I wanted to give you fair warning so that you are prepared to act accordingly when the time comes. We may only get one chance."

The feeling of being powerful returned. "Of course, whatever you need."

Chester gave a nod of satisfaction. "Thank you, Senator. That is all. We'll be in touch."

"What the fuck?" Manning thought to himself. That was it? He had more questions. What actions would he have to take? What kind of hole was he digging himself into?

The flash of anger was cut short as Chester started his engine. Manning knew better than to bring up his contention. It would be sign of his weakness and lack of understanding. It was best to maintain his composure. Without a word, he opened the car door and stepped out. The prick didn't deserve a goodbye.

He walked to his waiting SUV and security detail. He fought the urge to look over his shoulder. He knew Chester would remain in the dark until the Secret Service left the garage.

18

HOPE stretched and rose up from her desk. The clock on the bottom of the computer screen read four fifty nine. That was good enough for her.

She couldn't wait to get out of the damn cubicle and escape the grind. She was glad to get away from the loud mouth next to her, who blabbed on the phone about nothing incessantly.

For the last month she had played the part of an executive assistant for the VP, Facilities Division of Experfax. It was a thankless job, but at least her boss traveled often enough that she didn't have to deal with him on a daily basis.

A large proportion of the company's workforce was outsourced through temp agencies. No health coverage, 401k, or any other benefits for that matter. Just another way for the company to cut costs. It was also an easier way for Hope to get the job. The temp agency that had set her up was easy to convince that she was the most qualified candidate. It also helped that Reggie made sure she was the only one that passed through the pre-screen software. Her background check was spotless.

The person that Hope replaced had been an assistant her entire career. From what Hope could tell, she was a very good one. She was only five years from retirement when she was let go. Hope was being paid a fraction of what the former assistant made. Seemed like a good deal for the VP.

And it would have been, if it wasn't for the real reason Hope was there. She looked forward to the day that they were going to destroy the company.

She was also looking forward to never coming back to the god-forsaken place. 'Corporate America' wasn't her thing. She'd done her undergrad in art history with a partial scholarship for gymnastics. Even with the scholarship, she'd taken on lot of debt that she couldn't pay for when she was done with college. After a year of looking for a job, she'd taken the first assistant job she could. And, after a year of being underpaid and seeing what work-life 'balance' was like, she decided to never work again.

She would join her brother and friends in what they were doing.

After all, it was exciting. It paid her bills. What else could she ask for? Sure, she had to do odd jobs here and there between scores as part of her cover, but for the most part, she was able to take control of her life.

There was only one thing that made this job tolerable: that she wasn't there for the job itself, but that it was all a part of their next score. It was a score with no monetary benefit. But a score that would be worth more than they could ever steal for themselves.

She imagined it helping millions of people to have a fresh start, or to even get ahead in life. The potential of helping so many people made it easier to deal with the office space zombies. The ones that constantly badgered her with requests for this or that. Setting up meetings, answering phone calls and emails. Looking for this report, making that report. Making a presentation that amounted to no real value.

A lot of those people would lose their jobs because of their plan. She thought about Roman's words: "For there to be winners, there will be losers." All of these employees contributed to the success of the company. A company that made money providing the service that they were about to destroy. Did it make them deserve what was about to happen?

Hope couldn't answer that question.

She walked through the cubicle farm and said good evening to the receptionist by the elevator. The ride down the elevator was like a decompression from a deep-sea dive.

At five PM in Texas this time of year, the sun rose high and bright. She walked towards the visitor's parking lot. She enjoyed the brightness and the heat. She imagined it was the heat bouncing from the sands of a beach. Radiant and rejuvenating.

A red Jeep drove up to the sidewalk beside her. Hope's heart fluttered for a second. She loved it when Roman picked her up from work. Usually it was Burton, but he had been traveling a lot lately, preparing for the score. She hoped he would be traveling a lot more.

She jumped into passenger seat. She greeted Roman kindly, but forced herself to look out the passenger side window. She tried her best to hide a slight smile on her lips.

"Turns out, Burton is still in Chicago. The set up is taking a little longer than expected, but he'll be back in a few days," Roman said as he pulled out of the company parking lot. The air flowed freely around her, blowing her long hair back. "How was work?"

"Boring as always. I did a good scan of the access card for the high security zones," she said proudly.

She held up the card scanner that Reggie gave her a week ago. She had been trying to skim the access card that her boss kept on him at all times. She was finally able to slip it from him when he was heading to a meeting.

When she finished the scan, she dropped it on the floor next to his desk. He would think that it simply snapped off his belt. She beamed from accomplishing one of their milestones. It meant they were that much closer to their score.

He looked at her with that smile that she couldn't get enough of.

"That's great, Hope! We're right on track with the timeline. We're getting really close."

She couldn't hide her smile this time.

"I think we figured out how to access Equirian, and Burton is finishing the set up in Chicago." He sped up along the on ramp and then merged with the traffic on 635. His tone changed and he gently grabbed her hand. "We're almost there. Thank you for this, really. I know you hate going to the office every day, but I just wanted you to know that I really appreciate it."

Hope could feel him almost pull away, but she tightened her hand around his. She wasn't sure what overcame her. She couldn't even imagine what she was doing.

"You know I'd do anything for you." The words left her lips just before she knew what she was saying.

Living in the same house with him for the last few months had been both a blessing and a slow torture. She would fall asleep every night, hoping he would appear at her door. And then she would wake up disappointed every morning.

She was excited to come home and see him every night. She imagined it was their life together. Sure, there was Reggie and

Burton. But in that house, it seemed normal. Natural.

There was a loud silence for the rest of the drive home. All Hope felt was the warmth of his hand, even with the Texas heat. She watched his face as he concentrated on the highway. The sunlight made his eyes shimmer. Before she realized it, they were parked in front of the townhouse.

Hesitating, Roman slipped his hand from hers and turned the ignition to the off position. He kept his eyes on the street in front of him, but she could see that he was looking at her with his peripheral.

She could sense his thoughts. Probing. Waiting. Wondering. She had known him for so many years, but felt like she was finally getting to know the side that she had always wanted to know. She reached up and brushed his forearm with her fingertips. She could feel her lips slowly part as she leaned forward.

As if in a dream their lips touched, and they held each other in a tight embrace.

They hit a speed bump that signaled they had entered the neighborhood.

Hope snapped awake. She must had fallen asleep from the ride home. She checked to make sure she wasn't drooling.

"Have a good nap?"

"Mmmm," she sounded with a sense of disappointment. She wanted to curl up and nap forever now.

"It won't be much longer that you'll need to work there. I promise we're getting close to figuring it all out." Roman pulled up to the curb in front of the townhouse.

"What's for dinner?" she managed to say as she weighed the option of jumping on him right then and there.

"I think I'll make spaghetti."

The image of Lady and the Tramp with a bowl of pasta shot across her mind, making her tensions release. "Sounds yummy."

As they walked up to the front door, she bumped him lightly with her hip. He stopped and brought his hands up into a Frankenstein pose as she skipped inside, not really wanting to run away.

19

THE branded network utility van sat parked in the middle of the intersection. They were halfway between Chicago and Aurora, Illinois. A yellow vent hose ran from the back of the van to the open manhole. Greg Gonzalez was perched between the open double doors, keeping a lookout.

Burton was inside the manhole. Cables went from one side of the shaft to the other, each were about an inch thick. There were dozens of them intertwined in an organized mess; optical fiber cables that were used to transmit data across long distances at high bandwidths.

Burton twisted and turned the large schematic in his hands. He was trying to orient himself and confirm that he was in the correct manhole and that he was looking at the correct cables.

The internet age had been thrown together in a hurry. Every new technology added layers of complexity on top of the last layer of complexity. The schematic reflected these layers in the most confusing way.

Greg rubbed the sweat from his forehead. "Are we at the right one?" he said into his in-ear mic.

"Yeah, I think it is. Reggie really needs to make these easier to follow."

"This is our last one, right?"

"Yes. I am so sick of cables."

They had been doing this all week. After finding the correct access point, they had to make sure there was no other maintenance scheduled. Then they had to disable any access security, like sensors for alarms. And when they were finally in front of the cables, they had to make sure they were at the correct set.

There were hundreds of cable lines routed through Illinois. Some were documented well; others were not. If they tracked the wrong line, the last part of the job would fail. That wasn't an option. Burton had to be sure that each one they set up was correct. He found the codes Reggie noted with tiny arrows marked in pencil. He made a mental note to strangle Reggie.

The shaft was dark and the only light was coming from the open manhole above and his small led headlamp. The space was dry, but the air had a moistness that implied it had been recently filled with water. As he pushed around the cables, the grime made it even more difficult to find what he was looking for.

He didn't mind these kinds of tasks. It reminded him of his deployment in Afghanistan, working in tight, dirty places. Marines were built for this: to carry out tasks normal people wouldn't do to achieve whatever mission that was given them.

He tried not to think of those times. The things he did.

He tensed his entire body for a few seconds, his eyes closed. It was as if he was bracing himself for the impact of his memories. Sometimes he couldn't stop the recollections from replaying on a loop through his mind. He had no choice but to let the memories come, incoherent and painful, leaving him as breathless as a punch to his side.

"You okay down there, boss?" Greg voice appeared in his head.

As immediate as the feelings had come, they left him. His mind was back in the shaft and his hands were holding onto cables. He let his body relax and he refocused on the numbers he was looking for. Each cable had numbers imprinted on the side all along its length.

"Yeah, doing fine. Just a mess down here." Just as he said that, he found the four cables he was looking for. He pulled on each to release them from the larger tangle.

"I found them. Placing devices now," he said to his lookout. This was when things could go very wrong and Greg would need to either save him… or disappear.

He opened the plastic briefcase he had next to him on the floor. He slowly took out what looked like a six inch long, two inch wide plastic bag of gray sand. The gray sand was a combination of iron oxide and aluminum powder. Better known as thermite.

He wrapped the plastic bag around the cable like a collar, securing it by wrapping the entire thing with black duct tape, only leaving a magnesium ribbon coming out of it.

He did the same with the other three cables. He then carefully connected each magnesium ribbon to screws on the outside of a waterproof box. This was the remote igniter. He trusted Reggie's build, but did this as slowly as possible. He turned the device on and sat it in the middle of the bundle of cable where the thermite collars were. If everything went well, the igniter would be destroyed as well.

He stood back and looked at his handiwork. Satisfied, he took the schematic and shoulder bag and ascended the manhole steps.

Joseph Preacher

He called up to Greg, "We're done here. Let's pack up and go."

20

NO challenge was too great for Reggie Dymond. That's what he always told himself. There was no way that the problem in front of him would get in the way of getting the job done.

He was smarter than the problem. More determined. Coding this ingenious piece of malware was difficult, but not impossible.

Roman had engineered a brilliant plan, and everyone was doing their part. His was to sit in his chair until his beast was unstoppable. If he could not, then the plan would have failed.

And if it failed, it would be his fault.

As a child, he'd lived in Lesotho, a small landlocked country in South Africa. There, he had lost his entire family in one day.

In the back of his mind, he could still see his father shot through the neck. His mother and sister were slain away from his view. But his father's last breath was only ten meters from him.

Hidden in the tall grass, he was frozen as he watched his father's eyes look at him and then go blank. He was sure he would be caught. But the attack on his village ended as soon as it began, and he watched his father's dead body dragged away.

He had remained hidden through the night, unable to move out of fear. Out of loss. That moment was impossible. Alone. Hungry. Afraid. When he felt it was finally okay to move, he walked aimlessly through his destroyed village. He found food that would have been considered foul any other day. He drank water from the well. He promised himself he would figure out how to make it.

He did make it. He walked to the only other village he had ever been to other than his own. It took him a day, with no food and only a little water. It had also been attacked, but there were still villagers there, with aid workers and help.

He had made it. He missed his family. He never stopped missing them. But he kept going because he knew his father would want him to.

Even though there were people in the village, he was still alone. So he decided to be alone somewhere else. He heard stories of a city, and all that you could do there. Ways to do better. So within a week, once he had collected enough food and water from the aid workers, he journeyed to Johannesburg.

He was only eleven, but somehow he found his way to the city. He was soon hungry again, but there were other children like him. At first, he followed them, doing what they did: begging tourists during the day and sleeping in abandoned shacks at night.

He couldn't remember how long he did this, but this went on for a while. Maybe months. Maybe a year. Eventually, he was caught stealing from a shop. It was one he stole fruit from often, but this time the policeman was near enough to catch him. Instead of jail, the policeman brought him to an orphanage.

There were a few hundred children there, but there was food and a bed for each of them. They even had a school there. Teachers told them that if they learned well, they could achieve anything. So he started learning.

He would learn everything they gave him and would try to find more to study. After a few years, his teachers realized he should go to a better school, so they enrolled him.

Learning separated him from his peers even more. He taught himself english, math, and geography. But his favorite lessons were computers.

They were old and donated models. But it was where he learned BASIC and C. He started learning on his own, to the point that he surpassed what his teachers could offer him. Somehow, he took his skills further, making websites and working as a remote contractor on small projects. He was close to living in the classroom where the only three computers in the orphanage were housed. He didn't make much money, but he gained so much in experience.

He learned all he could about America, and what he would have to do to survive there. He figured out what he needed to do to get into a college, and spent his adolescent years filling in the prerequisites.

While his peers were having fun and growing into the city around them, he stayed in the classroom alone, trying to grow into a country far away.

On his nineteenth birthday, he was accepted to NYU and used the money he made from contractor jobs to get himself to New York and survive. It was an impossible feat, but he achieved it.

At NYU, he met Bryce and Roman. They were wild and funny and treated him like they had been friends forever. They didn't mind that he was quiet and kept to himself. That he was different.

When they found out about his talent for hacking, they opened up his mind to what he could really do. It was a possibility other than making the next website or app. It was more exciting than the potential job opportunities he saw before him.

He wanted to live a life of excitement, using the ability he had. He'd never thought of alternate possibilities before he met them. With them, there were endless impossible moments that he was able to challenge himself with.

This was one of those moments. How to create the perfect malware package, using every technique he knew of - and some that were nothing but theories in the hacker community. It had to be like a worm that needed no assistance to propagate, breaking through all connections and finding its targets.

Roman and Reggie even came up with a name. Jubilee. The more Reggie learned about it, the more it made sense.

For months, he worked with other hackers in the Darknet. Some were skilled, most were not. But there was no way he could have done it on his own. So he split the project up into a hundred tiny components, and farmed the project out to anyone that was willing.

The great thing about hackers was that they were passionate about solving problems through code. So passionate that most of them worked on their components for free. Within just a few months, all the components were complete. He'd been spending every moment since stitching it all together.

He had the framework, and it worked to a certain degree, but it was still flawed. It still needed to be unstoppable. He was close, but not quite there.

He could feel beads of sweat on his forehead as he worked. They only had a few more days to work on Jubilee. A few to make her as good as possible. Everything else was set in motion and it was up to him to do his part.

He thought of how Roman had just lost his father. It was different, but in a small way the same as him losing his own father. From a gunshot or through pressure, it was painful either way. Even though his work would throw the economy in turmoil, it would help the people who needed it the most. Roman's logic was sound. The financial world would figure out a way to fix itself. Reggie wanted to do anything he could to help Roman. To help one of his only friends in the world. That alone was worth it.

21

IT had been a longer than usual flight, but one he didn't mind making. Bryce hadn't seen his friends in a month, and was looking forward to being back in Texas. Bryce had plenty of acquaintances and many people that he enjoyed seeing from time to time, but there were only four that he enjoyed seeing more than his own family.

As they were working on putting the plan together, Bryce had stayed mostly in New York, doing his part. Making sure that he was establishing clients that needed access to the credit reporting agencies. Ones with a lot of money that wanted to buy a large lot of preferred stock in each company.

As they were planning, he received coded emails, sent to an anonymous address that explained where they were with the plan. He knew little else.

He picked up the rental car, an Audi A4, and plugged in the address on its GPS. He had driven to the townhouse a few times, but he always seemed to get lost with all the highways and then residential roads.

Being away from the planning was unnerving. He would have flown out a lot more, but that could have raised some flags. Now that the plan was in motion, his assignment was to stay for two weeks to do business. He had some prominent rich clients that happened to live in Dallas and would visit here and there.

They were few and far between, and he would strategically cancel the appointments, but it gave him a reason to be away from New York. He needed to escape the hustle of the place anyhow.

He parked the car and walked up to the entrance with only his leather duffle bag over his shoulder. Before he reached the door, Roman was at the entrance and waiting to give his best friend a welcoming hug.

"Welcome back, buddy."

"Been way too long. Start up the grill," Bryce said as he left his bag by the door and headed towards the workroom.

"So… is the plan ready?" he asked.

"It is," grinned Roman.

Bryce gazed at the perimeter of white boards that documented and linked every possible detail of the plan. Steps, and all its contingencies linked together by strings of yarn. It was like watching the investigation of a serial killer unfolding on a crime drama TV show, but more in depth. Reggie was where he usually was, stationed in front of his array of computer monitors.

Bryce squeezed the shoulder of his other roommate. "What level are you at with WOW?"

"You know I've been over that for a year now," Reggie answered without turning around.

"Yes, but I miss your social graces during that time." Bryce smiled at the familiarity of his friend.

"Is your meeting still on for tomorrow?" Roman said, as he looked at a position on the whiteboard.

"Yep, right on time," Bryce responded, following Roman's eyes to where he was looking. There was a small post-it taped on the board, with details of his meeting with Experfax investor relations at 10 a.m.

The board didn't have an inch that wasn't filled with a note, photo, section of map or some drawing. Along the top was a timeline that scaled the course of the next two weeks across three full-sized boards. At each interval of time were the steps that needed to be carried out during that time, and who was to execute those steps. Other masking-taped strings of yarn linked some steps to the boards on adjacent sides of the room. These were the contingencies for what Roman thought could go wrong and their backup plans.

It was beyond impressive. Roman always planned like this, but this was the most intricate plan Bryce had ever seen him do.

"Thought everything through, as always," Bryce said as he followed his steps and contingencies. It was as if someone had opened Roman's brain and looked inside at every nook and cranny. He knew most of the steps, but now he was able to see the entire picture.

After looking at a few sections and trying to follow the strings, Bryce stepped back and said, "I need a drink. Scotch?"

"Sure," agreed Roman, leading Bryce to the kitchen. They poured themselves drinks and walked out the back door that opened up to a fenced in yard the size of the apartment in New York. They sat down on the cushioned patio chairs and lounged, taking in the late afternoon.

"Are we ready?" Bryce asked for the first time.

"We are as we'll ever be," Roman answered before taking a nice swallow.

Bryce considered his next question. He hadn't seen Roman in a few weeks and wasn't completely sure where his head was.

"Is… how are you handling… everything?" Bryce asked.

With a sigh, Roman nodded, "I think I'm dealing with… it. It was one thing to lose Mom, but now that they are both gone…" he paused, looking at the sky turn a darker orange against wisps of clouds as the sun set. "I just feel like I'm really on my own now. It made sense when she died. Health issues can't be helped. But my father? There's no way to bring him back." Roman took a larger than normal sip from his glass. "But maybe something good can come from it."

"That's not what I was talking about," Bryce looked at him in earnest. He studied his eyes, noticing the darkness under them.

"Have you been sleeping enough?"

"Enough. At least four or five a night," he said, keeping his eyes to the sky.

Bryce knew that it didn't necessarily mean all at once. That it was broken out into an hour at a time at most. Hope had called him a number of times the last few weeks, voicing her concern.

Bryce looked out at the sky in the same direction as his friend. The colors were getting deeper and looked surreal, as if photoshopped to perfection. "We need you to be healthy, man. We can't get through all this if you're not in prime fighting condition. I brought some sleeping pills, in case you need them."

"I'm fine. Really. I've just been thinking a lot. There's so many areas where we could get caught." Roman rubbed his forefinger on his right temple. "The plan is sound. Just need to figure out all the contingencies. Too much is at stake to fail."

"It's always that way, Roman. You've never lost sleep before."

"It's different now. This could help so many people. Relieve them of so much burden." He took another sip, leaning forward in his chair, holding the glass with both hands. "I just wish I would have thought of this before he died." Roman closed his eyes.

Bryce leaned forward and placed a hand on his friend's shoulder, "Don't think that way. There was no way you could have known. We're going to make this happen. But you need to rest."

Just as Roman was about to respond, Reggie burst out the back door and ran up to them. "She's working!"

Both Roman and Bryce rose to their feet.

Reggie didn't let them respond. "Jubilee is breaking through the test environments. She's at seventy-five percent success rate."

Bryce looked at Roman. "Is that a good thing?"

Roman smiled. "It's going to work. There's no such thing as one hundred percent."

Reggie couldn't help butting in, "Seventy-five percent that one instance of Jubilee will succeed in bypassing any barrier. That's why she multiplies. The more tries, the more chances. We just have to have enough chances for her to get through and infect behind the barrier. It was the biggest risk factor."

"And seventy is passing. That means it's a green light," Roman said as he tapped his glass against Bryce's.

22

ROMAN kept his nerves in check as he drove the utility van up to the security booth. They had wrapped the van with Dailmin branding. It was a commercial heating and cooling company that was well known enough to be overlooked.

This was the first time he had been this close to the building, and the schematics of the entire facility began flashing across his vision.

The guards were in the middle of their morning shift change, so this was the perfect time to come. The sun wasn't blistering hot yet and the air still had a bit of crispness to it.

He pulled up to the guard booth and stopped short of the security barrier that made it impossible for anyone unauthorized to enter. This was the vendor's entrance, and everyone needed to stop here and be cleared. The employee entrance was just ten feet away but had speed bumps that severely slowed the vehicles down to provide the guards enough time to get a good look of the drivers and passengers. Employees had an RFID tag attached to their windshields that allowed them easy passage.

As soon as the guard noticed Roman pull up, he nodded at his partner and walked up to Roman's driver side window. He was a stocky man in his late forties. Roman lowered his window to greet him.

"How is it going?" Roman said with a cheerful smile.

"Good. Good. Do you have a work order?" the guard answered with courtesy, but not quite as much cheer.

"I certainly do." Roman reached down and grabbed the paperwork he had ready on the passenger seat. He handed it to the guard.

"Is this the first time you've been here?"

"Yes. Yes it is," another smile for good measure.

"Can I get your ID please?" the guard said, still looking over the paperwork. He would be looking for the requester for the work order, which was Hope's boss, as well as date, work order tracking code, and vendor rep name, which was all standard procedure. Reggie had meticulously incorporated all of it into the forged paperwork. The same records would appear in the HVAC company's database if the guard happened to feel like calling and verifying it's authenticity.

"Certainly," Roman said as he handed the overly competent guard his forged driver's license and company ID.

"Give me a second. I just have to set you up in the system and I'll be right back," the guard nodded slightly.

Roman returned the nod with another smile as the guard turned and walked into his booth where his partner was waiting attentively.

There was no one behind Roman. There were only a few vendors that came to this facility each day and all were equally scrutinized. Roman knew this would make him stand out, even with all the correct paperwork and IDs in order.

Two long minutes later, the security barrier lowered slowly and allowed Roman to pass. He could have sworn that the guard was still looking at him suspiciously.

He drove through the windy driveway that was carefully landscaped to look like one were driving in a pristine countryside. It finally led him past a few employee parking structures and he turned into the open parking that was for vendors that had a perfect view of the front facade of the main facility.

It was all glass, and well architected. He parked in the closest spot he could find, not for convenience, but so he would have a shorter distance to run if things went wrong. He could feel himself holding his breath as he walked up to the building. Taking one last look in the reflective glass before entering, he examined his look to confirm it was believable.

He was in a forest green polo with the company's logo emblazoned on his upper left chest and black khakis. The typical look of a vendor. He also pulled a large four wheeled cart that contained cases with the tools he would need for this part of the job. It looked like HVAC tools, instruments, etc. It would also work for their alternate use.

23

ON the other side of the building, Bryce was already sitting in a conference room with fifteen of Experfax's employees, going through another presentation on the company's capabilities. This was the third and final day of these kinds of meetings and he was very relieved that it was almost over. He had been there since early morning and was already on his second cup of coffee.

He glanced down at his watch and noted that Roman should be at the reception desk just at that point.

"So as you can see, your investors should not be worried about the security at our data facilities," said the junior technology security person, whose name he didn't care to remember. "All our facilities employ the most sophisticated security measures physically as well as virtually. This campus is just an example. Our data is an asset and we have the utmost confidence in our ability to secure it."

He kept talking as he went from slide to slide. Bryce ignored most of it as he kept track of his watch and thought through the next steps of Roman's plan. He tuned his hearing for anything that came across his hidden earpiece as well. He didn't need to hear anything that the security executive had to say. Bryce and the rest of the crew knew more about the data facility than any of the employees in the building.

"We have redundancy measures for all our major systems. Electrical, water, sewage, air. They are routed throughout the campus utilizing multiple paths. If one path of any system becomes blocked, there are alternate ways for the system to maintain a connection.

"We also have the best CCTV on the market, with minimal blind spots inside and outside the building."

The moment of truth was about to come and he could feel himself getting anxious. He was ready to carry out his part of the plan. Nothing else mattered.

24

THE security check after the reception was as thorough as he'd expected. The staff was well trained and they acted as if they were guarding an embassy, not a typical corporate building. Hope was already waiting for him from behind the metal detectors.

Roman's wheeled cart did not fit into the x-ray machine, so an overzealous security guard spent fifteen minutes inspecting each separate metal tool case. It all looked like normal tools of an HVAC repair man; screwdrivers, drills, and some complicated testing equipment. As the security guard inspected, Roman and Hope stood on the side.

"So should this inspection take very long?" Hope asked Roman casually, as she did her best to focus on his eyes. It was the easiest thing to do to avoid glancing at the security guard.

"No, it should be all done today. We just have to inspect for any wear and tear on the systems. Replace any parts if needed. It may take longer if I have to order parts, but I should have everything I need right in there," he said, pointing at his open cases. He kept his eyes on the security guard. This was normal for anyone getting their bags inspected. He was also looking for any expression of suspicion on the guard's face.

"That's good to know. I really have a lot to get done this week. Not that I mind escorting you. It's a company policy that I have to while you're in the building."

"That's fine. That's standard in places like this." Roman caught a slight puzzled look on the guard's face as he held an electronic device in his hand. "Please, be careful with that, sir. It's a delicate device to test the air quality."

The guard nodded and respectfully placed it back in its compartment. "I'm all done here. You can go ahead and close this up and you're clear to go," the guard said as he straightened up from the case. "You folks have a good day."

You had to love southern hospitality.

Roman quickly adjusted a few items and latched the cases closed. "Lead the way, Miss," he said as he rolled the cart ahead of him. They were still on schedule.

25

BURTON came to the edge of the wooded area and crouched down next to the trunk of a small tree. It wasn't much of a cover, but the cameras' fields of view ended at the edge of the clearing and there was no clear view from the road on the other side of the building.

"Okay, I'm at Bravo 1," he whispered. The mic would easily pick up his voice, and he waited for a response.

"Lekker. Standby," Reggie's voice sounded in his ear. Reggie was in a van parked in the small office complex, about five hundred yards on the other side of the wooded area. He was already in the wireless security camera system and every other system that controlled the building.

There was no personnel at this site, so everything was remotely controlled and monitored. It was Reggie's favorite kind of system. If anyone could control it remotely, that meant it was something he could tap into.

"How are we on time?" Burton said impatiently. He was starting to feel the late morning heat, sweat building on his forehead. He had a black bandana and black baseball cap covering his face. He knew that it was just going to get hotter. Too bad they couldn't have done this job closer to the spring or fall.

"Hold your horses," Reggie's new favorite term. "I'll be done just now. These things are not quite so simple, you know?"

"Okay, well hurry up. I'm not in an air conditioned van," he said as he looked down at his watch. Roman and Hope should have cleared security by now and would be in the main HVAC room in a few minutes, if they were not there already.

26

HOPE pushed the code on the keypad. A green light lit instantly and the lock released on the door to the HVAC maintenance room. She held the door for Roman to go in first with the equipment. The room was a large section of the building about two floors high and just as wide. It was all bare concrete floors and walls.

The room was filled with pipes and galvanized steel ducting and machinery. The sound of the blowers could be heard past the ceiling that led to the roof. This was one of two maintenance rooms and Roman had decided that it was the closest one to their target.

"Halfway there," Hope said with a smile.

"Not to be negative, but it's more like a tenth of the way," Roman said, smiling back. He scanned the walls and corners and spotted the two security cameras in opposite corners as expected.

The cameras were advanced high-definition which could pan the room remotely and were hidden behind a dome. This model sensed heat and was able to follow heat signatures around the room automatically. It also worked on backup power and had a casing that made it difficult to get to the wires. Difficult, but not impossible. There were one hundred and twenty two of them deployed across the office campus, and half of them were in this building. They were all monitored in the security room cycling on multiple screens every thirty seconds. The guards monitoring them would be alert and knew what to look for.

Even with such competent surveillance, there was always a blind spot in any given room. Roman found the room's blind spot instantly. It was in between two large evaporator and condenser unit boxes in the center of the room. There was just enough space in between the metal structures for both Roman and Hope to hide behind as they got ready.

"Let's start there," he said as he started to unload his cart. He pulled out two large instrument boxes that looked high-tech and sensitive. He carried them to the safe area and placed them on the floor. They were about the size of small suitcases. He released the hidden latches that looked like switches and opened them up to reveal their disguises and small tools they would need.

Without a word, Hope casually walked over to the safe zone as if she was just observing what he was doing. As soon as she was clear of the cameras' views, she began unzipping her skirt and letting it fall along her legs. Roman knew this was part of the plan, but when he saw her start stripping, his heart began to race, and he was frozen in shock.

It was for only a second, and he hoped she didn't catch him looking. He quickly turned around and pulled what he needed from his case. He had always thought she was beautiful, but seeing her take off her clothes sparked something in his mind that completely distracted him. He knew she would be stripped down to her lingerie at this point, and then putting on the black neoprene body suit.

He shook his head as he refocused his attention on what he needed to do. There was no time to have those kinds of thoughts.

"I'll be ready in one," Hope said behind him.

"Great. That makes us ahead by five. That will give you more time to get to the next spot." Roman pulled out a small hip bag and head mask from Hope's case and looked back at her. She was just zipping the final inches of her bodysuit. It would keep the cameras from detecting her heat as well as protect her from the extreme cold or hot air that was traveling through the vents. It conformed to her figure perfectly, and Roman couldn't help absorbing the image.

She rolled her long hair into a loose bun and reached out her hand. He handed her the head mask.

He had to stay focused. The only way this would work would be if they stayed on track. The building was built like a Faraday cage, blocking any outside wireless signals. Nothing could come in or out of the outer walls. Even cell phones were prohibited from being used within the building. This was also keeping them from being able to communicate with each other. They had to trust that the others were getting their tasks accomplished on time. A perfect coordination. He had their lives depending on him. They had followed him into this risky scheme, and he had to make sure they would get out of it safely.

After handing Hope the hip bag, he hit the button on a small camera sized box he had in his other hand. It radiated a heat signature that would cause the cameras to follow him. It was equivalent to five human bodies, and the programming in the surveillance system required the cameras to pan in the direction of a cluster of people.

He walked with the device back to the equipment cart. He pushed the cart to the farthest wall opposite the room's door and placed the device on top of it. The cameras should have panned and locked in on the cart's position, but there was only one way to know. If it didn't work, security guards would start showing up.

"You're good to go," he said as he walked back to Hope.

Without a word, Hope climbed on top of the condenser unit and maneuvered up the room, using the pipes as if they were rungs on a ladder. She looked like a majestic shadow floating among all the fixtures. She stopped at a large duct with a square grate covering it. Within seconds, she had the grate removed and disappeared into the opening.

"Good luck," Roman whispered.

It was time for him to do his thing now. He went over to his open case in the safe zone and took off his shirt, and replaced it with a t-shirt with an Experfax logo on it. From what Hope said, most of the IT staff in this building wore this to feel like they were part of some innovative, Silicon Valley company. Within minutes, he pulled on a realistic gray haired wig. It had taken him weeks to figure out how to put it on correctly. It made him look at least fifteen years older. He completed the look with pair of thick black rimmed glasses and an over-the-shoulder messenger bag.

He took a second to look at himself in the mirror that was attached to the lid of the case. He looked like a completely different person, complete with matching ID hanging from a lanyard around his neck. He latched the case closed and headed towards the door, pulling out a flat circular device from his messenger bag. The weight of it could be heard as it attached itself to door with heavy magnets. From what Reggie had explained, it released the bolt of the door so that it would open without triggering the sensor that told the security system when it was open. Anyone monitoring the area wouldn't know that they had left the room.

He slowly cracked the door open and peeked down both directions of the long corridor to see if anyone was coming. The only things in the hallway he had to worry about were ceiling mounted cameras, which were exactly like the ones in the maintenance room.

They were now all at the point of no return. If he got caught outside of the HVAC room, he wouldn't be returning to it.

27

THE warmth was intensifying as Burton waited for what seemed like forever. It was only ten minutes from what his watch said.

"Okay. Security cameras and electric fences are down," Reggie said, breaking the silence in Burton's head.

Burton rushed forward, using his mental and muscle memory to move the plan forward. He released the twelve-inch bolt cutters from his small pack and held them tightly by the grips. As soon as he reached the fence, the bolt cutters made positive contact and he snipped each link in a straight line, starting from about four feet up from the ground. He could feel his hands begin to sweat from inside his gloves. Within a minute he was done cutting his last link. He pulled the two sides of the opening apart and crouched through the fence, being careful not to get caught in the sharp wire ends he just created.

"I'm in," was all he said as he broke into a sprint towards the large paved area of transformers.

There were ten transformer step-down units, each one as large as two cars stacked on each other, neatly placed in rows and columns on a large cement slab. This one substation directed the power from the main transmission lines, stepped down the voltage to usable levels and distributed it out to hundreds of households and businesses in the immediate area.

Burton only needed to find one.

"Remember to look for six zero five eight," Reggie added.

Burton didn't feel the need to respond. He already knew the layout of this utility station by heart. He had pictured it in his mind as he studied the technical drawings and had already envisioned the course he would take through the simple maze. He knew every position of every number and used them to guide him to his target. He slowed to a jog and then stopped in front of six zero five eight.

It was a large metal box about ten feet tall. It had a weather protected access panel on its front which was locked by two combination locks. That was one thing they hadn't been able to find out: what kind of locks these were and what were their combinations. There were small seal tags that marked when it was inspected last. Breaking these seals would indicate that the box had been tampered with. They also didn't know what kind of tags would be used for these seals.

"Do we have the right ones?" Reggie asked, reading Burton's mind.

"Not sure. I'm looking."

He removed his bag and dropped it on the ground in front of him. There were a dozen kinds of plastic tags that were used to provide the seal for all industries that everyone used. The ones this utility company used were generic and Burton looked through his bag of tags to find the right ones. He also had a large bag of opened and ready combination and keyed locks. He grabbed two that were close enough to the ones that were on the access panel.

"I got them," he said, placing the items next to the bag. Now that he was sure he had what he needed, he picked his bolt cutters back up, snapped at the locks and seals and let them drop to the ground.

"How does it look inside?" Reggie asked.

"As expected." Burton took a minute to study the inside of the panel. The circuitry was laid out on a simple schematic printed on a large sticker on the back of the access door. Each of these transformers were replaced when needed and, over the decades, each had been upgraded with a different build and internals. For this one, it was installed only a few years ago. Most likely made specially for its main customer, the Experfax data center.

It was a high capacity transformer with redundant fuses. He grabbed his smartphone, snapped a picture of the schematic and instantly sent it to Reggie. He could read schematics just fine, but they were short on time and he needed to be sure he was doing the right thing.

"Sent you the schematic."

"I got it," Reggie said. There was a brief pause as Reggie scanned through the design, "You're going to change fuse four and fuse eight. That should do what we need. " A pause, then Reggie added, "Change four first."

Burton looked inside the hole that exposed some of the insides of the transformer. The fuses were round ceramic and glass components that were about the size of his hand. There were ten of them and they were neatly numbered with stickers on the metal panel they were installed into.

Burton found four and eight. He looked back in his bag and found the fuses that looked like the ones he would replace. There were a few different options for these as well.

He placed them next to the bag with the other replacements, stood up and stretched.

"Okay, I'm set."

All he had to do now was wait.

28

HOPE focused on each stretch as she went forward.

"Left hand, right knee, right hand, left knee, fifty-six," she said inside her head. It was a pace that she used to track the time and distance she had gone. In the dark vent with nothing but a small blue LED light, her pace was necessary to know where she was in the large map in her head. Every turn reset the count.

Her years of gymnastics training conditioned her body and mind to be resilient. To power through the discomfort. To be disciplined and focused. Every movement mattered.

She was in the exhaust venting system, and the heat was starting to get to her. Each server generated more than a thousand BTU an hour. Thousands of servers were in the building, producing the same heat. The ducting that she was currently in was one of a dozen paths that the heat escaped through, exiting on the roof with the help of large venting fans.

With her suit, head mask, and goggles, she didn't feel the direct heat on her skin. But even after the face mask's breathing system cooled the air, each breath was still uncomfortably warm.

The ventilation didn't have much need for security measures. The ducting was not a comfortable way to sneak in and out of the building. It wasn't very large either. She felt like a worm squeezing through a tight fit tunnel. There were certain areas that had simple motion sensors that she disengaged using a magnetic device Reggie had come up with.

She loved doing this. The thrill of using her body and focus to accomplish something big. If her life was nothing but doing her day job, she would have most likely killed herself - or someone else - a long time ago. She couldn't imagine living a mundane life, day in and day out. Go to work. Go home. No excitement. No challenge. She couldn't ever do it.

Her focus helped her deal with the heat. Her body was tuned to crawl through these tight quarters for hours. She had been training for weeks in a plywood maze they had built out in the garage. It was built with the same general dimensions as the ducting and she almost felt more comfortable in here than she would have at her desk in the office. She could have done this for hours, if it wasn't for the oppressive taste of the heat in her mouth. Fortunately, she reached her destination in twelve minutes.

The end of the ducting opened up to a compartment that was four times wider than the ducting. It also housed the exhaust fan and maintenance access. She could feel the air rush from behind her as it entered the compartment, being pulled by the rotating blades of the fan. She bent at a right angle, so as to not touch the fan. One false move and she could lose her skin. The compartment housed the motor for the fan and next to it was a door that allowed access to maintain it. It was also her exit.

She shuffled to the door, maintaining her low crawling technique. The access door easily snapped open and she peaked outside in all directions. After making sure no one was around, she pulled the rest of her body out of the fan compartment.

There were cameras on the roof, but they were all pointed at the roof access door on the other side of the building and at the corners overlooking the outside perimeter. She was free and clear to walk around and do what she needed. The roof was filled with similar fan compartments. There were a dozen all together, either exhausting hot air or taking in fresh air. She reached inside her pack and pulled out a metal box that was painted off-white, similar to the paint on all the fan compartments. It wasn't an exact match, but it was a good enough camouflage.

She took a second to stretch out her body and looked around for the other compartment she was going to have to access. She found it in another cluster of fan compartments on the opposite side of the roof. The intake fans were separated from the exhaust fans.

She pulled out a compact bundle of thin cable from her hip bag and plugged it into the metal box. She held the box next to the access panel and it instantly attached itself to the aluminum outer wall. Reggie really loved using magnets. She replaced her mask and crawled through the access door, holding the other end of the self-unbundling wire. She smiled behind her mask as she felt the cool air from the fans. This would be a much more comfortable crawl.

29

EVEN though Roman was well-disguised, it was best to direct the cameras away from him, rather than to give the security staff a recording to look back and determine that he did not belong. To do this, Roman pointed another Reggie gadget that looked like a flashlight. It did not produce light, but directed a spot of heat against any surface. Just enough heat to trigger the security cameras' heat sensors and pan them away from him. He held it in his right hand at his waist, close to a normal walking position. He just hoped he wouldn't run across someone that would notice, because it would be hard to explain why he was holding a flashlight.

He had to focus on his task at hand. He timed his pace in line with where the others were. He had to be at the server door no sooner than when Hope reached her point B.

This gave him time to walk past his target door a few times to scan its corridors for other personnel that might access it. This also gave him time to worry.

Were their schematics and specs correct? Could Hope have gotten stuck at any point? If anything was off, she would be trapped. Could there be sensors they were not aware of? The stakes were high and the consequences were grave.

Burton and Reggie were a few miles away, breaking into a utility facility. If they were caught, they could be accused of terrorism. Bryce was at the highest risk of detection, having to be completely visible and on his own. If they saw through his charade, there would be no way for him to escape.

If Hope herself became lost, she would exit the closest vent and get to the nearest ladies room. There were five in the building, and she had placed a small sealed bag in each of their waste baskets. The bags contained a tightly packed pair of slacks, button down shirt, and slip on shoes. She kept her ID with her, so she could change quickly, and exit the building after pulling a fire alarm. The fire alarm was her signal for everyone to abort.

Roman's heart beat faster in anticipation of that signal.

30

HOPE kept going. She knew that every second past her mark would worry the rest of the crew. She held in one hand the diminishing bundle of cable, using the other hand to guide the cable as she lay it down next to her. If it so much as tangled slightly, she would have to crawl backwards through the vent somehow and start all over. The plan would be screwed.

Thankfully, that hadn't happened. She was nearing the end now, and she was on time. She could see the vent outlet leading to the room she needed to be in.

Hope looked through the grated cover of the vent outlet. She could make out the dimensions of a large room, dimly lit. The room was filled with server cabinets, perfectly organized in rows and columns. They were evenly spaced and gave off a slight hum.

She guessed she was about fifteen feet from the floor of the room. The vent had a perfect view of most of the room, but there was a blind spot just below the ducting. The room wouldn't have security cameras, so that was one less thing to worry about. Access to this room was limited to only a few individuals in the entire company, so cameras only monitored the access door.

After she was sure there wasn't anyone else in the room, she took a small tool out of her hip bag. It was a small, battery-powered ratchet that had a one eighty degree flex head adapter. It was the only way she could unbolt the fasteners from inside the ducting. She slowly worked each bolt, letting the magnetic attachment catch each one from falling to the ground.

After about two minutes, she was able to release the grate. She used some five-fifty cord to temporarily suspend it from the opening. Even though the air was as cool as the inside of a refrigerator, she could feel sweat building under her hood.

She took another deep breath and lunged forward, hands first. She had tied the cable end to her wrist so that she could use her hands freely.

As soon as her body was completely free from the ducting, her hands caught on a solid metal piping that was well-anchored to the ceiling. It gave only slightly to her weight as she secured her grip like it was a bar.

Hope swung back, hollowing her body. She straightened at the bottom of the swing and tapped hard as she went forward, letting go as she went horizontal into a perfect flyaway and tucked into a somersault. Time slowed as she rotated in the air. Feeling herself descend, she extended her arms in front of her. She flexed her knees and leaned forward, sticking the landing perfectly on top of the box. She brought her arms up in a perfect lunge. She imagined a crowd cheering at her performance as she gave herself a silent congratulations, even indulging herself with a tiny bow. That routine had to have been a ten across the board.

Refocusing, she knelt down on top of the box. She counted the server racks by row and column and confirmed that she landed on the exact box she needed. She untied the remaining cable from her wrist and let the rest of it uncoil.

Suspended in the air were large wire conduits of network cables and other wiring, being guided and dropped to each individual rack. She found the cable path that led to the rack she was on and gently pushed her own cable's length into the bundle. It was easily buried and hidden.

She ran this down the entire drop until she reached the end of her cable and was looking upside down into the open rack. There was no door to the front, exposing all its connections for easy access. She took a moment and studied the boxes that were neatly mounted in the rack. She was looking for a particular box that Reggie needed. There were a few possibilities as to what it would look like, and she had to be sure that she chose the correct one.

She recalled her lesson on geek gear from Reggie. There were routers, switches, and bridges. Reggie had told her to look for a thin box that had nothing but ports with network cables plugged into them. Most of the ports would be taken, but hopefully one would be available for her to plug into. She found the one she needed in the mid section of the rack. She stretched the rest of her wire out and saw that she had just enough left to reach it. She tucked the loose wire along the path of another cable that ran into the rack. There were velcro straps every few feet, and she took the time to undo them and add her cable to the bundle. Confident she had done a good job at camouflaging the cable, she found an empty port and plugged it in.

She was still upside down, holding her breath and waiting for any indication that it had worked. It would be lost time if they had to go into the contingency plan. And she did not even want to consider that route. After a moment, she caught sight of a small green LED blinking rapidly in the end of the cable. Reggie had said that was what she needed to see.

Part of her imagined alarms going off at a security desk at that very moment.

Reggie had assured them that this was the least secure spot in the building. That was why they chose this room. It was one of the normal network hubs in the building. It was less secure than the highly mission-critical hubs that handled the high valued and secure data. This one handled regular internet traffic, voice over IP, and other considered normal business functions that did not need a multitude of firewalls of protection. It was completely separate from the more secure area that they needed to get to eventually, but it was the only way of getting into the building.

A minute went by and nothing happened. She stood on top of the rack with her hands on her hips. She tapped in her ear on her earpiece, hoping it was turned on and everything was set correctly. She checked the small radio the size of a pager that the earpiece was wirelessly connected to.

Just when she was about to give up and have a fit, a small repeating beep became audible. She began to grin from ear to ear.

The indicating beep stopped and she could hear a voice come on, "Testing, testing. Black Cat, do you hear me? This is Dungeon Master, over." It was Reggie.

"Dungeon Master? Really," Hope rolled her eyes.

"I told him it was dumb," Burton said.

"It makes sense that I am the Dungeon Master. I have a complete view of the battlefield."

"Fine, Dungeon Master. Do we have everything we need?" Roman interrupted.

"Comm signals are strong. We are tapped into their security system. We have eyes in the building." Reggie said as Hope jumped up onto the pipe she'd used to descend.

"I'm making my way back to point A," she said as she climbed back into the ducting.

As she began her slow crawl, she could hear Roman's voice say, "Okay, we're on track. Let's move on to the next phase. Dungeon Master, what do you see?"

31

THE inside of the van began to light up with screens and indicator lights. Reggie felt as if he was coming into sunlight after being in the dark for too long.

Experfax was much more security-conscious than many other companies. The powered antenna and relay box that Hope had connected into their network was the only way to get any kind of signal in and out of the building. There were even wireless signal sniffers that would have set off alarms if they'd used unmasked comms.

Now that they were connected to the company's network, he was able to hide their communications. He was also in their security system. It took him a few more minutes than he expected, but he was able to find a backdoor through the very system that was there to detect him. He was able to see and control every camera on the campus. It was go-time.

The AC was blowing cool air using the auxiliary battery to keep all the electronics at a cooler temperature and even though the inside of the van was cool, Reggie could feel the sweat building on his forehead as he feverishly typed commands in the terminal window. He studied the network structure and found the individual servers he needed to get into. He wouldn't be able to do much until Roman accomplished his task, but he had to be ready.

He looked over at the monitors that showed him the security system view. In front of him were the same screens that the security staff would be monitoring. There were no alarms or caution messages.

"Everything looks green," Reggie said, with a slight nervousness.

"Okay, Dungeon Master. Mark the time. Everyone, be ready to set," Roman said over the communication system.

Reggie looked at the red digital clock display set in the center of his screen array. Once he started the clock, everything had to go at a specific moment. Everyone knew their cues based on the master time.

He hovered his finger over the start button, "Marking time in three, two, one, mark." He pushed the button and the clock's millisecond position came to life, followed by the seconds. There was no turning back.

32

BURTON looked up from his watch after starting his timer. He had been waiting for what felt like hours. Now he sprang into action like a released coil.

The Texas heat was getting uncomfortable and it was amplified by all the metal and cement he was surrounded by. He looked in the opening of the transformer and, with his right hand, held onto the fuse marked four. In the other hand, he had their version of the fuse. He took a breath and twisted the fuse free. In a smooth motion, he replaced it with their fuse and twisted it in the locked position. After dropping the original fuse into his bag, he picked up the other fuse and did the same for fuse eight.

Just as he locked fuse eight into position, Reggie's voice alerted him, "There's someone walking around back there."

Burton crouched down instantly, trying not to curse out loud. In a whisper, he said, "Can you be more specific?"

After a second, Reggie said, "He just came out through the back door of the building. He must be a maintenance guy. He's not walking in a hurry or anything."

"Where is he exactly?" Burton said under his breath as he started closing the access panel.

"He's in charlie five," Reggie replied. When planning things like this, they applied a simple grid to every location. That way, they could always relay a location on the spot. Burton pictured the worker in the grid. He was just outside the maze of transformers. He wouldn't be able to see Burton or hear him. The problem would be that Burton had to pass him to get to the fence opening.

As Burton was thinking of a way out, he remained calm and went through the steps he had practiced a hundred times. He closed the access panel. He placed the locks he had ready into their new homes and secured them. He snapped the inspection seals in their place.

"Where is he now?" Burton asked under his breath as he secured his backpack on his shoulders. He pulled the shoulder straps tighter and snapped the hip support around his waist. He was most likely going to have to sprint it.

"He's still in the same spot. He must be taking a smoke break." Reggie responded.

Burton wiped a stream of sweat from his forehead. At least the guy wasn't roaming around. "I need a distraction."

"Already on it." Reggie shot back instantly.

Burton made his way back through the maze, being careful to back track exactly. The worst thing he could do was make a wrong turn and lose his way. He made it to the last transformer, where he would make his exit.

Burton crouched low, leaning against the warm metal. He was only ten feet from where the utility worker was standing, but was still well hidden as long as he didn't move any further.

"I'm waiting."

"Almost got it," Reggie snapped. Burton knew that Reggie was working as fast as he could, but he couldn't help pushing the guy. "Ready for your distraction in three, two, one."

Just as Reggie said one, Burton heard a sound coming from inside the building. As it repeated, he realized it was an alarm. A burglar alarm.

Burton coiled his body, hands in the launch position on the ground like a sprinter. He could hear the rapid rustling of gravel under the worker's feet as he scrambled back to the building. Burton waited for Reggie again, being sure to resist the urge to start running for the fence. Burton trusted Reggie with his life. He would tell him when it was time to go.

"He's almost there. Almost," Reggie paused for a second that felt like an eternity. "He's back in the building. You are clear."

Burton launched at the word "clear" and sprinted towards the cut in the fence. He had less time to get out of there and cover their tracks now that the staff would be forced to sweep the area for any issues.

He maneuvered his way through the cut opening. Once on the other side, he pulled out a hog-ring stapler that wrapped small pieces of wire to sew the cut sides together. It would hide the fence opening from a distance, and if someone did notice it, it could pass for a deliberate repair of a fence. Binding the last link, he took a quick look around to see if anyone was watching him. He was still clear. He turned towards the van and ran through the wooded area.

33

ROMAN walked towards the same door he had passed five times earlier. Using the heat device, he had been able to avoid the cameras, but he was ready to move on. He placed the electronic card that they had encoded with Hope's boss's credentials. After taking a moment to register, the box above lit green, indicating that a biometric handprint was needed to approve the credential.

Roman pulled a thin case from his messenger bag and opened it to reveal what looked like a surgical glove. Reggie had infused a handprint into the glove. Hope had been collecting it piecemeal from the boss's coffee cups for months.

This was a one shot deal. If the print worked, he would be able to get into the room and they would be closer to their goal. If it didn't work, alarms would go off and he would be greeted by the building's security.

He slipped the glove on, making certain that it was snug and didn't have any folds in the plastic. He held his breath and placed his hand on the biometric sensor. A second went by. Then another.

He imagined the security room filled with armed staff. The alarm going off, but only for them. They would rush to their armory and grab weapons and gear that could take down an army. Their security protocol was to treat any breach as a high-level one. And there was no way out of this hallway. No contingencies.

He could hear Reggie and Burton taking care of the fuses at the utility station. He could hear Burton getting trapped unexpectedly. He would be able to get out, Roman knew. Reggie just needed to provide a distraction.

Another few seconds went by. The small display over the biometric continued to blink, "Scanning, scanning." No matter how fast technology was, it could never be fast enough. He held his hand still and listened for any signal from Reggie that there was trouble.

If Roman was caught, at least he knew the others would be able to get away. Hope was most likely half way back to the HVAC room. Bryce would just ask to be excused and leave the building. As long as Roman was the only one caught, he could live with that.

He would go to prison for a decade or two. But at least his friends would be okay.

It had already been forty-five seconds and the display kept blinking, "Scanning."

Just as Roman was about to give up and make a run for it, the display read, "Accepted."

A heavy magnetic bolt could be heard releasing. Roman let his gloved hand down and opened the door to the central server routing room.

"I'm in," he said, just loud enough for the others to hear.

34

BRYCE sighed with relief as he heard Roman's words in his ears. He had been holding his breath off and on, waiting to hear Roman's statement of success. It was his signal to get out of this grueling meeting.

He had tuned out the presenter as soon as their comms were online.

He felt his watch vibrate, a silent indication that is was time for him to make his move. He looked up at the presenter and assessed where he was in his dry, pointless PowerPoint. Everyone else in the room was ignoring the guy as much as he was. All of their laptops were open on the round conference table and their focus was obviously on other business.

He pointed a question to the head of Technology Resources department, Director Jim Thomas. "Jim. I don't mean to interrupt. Great presentation by the way. This is a lot of information to take in. Could I get a copy to review in-depth later?"

Jim, slightly startled, looked up from his laptop screen. He was in his fifties, and looked to be a man that knew everything there was about networks and systems. He pushed his gold rimmed glasses up the bridge of his nose to adjust his sight. "Certainly. That shouldn't be a problem. We may have over-prepared the information for you. Tom," he looked at the presenter, "I think this is a good point to stop at. Could you bundle it up and have it emailed to Bryce when we are done here?"

Tom nodded, looking slightly peeved.

Bryce smiled slightly, "Great. Thank you. Looking at the schedule, we are going to cover the capital improvements to the existing network assets?"

The director nodded.

"Before we go over the proposals and the investment needed for those, I believe the investors would like my report of the current state of the existing assets. I know this is a bit unorthodox, but it might help me to see this physically. With my own eyes? Is any of it in the building?"

The director cleared his throat. He brought his fingers to his lips and thought intently of his options, looking thoughtfully around the room. "Raj, we can let him see section eighteen, can't we? He should be cleared for that area." He pointed the question to a younger Indian man.

Raj looked up from his laptop, blinking rapidly, "That should be fine. That will certainly be a good example."

Jim looked back at Bryce, "Okay then. Why don't we take this opportunity to walk around a bit. We'll show you our older systems. You'll see why we need to greatly invest in an update. It's in the next building, but it shouldn't be a long walk. Does that sound good?"

Bryce smiled wider and said, "That's perfect. Can I leave my laptop and briefcase in here?"

"Definitely. I'm leaving mine as well. The room is secured with a code, so things will be safe in here. Tom, please turn on the lights."

They all stood up from their seats. Bryce's play was working out exactly as planned. He looked around the room again and reviewed where everyone was sitting. He casually stretched. It felt like he had been sitting in the chair for hours. As they made their way towards the conference room doors, he took an assessment of who had left their laptops.

35

BRYCE walked next to Jim as they headed down a long corridor. As they walked, Jim shared which companies he'd worked with before and how he came to be a part of Experfax. It was through a merger and he was valued enough to be kept after the restructuring. He had been with the company for twenty two years and had seen it grow from a single server room to the international network of warehouses of servers it had become.

As Bryce listened to him, he was also listening to Reggie's progress. He also wondered if he should feel sorry for what he was about to do to Jim's long career. He was about to do something that would force this old man into early retirement.

What they were about to do could make this company nonexistent. The company, as a whole, was the reason the credit environment was the way it was. It helped some but subject so many more to a life of destitution. The individuals that worked for Experfax weren't bad people. Not all of them. They each just did their jobs and collected their salaries for the work they did. They would suffer for what his crew was about to accomplish. Should he feel bad?

Possibly, but the thousands of employees did not compare to the millions of people they were about to release from the invisible hand of oppression.

Just as they turned the corner to exit the building, he could hear a number of their cell phones go off. Some were silent, but a few sounded an alert that signified more of an emergency than a normal phone call.

One of the men tapped the director on the shoulder. "Sir... You might want to see this," the man said as he handed Jim his phone.

The entire group of men and women stopped in the middle of the hallway behind their boss. "What can be so important that I have to look right now?" Jim said as he raised his gold rimmed glasses and held the phone at a better distance for his eyes. After a few seconds of reading, a grim look flashed across his face. "How can this be? Is this confirmed?" His voice became deep with concern as he looked at all his reports' faces.

"It's in sector twenty five in the east building. It's happening right now, and I cannot seem to access it remotely," Raj said without looking up from his smartphone. He was feverishly tapping away at the screen.

The director looked up at Bryce. He was doing his best to put on a calm facade. "How bad is it?" he asked under his breath.

"Potentially... very bad. We should go there right away," replied Raj.

Jim closed his eyes for a moment and when he opened them again, he projected only control and order. "Bryce, I do apologize, but we are going to have to take a longer break before the next session. We have to address," he paused to think of the correct term, "an immediate issue. Should take no more than an hour or so. The team here will need to head there directly."

Bryce nodded, giving his best look of curiosity. "I wouldn't mind coming along. It will give me a chance to see your team in action."

The director let out a nervous laugh. "No, no. No need to come along. It's a high-security area. Would you mind waiting in the conference room? There's plenty of food and beverages set up. Here is the conference room door code. Do you know your way back?"

"It should be easy enough," Bryce said, taking the piece of notebook paper Jim scribbled the code onto. "I'll take advantage of the time and get some work done."

"Good man." Without another word the director turned, speed walking out the door. His team followed him closely, all while focused completely on their smartphone screens.

Bryce turned in the opposite direction, back towards the conference room. He unsuccessfully held back a smile.

"You should see their faces, Darth Vader."

"It's Dungeon Master. And they should be very freaked out. That is the appropriate reaction to what I just presented them with."

Reggie had routed his way into their enterprise website. It was the main gateway through which Experfax's clients accessed its services. Reggie had set up more than a hundred thousand robot drone computers all over the world the last few months. These were unsuspecting personal and corporate computers that could do whatever Reggie wanted at the drop of a keystroke.

The owners of these computers would never be aware of what he was doing, since it was all being done in the background. His command was for them to all access the Experfax's enterprise gateway at once, forcing it into a Denial-of-Service. It was a common enough hacker attack, but one that was effective at keeping networking security people busy. Busy enough to be distracted as they carried out the real attack.

Bryce walked back to the conference room, pacing himself carefully. He tapped the code onto the pad and the door unlocked. There was no one else in the room but him. All of the team's things were as they had left them, including their laptops. Bryce looked around and placed faces with names and job functions to each laptop.

"Okay, Dungeon Master. Which laptop do you want first?" Bryce asked as he reached into his laptop bag and pulled out three things that looked like USB flash drives. He placed them next to his open laptop.

"I'll need the network hardware guy's first?" Reggie said.

Bryce took one of the devices and walked it over to the seat of Jason Belkson, the company's network hardware engineer. He opened Jason's laptop and plugged the device in the USB slot. "Placed device one into Jason Belkson's computer."

"Got it. Now I need the head software engineer."

Bryce grabbed another device, noticing that his laptop screen was full of activity. Reggie was remotely in it and working so fast that it looked like the computer was possessed with opening and closing windows and scrolling type. He walked over to Raj's laptop and did the same. "Placed device two into Raj Batool."

"Got it. Last one I will need is the director's."

Bryce had remembered this one and was already in the middle of plugging in the last device. "Placed device three into Jim Thomas."

"Got it."

36

BURTON drove five miles above the speed limit, which was still much slower than all the cars that passed him on the main highway towards the Experfax building. There was no way he could risk getting pulled over right now. Even at this pace, they would get to their target position before they needed to.

Behind him, Reggie was typing on his keyboard with intent.

"Okay Goblin, just standby for a moment as I do my work." Reggie said as his eyes bounced from screen to screen and his hands tapped feverishly on his keyboard.

"Did you just give me the name... Goblin?" Bryce responded.

"Do you not like it?"

"I'm not sure if I should feel insulted."

"It's a compliment. Goblins are thieves. Thieves are boppin brah," Reggie said as the van made a lane change and he nearly fell out of his workstation chair. He repositioned himself and tightened the chair's seat belt.

He was buckled in tight and seemed to not even notice that he was in the back of a van. All he saw were the screens into the laptops and systems he was now in control of. He had less than five minutes to complete what he had been working on for months. Roman was in position and the window of time was small where he could remain. It was all up to him.

He could feel the tension building in his shoulder and neck muscles as he tensed up. His brain was going into overdrive and being pushed to the limit.

He was sending commands to a hundred thousand computer drones to continue the distraction attack of Experfax's enterprise system. He needed the network security team to be occupied with a serious issue. One that was trivial, of course, in comparison to what they were really doing. The system engineers were unusually competent and starting to subvert his drones, but he continued to send denial-of-service attacks, which was working for the time being.

He was simultaneously hacking into the three computers that would provide the access he needed to get them to the next stage. He had been able to break the encryption and log into the three computers Bryce had chosen. He exploited the company's password and two-step verification systems. He could access anyone's computer on the entire network as long as he had physical access to them. Bryce had completed that connection with the specifically designed USB drives. Through the dome antennae on the roof of the van, they had a direct connection to the communication unit Hope installed on the roof, via a hijacked satellite signal. This allowed him to be seamlessly connected to Bryce's laptop.

Reggie enjoyed the complicated nature of his solutions, but he had to admit that it wasn't his intelligence alone that had gotten him to this point. It required the whole crew; all five of them, to make his solutions viable. Most hackers and hactivists that he came across in the dark web were of a single minded sort, focused on the technology alone and what could be done through the wire. There were a few other contributors who focused on media attention and organizing, but it was the rare group that combined those skills with physical thievery.

Companies, after years of high profile hacks, were getting better at subverting attacks by remote hackers from around the world. And they also had many defenses that protected them physically. There was an opportunity to attack using both methods at the same time.

Now that he had complete control of the network's lead hardware engineer, lead software engineer, and lead network administrator, he knew where every network component was physically, what applications were on them and he had full administrative rights to access them.

Reggie searched all three computers and the network drives they had access to. All the pieces he needed were there.

"How are we doing, Dungeon Master?" Roman asked over the comm.

Reggie looked up at the digital clock in the middle of the array of screens. Its milliseconds were racing, like his brain. Below was a smaller display counting down, with fifteen seconds left, and counting.

"On track. Going dark in ten, nine," Reggie continued with the countdown.

He flashed his eyes across the screen, reviewing all the windows within windows. This was the moment of reckoning. He was ready.

"Power shutting down in three... two... one." Just as he finished saying one, he could see the screens showing the security cameras go dark. "Confirmed, power is down in the building."

"Confirmed. Ready when you are, Dungeon Master," Roman

said, with a tone of excitement that resonated through all of their ears.

37

ROMAN'S headlamp was one of the very few sources of light in the small server room. The fuses that Burton had set up in the transformer were set to break at a certain time, like a time bomb. It had worked as planned, cutting off power to the Experfax building they were in. The vital servers and control units were plugged into Uninterrupted Power Supply backup battery systems that kept them from shutting down, but other non-priority systems such as security, lights, and secondary servers were allowed to be without power.

There was a redundant power source that fed into the building, but the system took five minutes to switch over. That gave the crew only five minutes to accomplish what they had set out to do.

Roman looked at the server in front of him. It was the main software repository. This one rack of servers housed all the programs that would be duplicated and supplied to all other systems. It was protected from other systems and most outside connections. New software, software updates, and maintenance protocols were set up in these servers to be shared and distributed systematically to the entire company network. It was constantly processing distribution jobs from teams around the world, providing bug fixes and system upgrades to different software.

Everything else in the room wouldn't need to be on during a power outage since nothing provided operational support. There would be a stand alone UPS set up to keep what he was looking for powered on.

"Okay, I found the Mother," Roman said, referring to the server that controlled the repository. It was the only system in the room that still had indicator lights lit up.

"Okay, find network plug five." Reggie said in a rush.

Roman looked at the numerous network cables that were plugged directly into the server box. He recalled Reggie's short lesson on what plug was what on this system. "Found it," he said, placing his index finger on the spot.

"Go ahead and unplug it, but don't lose track of it in the mix. Plug in the laptop."

Roman already had the ten-inch-screen laptop ready next to him. He took the long network cable he had plugged into it and took the other end and plugged it into the empty socket. The laptop screen came to life with the buzzing handiwork and flying code signatures of Reggie's keyboard.

"Okay, I'm in!" Reggie sounded thrilled.

Roman was more nervous than anything. Everything was going as planned. That was supposed to be a good thing. His paranoid nature made him think of the twenty steps ahead of them. Once this was done, they would have to get out of there fairly quickly.

Right now, his friends were all on the line. Bryce was in a conference room, plugged into company computers. If anyone entered the room, it was over for him. He would easily be convicted of corporate espionage. Hope was crawling around the vents in the building, and if the wrong person was in the wrong place and heard her, she would be done for as well. Reggie and Burton were in a van that looked like a news van, but if the wrong police officer stopped them or questioned what they were doing, it would be hard for them to talk their way out of that one.

So many things could go wrong, and he had placed them all in those positions. They were playing a high stakes game for something that might not work.

"Be ready, White Knight. When I give the word, unplug the laptop and you're going to plug it into the slave," Roman recalled what the slave was and found where he would need to plug in.

"In three, two, one. Now," Reggie called out.

Roman pulled the plug out and seated in into the slave. "Done, Dungeon Master," Roman said. He could almost hear the smile over the air.

"Got it. I've implanted Jubilee into the Mother. She will distribute once power is on." Reggie paused to finish what he was doing. "I placed a log file in the slave that makes it look like a bug fix from one of their developers."

"Black Cat, how are you doing?" Roman said referring to Hope by her moniker. Images of her in her tight black outfit flashed across his mind and he hesitated, considering to simply enjoy the image versus not getting distracted.

"Almost back."

"Good, I'll meet you there. How is the drive, De Santa?" Roman didn't understand why Burton was given this moniker, but used it anyway.

"Will be in place in five," Burton responded.

"How are you doing, Goblin?" Roman asked.

"Other than being in the dark with nothing but the glow of these four laptops? Good to go," Bryce responded.

"Okay, everyone. We're not done yet, so stay alert." Roman applied the caution as he always did. This was not the time to relax. They were close to being done, but until they were on the airplane, there was still a chance they could get caught.

"You're free to unplug and get out of there in three, two, one. Now." Reggie relayed.

Roman unplugged the cable and tossed it and the laptop into his messenger bag. Without any hesitation, he slung it over his shoulder and walked out of the room. The hallway's lights flickered on as the power came back in the building.

38

ROMAN slipped into the HVAC room just as Hope finished fixing her hair.

"We're almost home free," Roman said as he pulled the wig off his head.

"Don't you mean, two-fifths of the way there?" Hope said with a smile. She looked at herself in the mirror as she adjusted her skirt.

Roman fought the urge to be distracted by the details of Hope's quick-change operation, focusing in on the next step in the plan. He moved towards his already opened case of clothes and began changing back into his vendor's uniform. "Dungeon Master. We are going with the first exit. Are we clear?"

"Looking now." Reggie's voice returned. Even though it was only in his ear, Roman was relieved to hear another voice breaking the silence. After tucking in his shirt, he gathered everything that was loose and threw it into the case. Hope was already placing her small travel case into his larger bag of tools and discarded clothing.

"All views show we are in the clear. Goblin, stand ready. The enemy is coming back to the conference room," Reggie directed to Bryce.

* * *

Just as the conference room door opened, Bryce lowered himself back into his seat. Seconds before, he'd been pulling the USB devices out of the three laptops they were controlling and placing each to sleep. He made sure they were in the exact state and position they were in before he had touched them. One had the monitor open, where another laptop was closed halfway. There was no room to miss any detail, no matter how small.

He looked intently into the screen of his own open laptop as if he was concentrating on something important. The director walked in followed by the rest of his team. They looked beaten and subdued, as if they had come from the battlefields of some great battle. It was clear they were not victorious.

"I was starting to get worried about you," Bryce said to the director, Jim.

Jim rubbed his palm against his own shoulder, trying to relieve a tense muscle. "I do apologize for making you wait so long, Bryce. We were caught up," he paused, choosing his words carefully, "solving an issue that needed our immediate attention." He took his massaging hand and rubbed his forehead, wiping away some sweat.

"I see. Anything I need to be concerned about?" Bryce raised an eyebrow. "Rather, anything my investors should be concerned about?"

The director did his best, unsuccessfully, to hide his nervousness. He showed his palms and smiled, "No, no, no. Nothing that is out of the ordinary on a typical day here. The normal troubles of a high-security business like ours. I assure you."

Bryce paused for effect and stood up from his seat. The director backed up defensively as if he was about to get smacked in the face. "Well, in that case, we can end the meeting here. I think you've covered all the important points. I know what I need to know. Why don't you have the rest of the PowerPoints emailed to me, and we can go over any questions I have through email or conference call next week?"

The director looked relieved and held out his hand, "That sounds like a good plan. If you are sure you have all you need, then I'm fine with calling it a day. Reach out any time if you have any questions, Bryce."

Bryce shook his hand, noticing that it was warm and slightly moist. "Will do. So how do I get out of here?"

He would be escorted out of the corporate headquarters before anyone was the wiser that they'd just been robbed of the most precious thing they kept within their walls.

39

IT was a good workout, but Steep could have pushed a lot harder. He wasn't in the worst shape. But he remembered when he could run twenty or more miles a week. Now he struggled maxing out the FBI PFT for his age group. How had age finally caught up to him?

The office was nearly empty. Most of his team was out at lunch or in the field. Ivan was in his cubicle in the far corner.

Steep opened his blinds, a signal he had made a habit over the years. It let his team know that he was in the office and available. If the blinds were open, any one of them could feel free to barge in whenever they needed something.

Before he turned around to his desk, he caught a glimpse of his boss coming through the main door. The SAC, Adam Pistone, wasn't alone. A clean-cut man in a suit that said "well-paid government contractor" walked alongside him. With a military build and impeccable posture, the man's swagger seemed to exaggerate Pistone's rounder frame. A visitor's pass hung from the man's suit jacket pocket.

Pistone rarely came by unannounced. Steep braced himself for an unpleasant interruption of his easy-going day. Forcing a smile on his face, he left his office to greet Pistone.

His boss reached out a hand. "Good afternoon, Tim. Hope you don't mind that I decided to just swing by."

They shook hands like old friends would. "No problem, Adam. You know you're always welcome. What's going on?"

Pistone gestured to the visitor. "Let me introduce you. This is Mr. Chester Smith."

"Just Chester, is fine. I've heard good things about you, Tim."

They shook hands and continued the niceties, Steep offering coffee. Steep led them into the conference room adjacent to his office. They sat together at one end of the table, trying their best to seem casual. Steep tried his best to hide his curiosity.

Pistone finally got to the point. "So Chester here is from the outfit TRM. They assist us with resources from time to time."

Steep had heard of TRM before, but couldn't have explained what they did exactly. Despite the large quantities of information he analyzed daily, Steep's memory was like a steel trap. If he couldn't remember the specifics of something, chances were it was because he'd never been filled in on the intricacies of it.

Pistone was obviously not going to overshare, either. "In any case, not sure if you've heard. There is a major cyber attack going on right now at the credit reporting agency, Experfax. It looks like there are multiple attacks going on and they are being persistent."

"I saw the bulletin coming out of the Dallas office while I was at the gym." Steep pulled his smartphone out, scrolling through his emails. "There wasn't much detail yet."

"There won't be much more coming across the wire. I'm assigning it to your team. But, before I sign it over, I wanted to introduce you to Chester and give you a heads up that TRM will be assisting your team on this case. He has some background information and the resources you'll find helpful."

Steep turned his attention to Chester, "What background information exactly?"

"You may not know, but we have an ongoing study that reviews FBI cases. We've been researching with algorithms to find connections in case files that may not have obvious links to each other. Almost like a search engine for investigations."

Chester paused to see if Steep understood. Of course he did. He studied Chester, looking for any facial micro-expression that might give him some more insight into who this person was. Either Chester was supernaturally good at keeping his expressions neutral, or he was an actual robot.

Chester continued in his cadenced, almost rehearsed sounding tone. "One of your recent cases. The one that involved hacking of ATM machines in DC, Boston, and NYC?"

Steep nodded. He and Ivan had been secretly scouring the case files he had covertly smuggled out on the USB flash drive. The case was as fresh in his mind as the day it had been taken off his desk. It didn't bother him that he still hadn't been able to find any suspects. But he wondered often why the case had been dismissed without a tangible explanation. At the edge of his thoughts, he started to realize maybe this man Chester was a part of the reason.

"There is a high probability that the ATM case is linked to the attack on Experfax right now. It looks like it could be the same hackers."

Now Steep was intrigued. "How can you find a link when there wasn't even enough evidence to build a TTP profile? And what kind of research do you have that you are able to determine this on a case that isn't even active?"

Steep's natural curiosity was only intensified by the mysterious and impassable individual that had suddenly appeared to work alongside him. Whatever the solution to this puzzle was, Chester Smith - as if that was his real name - would play a big part in figuring it out.

One way or another.

Chester displayed his first hint of human emotion when he heard Steep's line of questioning. He raised an eyebrow, while the rest of his face remained stoic. "That's the whole point of our research, Tim. Our algorithms found similarities that are nearly impossible to identify using traditional investigative techniques alone. We do not mean to question you and your team's ability. You handled the ATM case perfectly."

Steep held his tongue. Chester must have sensed that he was tensing up and was trying to appease him.

Pistone leaned forward. "Tim, I know this may seem unorthodox. I don't quite understand it myself. It's all computer stuff to me. I want Chester to work with your team because you're the most capable in this area. He'll need to observe and gather more information for his research, so I'm giving him full clearance. Initiate this Experfax case and find out what's going on. Chester should be a good resource. The Dallas Division knows you're taking the lead."

Pistone finished speaking and shot Steep a covert look that said, "Be careful." It was the glance of a friend looking out for him and telling him that this wasn't the time to rock the boat.

Steep took the sign in good faith. "Of course. Chester, you can use this conference room as an office for now. I'll ramp the team up and we'll be in the air before the end of the day."

They shook hands as Pistone said goodbye.

After making sure Chester was settled, Steep went into his office and closed the blinds. He sent a group text to his team, "Office. Now."

40

REGGIE'S eyes gleamed as he watched his work take hold. He was zoned into his creation and marveled that it was working.

He had stopped paying attention to his army of zombie computers that were still hacking away at the Experfax network relentlessly. Eventually, he knew the Experfax IT team would shut them out completely. The zombies would stop assaulting the system on their own within the next twelve hours before disappearing from their hosts without much of a trace. Only a blank log of the hours the computers had been active would be left behind.

Now Reggie shifted his focus to Jubilee, which Roman had strategically implanted into the central repository system just an hour earlier.

He didn't notice that Hope was now in the passenger seat of the van after her brother had picked her up from 'work'. He didn't notice anything. He was in a trance, watching the visual interface he had developed to monitor Jubilee's movement as she went from system to system, from backup to backup. He was still tapped into their networks through the comm link Hope had installed. Each piece was working together seamlessly.

Anyone looking for Jubilee would not realize what she was. On the surface, she was nothing more than a hash function that ran from a hidden rootkit, attaching hashes to each and every record in the system.

Hashes were bits of code that were commonly used by databases. They made searching data faster or were used for data integrity. But these hashes hid the code for Jubilee.

There were no tracers or any indication that she could be a hostile code. She used all the necessary licenses and access certificates that he had been able to get from the software engineer's laptop. Only Reggie was able to watch her, because only he knew what to look for.

The first thing that Jubilee did was multiply. She created three hundred and thirty three polymorphic mirror images of herself before looking for her first stop, which was an individual's record in the vast databases.

In each person's record was a social security number or equivalent that gave the system the ability to link all incoming records for that identifying number. All the debts and pieces of information were linked this way and stored on the databases that spanned the globe, yet linked to this single individual identifier.

Together, all these distinct pieces of data made up a person's credit record. A search by a credit-giving agency would run the information through a number of algorithms and presentation formats to aggregate a person's credit score and assemble a report. Agencies used these reports to judge if this person was creditworthy or not.

What Jubilee did was find all of these pieces and work backwards. All she looked for was the person's identifier, the record of debt, and where the source of the detail was coming from.

From there, Jubilee acted as a detective. She used the source data from each record to trace her way back to the creditor's system using the secure connection Experfax had with them. She would then scour for the data on the creditor's servers.

Once she found the source data on the creditor's databases, she kept looking for any other information that was linked to the person's identifier. As soon as she found an instance of the person's information, she multiplied by another three hundred and thirty three to find other instances.

Jubilee kept doing this until she could no longer find any other instances of the individual. If she didn't find anything, she started looking for new individuals to link to. New individuals to free from the record of their debt.

And then Jubilee would sit there. And wait.

The code was programmed to activate at a certain date and time. When that time came, the records would be erased. All of them, all at once.

She was able to break through any firewall by going through the same route that the creditor had sent the information from. Nearly all banks and institutions had systematic links that sent information to the credit reporting agency. Experfax paid for these to be sure they always received the latest information.

Creditors wanted this so that there was always up to date information on the debtor. This was a system to always keep the individual in check. To keep them oppressed and subject to their debt.

Reggie was excited to use this need against them.

41

THE back door of the van opened up, bringing in the evening sunlight. The hot air rushed in, hitting Reggie on the side of the face. He didn't turn his head from the display he was focused on; the image of a growing web of connecting dots. Each dot represented a name or record that connected it to another name or record.

"Hey, Dungeon Master. We're here," Burton said gruffly.

The sound of an airplane taking off could be heard from above. They were in the airport's long-term parking lot.

"I just need a few more minutes. I have to make sure she's doing what she's supposed to," Reggie pleaded.

He dreaded being on the plane. He would have such limited access while he was up there. Even with in-flight wi-fi, there was no way he could monitor Jubilee over it. He would have to refrain from accessing the internet at all. Maybe he would catch up on Battlestar Galactica?

Jubilee's web on his screen was still growing. It was already covering eighty percent of all the records at Experfax. He looked at a few other systems. They were still home-free. No one was close to detecting anything had happened.

Burton looked at his watch. "Fine. You have ten minutes. Hurry it up, or we'll miss our flight." Burton closed the van's door, and the space returned to darkness.

Jubilee started spreading to other systems around the world, carrying with her the targets she needed to find.

Someone would find her eventually. It would take weeks before that would happen though. By then, it would be too late. Jubilee was unstoppable, and far too robust to ever be completely eliminated or stopped. It would take months to even figure out how to start decrypting her.

Reggie's stomach started to growl. He hadn't eaten anything for at least a day. This wasn't a rare occurrence for him, and it was par for the course during a big job. He imagined a world completely affected by what he and his friends had just accomplished. Were going to accomplish.

Soon, millions of lives would be lifted out of poverty... or, at the very least, relieved of a burden that kept them from living the life that they were destined to. The millions that took jobs that squandered their talents so that they could keep up with the student loans and credit card debt required to afford going to college in the first place. The millions that were forced to carry an overweight mortgage because the market defined an overweight price for them to live in a neighborhood they felt safe in.

He wasn't so naive to think that there wouldn't be negative outcomes. The financial world would receive a reckoning. A meltdown would occur like none other in recent memory. Reggie had thought about this, examining it from every direction he could think of.

Who would be affected most? Anyone that had let greed encourage them to invest, knowingly or not, in oppressive values. They had made money while others spent their lives trying to pay it back.

The more research he did, the more he realized they had to succeed in this. He imagined people everywhere begging for him to work harder. To work longer. To make it even more foolproof. He had to give this to the world... no matter what.

He enjoyed working with Roman and the rest of the crew. Growing up as an outcast and a tech nerd, he'd thought he wouldn't ever be able to relate to other people. When he met Bryce, he thought Bryce was a privileged golden boy and had dreaded being his roommate.

After a few days of getting to know both Roman and Bryce, he realized that they were much more than they seemed. They had a real world sense of adventure that he'd only seen virtually. They didn't know technology like he did, but they were smart in a way that he never thought normal people could be.

Not only that, but they were good to him. Not like people that would try to use him for his knowledge. But like two guys that really just wanted to get to know him and be there for him if he needed. With no ulterior motives at all.

The scores in college started off small and became more complex over time. They trusted him and he trusted them just as much.

The first few didn't require much effort. A few searches on good targets or details of how to break into a small warehouse. He was an avid tinkerer, so he reveled in the prospects of creating really amazing tech that didn't exist or were nothing but theories until he created them. He imagined himself as the Q in a James Bond novel. Always coming up with spectacular tech to assist his guys.

Burton opened the door again. "How does our baby look? Here, eat something while you're working." Burton handed him a slice of pizza. It was his favorite kind. Hawaiian.

"She's everywhere," he replied with a smile. "She's already hit servers in London, Tokyo, Hong Kong, and anywhere else there's a link. The creditors all think it's trusted updates from Experfax, so there's no resistance. She will have complete saturation within forty eight hours."

Reggie bit into his first slice, the sweet of the pineapple mixing with the salty ham making his mouth water. He was so much hungrier than he'd realized.

"If it's already everywhere, do we still have to hit the other two companies?" Burton asked as he ate his own slice.

"The one we did today will eliminate about eighty percent of the records, but it won't get everything. Also, there's always a chance that some of these larger banks will go to the other two agencies and grab their records. If that happens, this would have been for nothing. The creditors may not be able to get all their records back, but they'll have enough where there will still be too many people on the hook. There will still be too many losers compared to the winners."

"Reggie is right," Roman said, sticking his head in the door. "We want this to help as many people as possible. The creditors need to be wiped out completely, and we can't chance that they'll survive this."

Burton looked at his watch again. "We'll need to get out of here soon. Our flight's in an hour."

Roman looked over at Burton. "The house is done?"

There was a temporary storage service that was scheduled to pick up all their things and move everything into storage. When they left the townhouse, they wouldn't be returning.

All of their things would be shipped cross-country in a storage pod to one of their break away houses in New Jersey. The townhouse would be cleaned of prints and the keys would be left on the kitchen counter by the service they hired. The lease was paid for the next month, but the landlord wouldn't mind them leaving a little early. The other locations already had all their gear and tech set up, so all they needed with them were their carry-ons.

"Yep, just confirmed. They are already done."

"Reggie, you good to shut down and get portable?" Roman asked.

Reggie nodded, finishing his slice with a reluctant sigh. "All ready to go."

"Good. Atlanta, here we come."

42

STEEP didn't normally like flying but this trip was especially unpleasant. They had been able to get on an Air Force Gulfstream V from Bolling Air Force Base, so at least it was a comfortable flight to Dallas for the rest of the team.

It was Chester that made him uneasy.

The man seemed like he was on a different plane of existence. Or on the borderline between sanity and serial killer.

Even so, Steep needed to somehow pump some more information from Chester. He had Ivan look up TRM and found the incorporation documents, but nothing else. Nothing official or unofficial. The company was a ghost. They were obviously vetted by his boss and the Bureau, but that did nothing to appease Steep's suspicions.

The crewman for the plane passed by to check on them. For a flight this short, all they received was a bottle of water. As he walked back to the crew area, Steep left his seat and followed him down the aisle towards the front of the plane where Chester was sitting. He took the empty seat across the aisle.

Steep greeted him, but only received a nod as a response. "I'd like to go over the case some more. Before we land."

"Didn't you write down what I already told you?" Chester responded.

Steep held his clenched fist to his lap. "Of course, but maybe if we put our heads together, we can come up with a way to apprehend these guys."

"Why do you think so? I have reviewed your entire case and all of the evidence. Unless you have more information than that. Which would mean you are incompetent."

Steep could feel his nails digging into his palm. "What about the information that you have not given me? How sure are you that this is the same hacker? If I had some data files or whatever you have that allowed you to come up with that, then I'll have my team run some scenarios. Before we land."

Chester turned his face to look into Steep's eyes. "I have given you all the information that I plan to. Don't misinterpret this working association we have. You are tasked to help me with finding this suspect or suspects. Not the other way around. If you have a problem with that, I suggest you discuss it with Pistone." He returned his attention to the plane's window.

Steep lunged off his seat. As his foot hit the aisle, he swung his arm through the air, but opened his palm and continued the motion to walk to the back of the plane.

Disrespect, he could handle. Dishonesty, he could ignore. Belligerence like Chester's... something about it poked a nerve in Steep. It stirred up a reaction he did not know how to suppress.

Most of his guys had their eyes closed, but Pickles and Summers were looking at him and must have seen the awkward interaction.

He took a deep breath and regained his composure as he walked to the back towards his seat. He stopped short of where Ivan was sitting next to a snoring Padilla. Ivan was hunched over his laptop, which was too heavy and big to rest on the fold-down tray table. The glow of the LCD monitor bounced off his face in the dark. Steep leaned down closer than he knew Ivan preferred.

"Can we talk?"

Ivan seemed to forgive the intrusion and also kept his voice low.

"What is up?"

"Before we left, I had you stop your progress on the ATM case. But we didn't get to talk about it yet. Were you able to come up with anything?"

Ivan looked over at Padilla and then towards Chester. His eyes widened.

"I didn't find anything in the files, but started looking around it. I searched the hacker boards for any discussions on backdoor tools. The kind that would have created the ones in ATSI. There were hundreds of results during the past two years, but I kept a list of all the users that were discussing it."

"So what can we do with that list?"

"I started looking at the attack that is currently underway at Experfax. It's a simple DDoS using a botnet of zombie PCs."

Steep defined for himself botnet as a coordinated group of compromised computers, or zombies, attacking through an internet connection.

Ivan continued, "I traced one of the attack IPs to a zombie PC, and it's infected by the classic Stacheldraht."

"Remind me what that is again?"

"It's a tool that is used launch the DDoS attack."

Steep remained focused and pushed aside his lack of technical knowledge. "How does that help us? If you are not able to find the tracker?"

"I am assuming that the hacker did not start this attack until after they finished the ATM job. So I did another darknet board discussion search for 'Stacheldraht DDoS' for just the last four months. "

"Because you want to see if any of them match the backdoor list?"

"Yes. There are two hundred and thirteen matches."

"That doesn't sound like a narrow search."

"I know. I have to figure out another way to narrow the list down." Ivan rubbed his chin like he usually did in puzzling moments. "What I cannot figure out is what they are trying to do. This DDos is only distraction. They may be stealing private information. But they seem too smart to even want to do that. The sale of that much information is always traceable."

Steep hadn't even thought that. Why would a credit reporting agency be the target? Ivan was right. There wasn't money buried in the servers. There was private data of individuals.

"Keep looking, Ivan. Maybe you'll come up with something."

Steep looked to the front of the plane where Chester was sitting. Maybe he already knew the motive. He didn't seem to be the kind of person that would be going after a hacker for no reason.

The very image of Chester, cold and unmoving against the window of the plane, sent an involuntary chill down Steep's whole body. If Ivan couldn't make a connection even knowing what they knew now, what kind of diabolical technology did TRM have at its disposal?

43

THE weather was a bit steamy in the summer morning. It looked like it was going to rain. They had started at dawn, still tired from the flight, but they had to keep going.

Roman knew that even though this next part of the job was going to be much easier, they had to keep on their game. Reggie was monitoring Washington for any network chatter that indicated the Feds could be on to them. He would be able to tell if there was some burst in activity. He would then have to determine what it was related to.

He wouldn't have much of a problem figuring it out, but right now, Roman needed Reggie to focus on the tasks at hand. If the authorities were alerted, Roman would need to make some significant logistical adjustments.

Either way, they would have time to assess the threat level once they landed in the next location tomorrow. No matter how good a security agency was, it would take them more than a day to connect the dots.

They were in an open loft that they were subleasing in the middle of Atlanta proper for three months. The previous tenant had to skip town, so he had placed this gem on Craigslist. He had needed someone to finish up the lease through August.

As long as they had the cash and didn't trash the place, he didn't care who they were or what they did. The large deposit guaranteed their privacy. It was much smaller than the town house with no rooms, so they had air-mattresses lined up along one of the larger walls.

Between Roman and Burton flying in to work some surveillance and setup, they had been able to set up all the computers and equipment around a large kitchen island that took up a quarter of the apartment. There was a blank wall in the living area they used as a planning board with detailed outlines of the current part of the job. Just like in the townhouse, strings of yarn connected each step and contingency.

They all stood in front of the wall, reviewing their next moves. They each knew what they had to do by heart, but it was always good to review everything up to the zero hour.

"I think Plan A is still valid. Let's stick with that," Roman said.

Burton took a sip of his energy drink and grimaced at the taste. "Everything is set up. I double checked everything last Friday when I was here."

"Good good," Roman said, bringing his attention to a lone picture of a security guard. This guard, Christian Feltch, had been on the job for just over three months and wasn't very experienced. But he had a college degree, so even with his lack of experience, he was given much more responsibility than he was capable of.

The company Christian worked for was an outside vendor that Equirian contracted for security. As a way to save money, the security company hired only temporary, part-time guards and their training was minimal. Their presence at the facility was a measure that gave the illusion of precaution, without much physical capacity to guard the place.

The building they needed to get into wasn't a data center this time, but one of the corporate offices in the middle of Atlanta Midtown, in between shopping centers and a good selection of happy hour spots. There were other companies in the same building - major vendors of Equirian that had chosen the location for its proximity to the credit bureau. They were companies that did the application technology, data warehouse programming, and everything else that kept Equirian functioning as the powerhouse of data it was.

The security company that Christian worked for also supplied the security for all these companies.

The technologists in these offices didn't maintain the servers, but were tapped into the data warehouses around the globe remotely. In the company's estimation, being in this one office was like being in the data center itself. And since the data was safely off-site, they mistakenly didn't think that anyone would try and break into this discreet site.

No one would, except for Roman.

44

CHRISTIAN Feltch stopped in at this independent coffee shop every time he was on his way to work. He would sit in the coffee shop and drink his coffee while scrolling through his cell phone, looking through sports scores and video game websites. Hope knew this, because Burton had followed him for weeks and memorized his schedule.

Today, Christian was on the night shift, so he would be getting his coffee at around five PM. Hope knew this because Reggie also had complete access to the security company's network. He was able to access the building's scheduling application that not only provided the schedule of all the security staff, but also controlled all access points depending on who was on shift.

That night, Christian would be on shift from six pm to six am. Most of the time, there would be another guard with him, except between eleven PM to two AM, when he would be by himself. During those three hours, he would be the only person able to access any part of the building.

Hope sat at one of the two seat tables that were lined up along the wall of glass. There were only five other tables and a few arm chairs. Most of the coffee shop was full of other patrons, all staring at their laptops, smartphones, or engrossed in quiet conversations. Two of the tables were occupied by Reggie and Burton. Reggie was facing her, working on his laptop on the small table behind the empty seat of her table. Burton was sitting directly behind her with his back to her.

This made it so that the empty seat at Hope's table was one of the few open seats at that moment. She sat facing the barista station and flipped through a video game magazine. She couldn't wait to get through this part of the job. She had been playing first person shooter games for the last few weeks, and reading all about the latest news on upcoming games. It wasn't her favorite research assignment.

She was wearing a pair of ragged extra short denim shorts, sandals, and a loose t-shirt that had a neckline that was low enough to give a lucky guy a hint of her perky, braless breasts. A pair of stylish sunglasses allowed her to study the rest of the room.

It was about time for her to work her magic. The key was to be in character. She let her mind drift to thoughts of Roman. Would he ever consider her as more than Burton's little sister? Every now and then, she felt like she caught a possible glimpse from him: a tender look, a touch that lingered a moment too long, or a smile that seemed meant just for her. She couldn't be sure if it was just her mind playing tricks on her.

She let herself think of him now though. Of his smile. Of his strong chest and arms. His quick intellect. She used this feeling to make sure she exuded the aura she wanted to convey.

She was still daydreaming when she heard a voice in her head, "Game on. He's at the cashier," said Burton. Ugh. It would be her brother to interrupt her fantasy moment.

She looked up and saw the man she had so far only seen pictures of. He had already paid for his coffee and was walking to the barista station. He was wearing jeans and a t-shirt with a large picture of a video game image she recognized, but couldn't quite remember at the moment.

"It's Ghost Com on his t-shirt," Reggie said, as if reading her mind.

She looked at Christian to the point where she was openly staring, waiting for her opening. After a moment of watching the barista making another customer's coffee, he scanned the room, possibly looking for an empty seat. Just as his line of sight crossed her path, Hope casually brought her hand up and lifted her sunglasses to rest it on her crown like a loose hairband.

She imagined she was looking at Roman catching her eye, and she genuinely smiled slightly. She could see that he caught her signal, and she slowly let her eyes lower to her magazine. Her legs were crossed at the knee and she let her raised foot dangle gently. After a count of five, she looked up again at him. He wasn't looking at her, but she could tell that he was trying to use his peripheral to see her. He wasn't doing a very good job of hiding it.

He eventually caved in and turned to her again. This time, she held his gaze and smiled unmistakably. He smiled back, nervously. It seemed like he wasn't sure what to do next.

He snapped out of his daze at the sound of the barista calling his name. He grabbed his coffee from the service table. As he turned to Hope's direction, he nearly stumbled, knocking into a low wall that separated the sitting area from the rest of the shop.

He looked at her as if waiting for a sign. She didn't break her line of sight, but didn't show any other signs. It was best if he made the decision himself. Too aggressive a move might make him suspicious, but too subtle a move would make him think it was just his imagination that this girl was looking at him.

He slowly walked towards her. It was only a few feet, but he made it seem like she was a football field away.

When he reached her table, she could see him tense up before asking, "Is this seat taken?"

She widened her smile and hoped that a sudden clenching of her abs was making her cheeks blush. "No, sit with me," she said in the breathiest voice she could muster.

His face relaxed as he let himself breathe again. He sat down in the chair and sat his coffee down. It seemed he didn't know what to say after that. He may have used up all his bravery for the day. Hope would have to help him the rest of the way.

"That's Ghost Com, right?" she asked pointing to his chest, centimeters from touching it. The table was very small, so their faces were only a few inches apart. "I love the campaign, but can't get through it all." She giggled, making sure her shirt was doing its trick. As if trying his best not to get caught, his eyes snapped from her chest to his own. It seemed to take him a minute to register what she asked.

"Um, right, it's a great game. I've already beat it at the Elite Level," he said, slipping in a few looks at her chest between every few words.

It was a socially awkward boy's wet-dream. A girl that was hot, loved video games, and was easy. She tried her best not to gag. "Maybe you can show me how to play sometime," she said, as she rested her hand on his forearm.

He responded with a sort of uncontrolled combination of a giggle and a grunt.

The role was feeling stale to her already, and Hope wondered how much longer she could keep it up. The sound of Reggie in her ear had never sounded better. "We're good. I have his credentials from his RFID card."

She was so relieved that she could have jumped up and given Reggie a hug right there. Thank God he was fast.

She took a large sip from her blended ice coffee drink. She looked at Christian while she had the straw in her mouth, being as seductive as she could. She got to the last sip and it made the distinct empty sound. She let go of the straw and made an exaggerated pout. She couldn't believe she had to act this way.

"Oh, you want another one? I can get it for you," Christian said as if on cue.

As she rubbed his forearm, she smiled, "Would you really? That is so sweet. It was the caramel flavor."

He jumped out of his seat, so happy he could be a hero. "I'll be right back," he said as he was halfway to the register.

She watched him as she grabbed his coffee with her right hand.

She scanned the room quickly to make sure no one was watching. Reggie would take care of the security camera, but an eyewitness would ruin all her effort. When she was sure no one in her field of view was watching, she said, "Clear."

Burton replied, "Clear."

In one fluid motion, she lowered Christian's coffee down to her right side and readied her left hand on the other side. In less than a second, she felt that Burton had held onto Christian's coffee, and had placed another cup in her left hand. Once they were sure they both had a secure hold, Hope lifted the new coffee and released the old. She laid the new coffee in the same spot Christian had left it.

The new cup held the normal latte that Christian got every time he came here. But this one had a special blend of tiny gel capsules filled with Triazolam that would start to time release in about six hours. The Triazolam would make Christian increasingly drowsy. Eventually it would be physically impossible to stay awake. Roman was counting on that happening at just after eleven PM tonight.

Christian was already at the barista counter, giddiness in his posture. He turned to her and smiled, as if he was the luckiest guy.

She smiled back at him, and thought the opposite.

45

STEEP didn't like this situation. He didn't like it one bit.

His intuition, which he'd learned to pay close attention to over his decorated career, was screaming in protest as he waited in the large conference room. He had been waiting for forty minutes.

That was forty minutes longer than it should have taken to be in front of the head of technology. They should have been ready for him.

Chester was somewhere else in the building. As soon as they had arrived at Experfax, he had their staff assign him his own small conference room. It was on the other side of the building and Steep was relieved that he wouldn't be in the same room.

It wasn't like Chester's brand of 'help' was any use to him.

Ivan and the rest of the team were set up around the conference table. Summers and Pickles were calling the local station and the home office, keeping all the powers-that-be up to date with where they were with the case. Which was currently... nowhere.

The door opened and five men walked through the door. They looked like they had been dressed professionally at one time, but now they were disheveled. Their ties were either comically loose or just gone. Their sleeves were rolled up and their shirts were untucked and mostly unbuttoned, showing their white undershirts. The person in the messy group who looked the most authoritative walked up to him and held out a hand.

"Good morning. Jim Thomas, Director of Technology Resources." He forced a smile. "I do so apologize about making you wait all this time. We have been... trying to address the issue."

Steep shook the director's hand. "We're here to help, I assure you. Why don't we have a seat and catch up? I'd like to know everything you've found."

After everyone was able to grab coffees, the newcomers sat down in chairs opposite the FBI agents. Steep and Jim sat at the head of the table next to each other. One of the IT guys set up a laptop to project onto the screen and remained standing, waiting for his cue. This took longer than Steep liked, but he could see these guys were worn out, so he held his tongue.

Jim started, "We've had numerous DDoS attacks since yesterday early afternoon. Every time we reset our servers, and came back online with the source of the attacks blocked, there's other sources that take its place. It's relentless. It's coming from every direction."

"Have you tried to find all sources before resetting?" Steep asked, in the least condescending tone he could muster.

"It's impossible to find them all. It's as if there are attacks on standby, waiting in line for the one before them to be blocked before they appear. Wave after wave of attacks are set up."

"Then you'll have to keep shutting down and resetting until it stops. There's always an end. Any idea where these could be originating from?"

"It looks like IPs from China and India are doing the heavy load. There's been no ransom notes or indication of anyone taking credit on the darknet. It's as if it was unleashed for no reason. It's a simple enough attack to address, yet it's relentless."

Ivan gave Steep a knowing look. Steep almost thought it was more like he was rolling his eyes.

"Is there any sign of anything that is piggybacking? Something more evasive?"

"Not that I know of. Let me defer to Raj Batool. He is our software lead, and has been heading up the effort to address these attacks. Raj," Jim said as he directed his attention to the front of the room.

Raj was apparently the person standing in front of the projector screen at a podium with his laptop set up in front of him.

"There are multiple attacks going on. UDP floods, TCP SYN floods, ICMP floods, and Smurfs. Each is very distinct but they are attacking persistently, making it impossible for any of our stakeholders to access our portal. This portal is vital to our business, allowing access to the services we provide our clients."

"What kind of services? Just getting credit reports on individuals, right?"

"Not necessarily. We have all sorts of information. Demographic, historical, habitual..."

Steep's interest piqued, "Habitual...?" He gestured for Raj to elaborate further.

"We gather information from many sources. Legally, of course," Raj said hastily. "From other information companies. Purchases, data requests, social media. It's all gathered here. Then we provide marketers and clients of that sort these details so that they can make strategic decisions."

"You mean... you have very personal details on nearly every citizen in the US?"

"It's all very legitimate and legal, I assure you. We take privacy very seriously. Every term and usage agreement has been agreed upon for us to use this information."

Steep was surprised, but only partially. The business of taking people's information had become the new gold rush. Every business, of every size, was out to gather the most intimate details of a person's life and exploit them to the fullest. They offered opportunities to be social, games they could play with friends, and shopping services. Things that people felt that they couldn't live without. All the while, sucking valuable private data.

And everyone knew this. They volunteered their information freely, not seeing the repercussions. They didn't realize they were trading their lives for easy access to money, to friends, or a cheap deal. They were in a system that would squeeze every penny out of them before they realized it.

Raj continued, "Also, I would like to clarify that this information is global, not just in the US."

Great, thought Steep. That's not a bad idea at all. "So is every data hub affected by this, or just the one here on this campus?"

"The portal is evenly distributed on our network... globally. We address all of the issues in-house, but every node that handles the portal is affected by these attacks."

Steep leaned all the way forward on his chair, his elbows on the table. He covered his mouth with his folded hands, holding back any comment as he was thinking. He thought about the attack and its nature.

There were a number of ways to take this. To be able to take down a multi-hub global web portal was no small feat. The only problem he had was that it was too obvious to be something that his only suspects, the ATM crew of thieves, would do.

He looked over at Ivan, "What do you think? It's too conspicuous to be our guys, isn't it?"

"It is overt, but the code structure that was released to me from the zombie systems matches our hacker's techniques. I'm eighty percent sure of it."

"Eighty percent?"

"There's always a chance that there is another very smart individual that is able to refrain from leaving signatures as well. The odds would be slim, but it's possible."

"So what does that mean? If this is from our crew, why would they do it this way? What would they gain?"

"A distraction, possibly?"

Steep paused for thought and then redirected his attention to Jim next to him, "Are there any indications that anything else outside of this attack was happening at the same time?"

Jim thought for a moment. His brow raised at a revelation, "The power did go out for a minute. The power company said that a fuse had blown at one of the distribution centers. But we had a redundant system so everything came back online very quickly."

Steep closed his eyes, not caring what the director or any of them thought. He needed to focus. If the power had gone out, there was a reason for it. It wasn't a coincidence. So the DDoS attack was definitely a distraction, but for what?

He opened his eyes and directed his question to Raj, "I need to know every system that was affected by the power going out. I want CCTV footage of all areas that would go dark at that time. I also want to know what happened when your systems came back online."

Jim raised his finger, already knowing some of the answer. "There's one small problem. After the power failure, all of our CCTV servers lost any footage they had for the day. The power surge initiated a reset of the security system."

"That's not a small problem," Steep said.

The hunt was on.

Steep couldn't help but think of Chester, hunkered down somewhere in another conference room with whatever secret algorithm software he had. A big part of him wanted to prove that he could beat Chester to the punch. But if he wanted to do that, his team would have to be faster, smarter and more focused than they had ever been.

46

ROMAN and Bryce walked up to the front of the office building, dressed in the security guard uniforms that Burton had procured from the same uniform company that the security company used. Roman was glad that the uniform included a baseball cap that they could use to cover their faces. Reggie already had control of the security cameras, but it was always better to keep their faces shielded in case of eyewitnesses. He walked straight up to the all glass door and swiped the key card that Reggie had made using the credentials he had sniffed off of Christian earlier that day.

It was fifteen after eleven and Christian's digestive system should have gotten through the coating of the tiny pills he had ingested with his coffee and released the sedative just moments earlier.

Roman walked up to the front security counter set in the middle of the empty marbled lobby. Christian's face was on the desk, the only thing keeping him from falling off the chair. His arms were hanging straight down at his sides.

"Is he drooling?" Bryce asked.

Roman didn't answer, but came up behind Christian and hooked his arms under Christian's and lifted him up. "Let's lay him flat under the counter. That should be enough out of view."

Bryce grabbed the guard's legs and they lifted him up gently and laid him down on the ground. They rolled him until he was completely hidden under the deep wrap around counter.

Roman looked at his watch. "I'll be back in ten," he said as he hurried to the bank of elevators.

Bryce took Christian's place at the security desk and made himself comfortable.

Roman walked into the elevator and hit the button for the fifteenth floor, the second to the highest floor in the building. He had to swipe Christian's credentials to get the elevator to move. It was where the top network and programming personnel did their work. This was where they managed their global network of server farms. It was completely a hands-off process. Most work was done remotely through the cloud, all in the effort of saving money, and being more efficient and flexible. That corporate need was also their weakness.

The elevator door opened into a darkened space. The main room lights were off, but there were dim lamps that provided a soft glow every twenty feet so that it wasn't pitch black. He could see the city's night lights through the floor to ceiling windows that wrapped the entire floor. The center of the floor was lined with small, glass walled conference rooms, each with whiteboards covered in stickies and colorful writing. Roman thought of his own work room.

The rest of the space was filled with short walled cubicles that provided a separation with very little privacy. It must have been to provide an open environment for team collaboration, but really most likely made everyone weary from the lack of privacy. There were small offices around the perimeter, all glassed in as well, that provided even less privacy, but a better view.

Spaces like this gave Roman a cold feeling. The idea of coming to a place like this to work every day would have been like serving a long sentence on death row for him. He had tried the office job as a cover from time to time, but he'd never lasted more than a few days. It made him feel claustrophobic, as if the office walls were crushing his spirit an inch at a time. There was also the fact that bureaucratic nonsense and inefficiency drove his well-ordered mind mad.

He used a high beam flashlight, pointing it at an angle towards the floor a few feet in front of him so that the light couldn't be seen from outside through the windows. Roman oriented himself with his mental image of the floor plan and the seating chart that Burton and Reggie had been able to swipe from a small consulting firm that had helped the company rearrange the space a few years ago.

According to the seating chart, his first stop was one of the offices on the south corner. The building was completely empty and would be for at least the next three hours. Even the workaholics had to leave to eat dinner and sleep for a few hours before coming back extra early. Still, Roman walked with caution, peering into every corner of the space with each step.

As Roman walked, he pulled on a pair of surgical gloves. When he arrived to the glass office, he used Christian's keycard to open the door. The door made a thumping sound as the magnetic locks released. The space behind the lock was nothing more than a glass box with a composite desk and matching shelving. There was a mesh executive chair behind the desk and two small guest chairs in front of it.

He went directly to the desktop computer tower, sitting in its special cubby built into the shelves. He gently pulled the box out to get to its back ports. Even though the monitor was off, he could feel the power supply fan running, indicating that the computer was still on. There was a thin layer of dust that implied the computer had not been moved for some time.

Roman reached into his bag and pulled out a small black plastic case the size of a cigarette box. It had a wire coming out with a USB connector at the end. He found an empty port and plugged the device in. He then replaced the computer box back into its cubby, making sure that it was in the exact same position as before. They only needed the device to stay there undetected for a few days, but anything that made the user curious about it could cut their plans very short.

Without touching anything else, he slipped out of the room and swiped the card to lock it. Just as he headed to the second target, he could hear Bryce's voice over his comm.

It sounded like he was having a conversation. "Oh yes, I'm new. What was your name again, sir? Just need to see your ID, if you don't mind."

Someone was in the lobby?

"Here you go, Mr. Cassidy. What floor were you going to? So I can release the security and turn on the lights for you."

Roman stopped in his tracks. Please, don't be the fifteenth floor.

"Floor fifteen? Great, I'll take care of that for you."

Shit.

"There, you go. Will you be long? Not sure? Have a good one then."

Cassidy. Roman recognized that name. Closing his eyes, he envisioned the seating chart: each cube labeled with a last name. His photographic memory buzzed as Roman searched his mind for the answer he needed. Cassidy...

Cassidy sat in a cubicle directly in front of his fourth target office and a few desks away from his third target's cubicle.

Roman would have to skip his second target. Otherwise, he would be blocked from reaching the one right next to Cassidy.

47

HE let go of caution and sprinted to the other side of the floor. He had exactly ninety seconds before the elevator reached the floor. Another thirty for Cassidy to reach his desk from the elevator.

"Reggie, can you slow the elevator down?"

"You mean Dungeon Master, right?"

"Dungeon Master, slow the elevator down!"

"Already on it, baas. He will be taking a few stops along the way up. He won't know why, but should give you an extra sixty seconds."

That wasn't much time, but it would have to do. Roman ran full speed towards the fourth target which was an office on the far side of the floor. It might as well have been in a different building. His flashlight's beam pulsed around the space as his arm pumped for more speed. He could barely see anything, and scraped by a few cubicle corners as he ran.

He finally reached the office door and was out of breath. He didn't know how long he had left, but couldn't stop to think about it. He unlocked the door with his keycard and the magnetic lock clunked open. He shone his flashlight across the room and found the computer where it belonged, in the same type of cubby as the one in the other office.

"He's three floors away. Will be there in twenty."

He didn't pause to respond and went for the computer. He studied its position. This was no time to forget proper procedure. He leaned the tower box forward and without looking, felt for a free USB port. His sense of touch was enhanced by the adrenaline that was pumping through his body, but the sweat underneath his surgical gloves made him clumsy.

"He's on the floor," Reggie said.

"I'm at target four."

He clenched his fist and took a deep breath to calm his nerves. Reggie would be able to figure something out. He had to trust that. Roman just needed to do this one small thing that took very little effort. He was already there and was so close to accomplishing it.

He turned off his flashlight and felt again for the USB port. He let his gloved fingertips press along the area where it should have been. He kept feeling until finally, he was able to feel the correct shape and size of what was an open USB port. He took a second device from his pocket and plugged it in.

He took another breath to keep from rushing. He gently maneuvered the tower back into its position. His night-vision was starting to set in, and he was able to decipher shapes and shadows. He studied the space to make sure he didn't miss anything.

When Roman was satisfied, he stepped back and crouched behind the office chair, hoping that it was dark enough and the mesh was dense enough to hide him from unsuspecting eyes. He looked through the glass, out into the main office space where assistants and other subordinates must have sat.

The longer he looked, the better his vision became. He was able to make out the cubicles and desks and chairs. He could see the layout. He determined that Cassidy's seat was the cubicle directly in front of the office he was in. The only separation was a short partition wall that covered a foot above the desk. He tried to remember what direction Cassidy would be facing when he sat down.

As he was thinking of his possible options, he saw a shadow move in the darkness. It must have been Cassidy. The faint night lights were barely creating a shadow.

"I'm stuck in target four. Cassidy has reached his desk."

"Looking at the floor layout, it looks like he will be facing the office," Reggie reported, the exact opposite of what Roman was hoping for.

A bright glow appeared behind the glass. Cassidy's face was now in clear view from the light of his monitor. He was definitely facing directly toward where Roman crouched. Any movement would be noticed instantly.

"I need a way out, Dungeon Master."

"Working on it."

Roman resolved to wait. If Reggie was already working on something, it was best not to distract him. He focused on staying calm. As long as he stayed behind this chair and didn't move, he would be safe. He tried not to think of the possibility that Cassidy would access the office. That he was an assistant who would need to get in the exact one he was in.

The seconds crawled by as Roman envisioned countless scenarios and how they would play out. The last thing he wanted to do was hurt an innocent man who was obviously working hard at his job. But if it came to that... he shuddered. Roman's moral sensibilities made him incapable of coming face to face with another man and killing him. Besides, an act like that would negate any good that Jubilee was doing, and make him a huge hypocrite. But if it was between hurting this poor office drone, or letting this whole plot go to waste...

Reggie's voice on the comm brought Roman back to his tense reality. "Okay. I've got it. In ten seconds the fire alarm strobes will start flashing. I'm making the floor cycle through a fire drill test. That should give you enough of a distraction to get through the door at least."

"You're a genius."

"Jy weet mos. Okay, five… four..."

Roman crawled from behind the mesh chair to the glass door. He watched Cassidy's face, and there was no indication that he saw anything. He was focused on whatever he was doing.

"One."

Just as he reached the door, the floor lit up and the fire alarm strobes that were spread around the floor began blinking brightly in quick succession. Roman kept his eyes on Cassidy and saw a startled expression. He looked up at the nearest strobe and gaped trying to comprehend what was going on.

Roman smoothly opened the glass door by its handle just enough to fit his body. He shimmied awkwardly out of the office and held the handle on the outside, easing the door closed. He watched Cassidy, now standing up facing the elevator and looking at the strobes helplessly. He was still trying to figure out what to do next.

The alarm was silent, so Roman considered not locking the office door. He looked at Cassidy and decided to risk it. He took a deep breath and swiped the card across the keypad. At the same moment the door made a clunking sound of the magnets engaging, Roman shuffled as silently and as quickly as he could across the walkway hiding behind Cassidy's partition. He was now looking at Cassidy's reflection in the office glass, the strobes giving a bright image every second. Cassidy turned his head slightly as if hearing something, but thought nothing of it.

Roman let his breath return to normal and began moving slowly, crouched down to keep his figure below the top of the partitions.

"I'm clear of the office. You can shut the strobes off," He whispered when he felt he was far enough away from Cassidy.

Instantly, the strobes went off. He peeked from behind a partition that was shrouded in enough shadow that he felt secure. Cassidy sat back at his desk and went back to working on whatever he was working on. "Good boy," Roman whispered to himself.

"Heading to target three." Crisis averted. Roman had two more devices to install before he could get out of there.

48

THE conference room was starting to reek with the mixture of pizza, coffee, and body odor. Steep really wished the room had outside windows. The Experfax team had settled with their laptops as close to the FBI team as they could. There were many conversations going on and Steep decided he didn't need to hear every one. It seemed like they were finally getting the portal attack under control with the help of Ivan.

Steep stood up from his chair and stretched. He looked at his watch but didn't register the time. It was the middle of the night and it looked like they would be working until dawn. He would let the guys get a rest in the morning.

"Ivan, let's go take a walk," Steep looked over at his comrade.

Ivan seemed to be the only one that wasn't phased by the long hours. It was already part of his being to work non-stop. He looked at Steep as if considering whether or not to share something. He rose from his seat, laid down his laptop and grabbed a tablet PC he had laying on his table.

They walked into a large, courtyard type area that was in the center of the complex, using directions from the company's staff. They grabbed a bench in a lonely corner. There was a full moon and the stars were bright, but the air was still hot from the Texas daytime sun. It felt good coming from the air conditioned confines of the building, and Steep almost felt as if he was melting.

"So what do you think this is really all about?"

Ivan scanned his tablet, tapping and swiping around until he found the screen he was looking for.

"Well, I thought it was strange that a power failure occurred right when the portal attack was happening. I have a feeling that the attack was just a distraction from what they were really after."

"Okay, that makes sense. But what were they after? And why a power failure? Wouldn't that make whatever they do electronically difficult?"

"That's true. Unless they were already onsite and were trying to access something that was on a UPS."

Steep thought about it for a minute. There must have been certain systems that were on an Uninterrupted Power Supply, or a battery that was plugged inline of the power, so during a power failure, the system would stay powered on. "Do we know which systems are on UPS power?"

"The head guy gave me a list of them. A lot of them are very limited access and they don't want us even to ask about them," Ivan said, showing Steep the list on his tablet.

"Well, he's going to have to cooperate if he wants our help to figure out what this is. The crew could be after the exact things they are trying to hide. Run this list against the logs. There must be a connection."

"I think I already figured it out. There were a number of maintenance actions that occurred right after the blackout."

"What kind of maintenance actions?"

"It looks like a massive change in records."

Steep was just forming a thought, when he saw Chester walking up to them from across the courtyard. He was coming straight at them. It reminded Steep of a soldier marching in ceremony. Or an evil warlord walking through a battle. He had a confidence in his posture and a firmness in his expression.

He wasn't sure why, but as Chester came up, Steep and Ivan stood up automatically. It was nothing more than an automatic courtesy, but Steep hated himself a little bit for doing it.

Without a greeting, Chester started, "Has your team made any progress?"

Steep clenched his fist. "Some. We are looking at any possible vulnerabilities caused by the power outage. We suspect it was related. There must have been an action hidden by the DDoS being used as a distraction."

"Of course there was. Any idea what?" Chester looked bored.

"Like I said, we're looking into it."

"Well, don't take too long looking. We need results fast. Every moment that passes makes it less likely that we will find them."

"There's no need to teach me how to investigate."

Chester paused at the comment. It was as if he was registering how to put Steep back into his place.

Steep didn't allow more time for a response, "What have you been up to, Chester? What have you been doing hidden away?"

Chester seemed to enjoy the confrontation. Steep could have sworn that the corner of the man's mouth raised slightly into a smile. "That is none of your concern. But, I have been working closely with my analysts in D.C. They are reviewing some video and data that might help us. We are looking all around the time the attack began."

"Wait a minute. You have video? Jim said that he couldn't provide any for us. That the security video for the day had been wiped during the power outage," Steep said.

"I'm sure a lot of their key systems that could identify who was in the building were wiped. But what I have access to is above Jim's level of responsibility. TRM has been working with Experfax for a long time. Let's just say that we now have access to the video and data for the twenty-four-hour period surrounding the attack."

This didn't make sense to Steep, and he doubted any questioning would provide answers from Chester at this point. "So when can we take a look at that video and data?"

"You're not. It's highly classified and private information. Only TRM is allowed to review it."

"How the hell am I supposed to do my job if my team has no access to the evidence?"

"Do not worry, Tim. I will disclose anything that will help in the investigation. My team is more than adequate at determining if anything will help."

"This is bullshit," Steep couldn't hold his temper any longer. It was one thing to roadblock, but this prick was actually withholding evidence? He could feel Ivan take a step back. Both of Steep's fists were clenched now. If this guy wanted a fight, he would have it.

As they stood there, Chester remained emotionless. Wasn't it obvious to him that Steep was about to punch him in the face? He just had to say one more condescending word.

The prick just stood there. Moments passed. Steep wasn't sure how many moments, but enough where the pressure in his temples started to subside. Enough moments for his anger to lower enough for him to think. To wonder what Chester was capable of. Chester knew what he was capable of. That was why he stood there. He was untouchable. There would be unequal recourse.

A good punch would have made Steep feel better. Just one. It would be satisfying just to see a bruise on the man's face. But that would be all Steep would be able to do. One punch.

Chester would retaliate, there was no doubt. But he wouldn't do it with a punch. From what he had seen so far from how Pistone acted, how Experfax gave him priority... even just standing there, confronting Chester as he was doing now, could warrant some harsh effect on his career.

But if Steep took his fist and ground it into the man's face, there was no doubt that the end of his FBI career would just be the beginning. He didn't know all the connections that Chester really had, but Steep could only guess that he could make it impossible for Steep to get a job anywhere, no matter how small.

Yes, in those moments, Steep could see in Chester's face the future. His stoic ass face, taunting him, but also warning him. Chester welcomed the shot, but Steep knew the blowback would be so much more devastating.

He regained his composure, and unclenched his fists. He made a slight turn towards the entrance back into the building. As he took his first step, he only said, "Let me know when you have something for me."

He didn't hear what Chester said in response, but it sensed

something like, "Very well."

Steep could feel Ivan's steps behind him. As they walked through the door and entered the hallway, Ivan rushed up next to him. "So I guess we're not going to mention anything to the team about the changes in records?"

49

ROMAN rushed from the elevator bank to where Bryce was at the security desk. He helped Bryce position Christian back into his seat and set his head on the desk. He would wake up remembering nothing, thinking that he fell asleep. He would be awake in an hour or so. Hopefully Cassidy would be working through the night.

The second part of the score was nearly done. There was no question that Reggie's Jubilee would do her job and wipe out a lot of the information that were in these two companies. It was only a matter of how thorough she was going to be. If she wasn't thorough, there would be an unlucky few that would stay on the hook for whatever debts they owed. Roman couldn't bear that. He didn't want anyone to be even close to feeling the pressures that they fell into unwittingly. Everyone needed a Jubilee.

Burton pulled up to the sidewalk in a tinted window van as Roman and Bryce walked out the front door. They had done what they needed to. Now it was up to Reggie.

"Did you enjoy the close call?" Burton asked through the open window.

Roman and Bryce got into the middle passenger bench. Reggie was in the back row seat, focused on his screen with his large over the ear headphones on. The faint sound of classical music could be heard coming from them. Hope was in the front passenger seat.

Hope looked back and smiled. "Bet you had fun with that."

Roman smiled at her, "Not too bad. Could have been more exciting."

"Are we all set to leave?" Bryce asked.

"Yep. Place is cleaned out. Bags are already in our rooms at the airport hotel. The flight in the morning is on schedule," Burton said.

"Great. Reggie will probably work through the night in the van. Let's go get a few hours of sleep. We'll need our rest."

50

ROMAN rolled around in the hotel bed, not thinking about anything particular, but at the same time, thinking about everything. He always felt like this before the end of a job. They had come so far, and the next and last part would complete what they were trying to accomplish. All the jobs they had done together never had anything to do with the money they would make. He had come to realize that now. Even without a payday, the thrill was still there.

Any mistake at this point would make it all for nothing. The smallest misstep would get them caught.

He couldn't sleep. He had taken a long hot shower, stretched his muscles, and even meditated. Now he was staring at a silent television, the picture showing advertisements for the pay per view movies. If he fell asleep now, he would be able to get at least a few hours. Maybe he would sleep on the plane. He always slept well when he was en route to someplace new.

He still felt wide awake when he heard a knock on the door. It was a faint tapping, but it was definitely his door. He jumped up from the bed and didn't bother to put on a robe. He was in nothing but his boxers, but thought nothing of it. It was probably just Reggie, wanting to give him an update. He had told Reggie to come up once he was done hacking into the system no matter what time it was.

He looked through the peephole and lost his breath.

Hope was standing there with a bottle of red wine. She was still wearing the denim shorts that showed off her bare long legs and loose white t-shirt. Her smile was as irresistible as ever.

"I couldn't sleep. Feel like a night cap?"

Roman swallowed hard and couldn't find the words. Instead he took a step back and opened the door wide to let her in. She walked in without a hesitation.

Should he call the others and invite them over? No. That was stupid. Why was he like this with her? He wasn't a womanizer, but he'd had his share of girlfriends and casual encounters. He was never nervous around them like he was with her. Maybe because there was more to lose. Maybe because he felt like he was taking advantage.

When she passed him, he could feel her body heat radiate against his skin. He became overly aware that he was only in boxers. He grabbed the white bathrobe that was hanging in the open hallway closet.

She sat on the bed, already pouring wine into two hotel glasses. He sat next to her, not knowing what to do next. He accepted the glass, their fingertips touched knowingly.

"Here's a toast to everything going as planned," she said, smiling again.

He still couldn't say a word. Why couldn't he talk? They tapped glasses and he swallowed the entire pour in one sip. When he lowered the glass, her face was right in front of his, centimeters apart. Her gray hazel eyes stared back into his. He could smell her faint perfume of flowers, or something sweeter.

He couldn't help himself anymore and leaned into the inevitable. Their lips met and it seemed like the world around them disappeared. The hotel and where they were, the time, even the job, all melted away.

She pulled back his robe and her soft cool hands felt wonderful rubbing against his bare chest. He helped her pull her t-shirt off, then her shorts. Her bra and panties came off instantly. He realized that his boxers were no longer there.

Their bodies fell onto the bed, not caring to hide under the covers. He couldn't hold her close enough.

He felt like he was in heaven. He had wanted this moment for the longest time, but not admitted it. His eyes closed and he enjoyed the feel of her skin against his. All he could feel were their tongues dancing against each other.

And then he drifted away. His mind relaxed as everything became dark.

Another knock at the door. It was nonstop, almost annoying. He sat up from under the covers, looking around in the darkness. Thin strips of light broke through the cracks of the blackout curtains.

He realized he was alone in bed. He felt the emptiness next to him. He pulled himself out of bed and went to answer the door. The light from the hallway was much too bright and his eyes took a few seconds to adjust. Burton was looking back at him, his body tense with anxiety.

"Roman. There's a problem. The van isn't in the hotel parking lot."

Joseph Preacher

"What?" Roman's mind was foggy with sleep. He struggled to understand what was taking place, admitting to himself that his perfect moment with Hope must had only been a dream.

Burton's expression stayed grim as he delivered the rest of the news. "There's more. Roman, Reggie is missing."

51

REGGIE wasn't the best at driving, but when he drove, he was extra careful. He thought this the entire way from the hotel to the convenience store only two blocks away.

He had been working for a few hours in the hotel parking lot, when he had a sudden craving for beef jerky. Usually he would have waited for Burton or Roman to check on him, but he couldn't wait any longer. When his cravings were this strong, he couldn't concentrate on what was on the screen. He had already gone through his entire snack stash, and all he wanted was a value pack of hickory flavored beef jerky. He only hoped they had the brand he liked.

He looked around, examining his surroundings like he'd seen Burton do a million times. Never just walk right in. The parking lot was empty and the only other car was at the gas pump. There was a young man pumping his gas, mostly staring at the pump's readout. It was the middle of the night, so there weren't many cars driving by on the street. There was no one else in sight. It seemed safe enough to walk in.

He took a spot on the side of the small building, out of view of the cameras watching the store's entrance. He turned the engine off and got out of the van. As he walked up to the store, all he could think about was the beef jerky. He should get three bags. Just in case. Maybe a big slushy would be a good idea too. He didn't want to get thirsty while he was working.

As he walked through the sliding glass doors, he sensed a fast motion behind him. It was a rush of air or someone coming up behind him. He could sense something behind him, but didn't make much of it. He turned down the first aisle and looked for his beef jerky. It only took him a moment to find the red labeled package. He could almost taste the smoky and salty dried meat in his mouth.

Suddenly, a loud boom erupted from the opposite end of the store. Reggie jumped. Was it from the direction of the cash register?

He didn't want to accept that he recognized the familiar sound. One moment, he was salivating at the thought of snacking. The next, adrenaline rushed through his body because he knew exactly what he'd heard. A gunshot.

He inched forward along the aisle. When he reached the end, he remained crouched behind the candy section. Something very bad was about to go down. But what?

"You better fucking listen up," said the man with the gun.

Reggie realized that it was the man from outside by the gas pump. The man was wearing a hoodie, and when the hood covered his head outside, he had looked like a black man. Now, with the hood down, Reggie realized that the man was wearing a black ski mask. The kind with eye and mouth holes.

"Just cool it, man. I'll give you the money," said the cashier. He was a bigger guy. Looked like he ate a lot of free snacks on the night shift.

The burglar waved his gun frantically. He was nervous and paced around as he looked in every angle. Even though he was searching, it was obvious that he wouldn't notice Reggie. He was sloppy, nervous. Terrifying.

"Just listen, fucker! Open the cash register!"

The cashier complied, working the register with one hand and waving the other to keep the burglar from thinking he was reaching for a weapon.

"Now put all that money in a plastic bag." He pushed forward, nearly shoving the gun into the cashier's face. "Hurry the fuck up!"

The cashier placed the money in a thin plastic grocery bag and handed it directly to the burglar.

Without waiting another second, the burglar turned around and ran to the sliding door. He passed Reggie as he did.

Instead of cowering, Reggie did something he never thought he would do. He never thought of himself as a hero. If anything, he thought of himself as a coward. One that hid in the grass as his family and village were destroyed. But at that moment, he wanted to chase the burglar. He wanted to catch him. The man was dangerous and needed to be stopped.

When he thought back to this moment later, Reggie would be baffled by his own reactions. Certainly it would have been better to just let this guy go. He could have grabbed his beef jerky and a slurpee and headed back to the van to monitor Jubilee in peace. Maybe this robber was some kind of kindred spirit to him, after all. Just another crook, a thief, like Roman and the rest of them.

But there was something about the situation that struck Reggie's sense of injustice. Maybe it was the trauma of his past. Maybe it was a sense of regret, long-buried but triggered by the sound of the gunshot. Maybe it was all the thinking he'd been doing about the grave unfairness between the winners and the losers of this world.

For whatever reason, he just couldn't. Let. It. Go.

As the burglar ran past him, Reggie jumped from his hiding spot. The burglar was already outside the door and didn't even notice Reggie following him. Just as Reggie got past the sliding doors, he paused, watching the burglar sprint for his car door.

In that brief moment, Reggie felt his arms squeezed and pressed against him. He was intending to move forward but he was stuck in place. His lungs had trouble taking air in as his ribs pinched together in his chest.

"I got you, damn it!" the voice of the cashier yelled behind him.

Reggie felt the cashier's large mass against him. The cashier seemed larger up close, and felt like he was towering behind Reggie. The cashier had him in a bear hug that felt like a vise grip.

"Your friend got away, but I'm not letting you go. The cops are already on their way."

"Ag, what are you talking about, man? I'm not with that chop!" Reggie squirmed, trying to loosen the man's hold. He had to get away. The van and all of their equipment was right there. There was no way that he could allow the van into the hands of the cops.

The cashier tightened his hold in a way Reggie wouldn't have thought possible. "I saw you come in with him. I knows people like you. Need to teach people like you a lesson."

This was bad. This was really really bad. How was he going to get out of this mess? The crew would never forgive him. He wouldn't be able to forgive himself. He struggled, and tried his best to get a stable footing. He squirmed and pushed, trying to get the huge man to let him loose.

Reggie watched the burglar's car pull away from the gas pump and swerve onto the main street, its tires screaming that it was going full speed. In seconds, it was out of sight.

Reggie was finally able to get his feet planted firmly to the pavement. He could feel the man's arms relax slightly. He readied himself for a definitive move. A head butt. Maybe a firm shove that could knock the man off balance and allow him to get away.

Reggie felt the man's right arm give and released him on that side. He didn't realize soon enough. He felt a large fist impact his right temple. The blow was so hard that it made his legs give way. He stumbled for a split second and then everything went black. He didn't even feel himself fall to the ground.

52

WHEN Reggie open his eyes, he was flat on his stomach. His arms were pulled taut behind him and there was a knee buried in his back.

For a moment, he assumed it was the fat cashier, but the knee wasn't heavy enough. It was still enough weight that made it impossible for him to get up.

Then he felt something stiff around his wrists. Plastic cutting into his skin. A zipping sound.

Reggie turned his head slightly to see a leg of a navy blue uniform. A cop. The police officer was placing plastic handcuffs on him. Was he being arrested?

He made a muffled noise, his speech slurred with his hazy consciousness.

He could hear the cop on top of him, "Whoa, there guy. Don't move."

He could feel the pressure - now a pain - from the knee between his shoulder blades increase.

The fear set in as he realized the situation he was in. This could not be happening. He couldn't be getting arrested. Not now. Shit. What was he going to do? He turned his head and saw the fat cashier talking to another cop.

The cop was writing in a small notepad. "So another black male was actually holding a gun, pointed at your face. That one got away?"

The fat cashier nodded. "Yes, sir. That's right. He just took off. I was lucky to catch this one by surprise. He didn't look like he had a gun, so I figured it was safe enough."

"And you're sure he was with the other suspect?"

"Yes, no question. They came in at the same time. He was hide'n behind the aisle. Guess cuz he didn't have a mask, too."

"Right, because the other one had a mask." The cop paused as if he had another question. Instead, he just wrote it down. He wasn't even trying to understand the situation.

Reggie felt his voice come back. "I was not a part of that. I was not with the chop."

The pressure on his back increased further. Any more and his back would be broken. "Don't make me smack you in the head, boy! I'll give it another knock if you don't settle."

"I'm trying to tell you. I wasn't a part of this. It's a misunder-..."

The cop slapped the back of Reggie's head. His face hit the ground. "Shut the hell up! What are you? Some kind of African? I have a taser with your name on it."

The other cop closed his notebook and stuck it in a case on his belt. "That was real brave of you risking your life like that. I think that's all we need for now." He turned to his partner.

"Bob, put him in the back. We'll take him in."

Bob raised Reggie to his feet, twisting his shoulders. This just was not happening. It could not be. He needed to get back to Roman and the crew. They needed him. He couldn't spend any time in jail. He thought sadly of his ill-fated craving.

"I was just here to get beef jerky!" He yelled it louder than he meant to. His adrenaline was pumping through him like a trapped animal. Reggie had to get away.

Without even realizing what he was doing, he pulled away from the cop. He must have done it so suddenly that the cop lost his grip and Reggie flung forward. He turned to look at the cop. He was angry and there was no hiding it.

He didn't know what to do next. What could he do? His hands were bound so tightly he couldn't move his arms. He couldn't run away. So he ran towards them.

"I didn't do..." he tried to yell.

A loud pop sounded and a cloud of confetti exploded from the Bob's hands. He didn't even see it happen, he just felt it. Two prongs stuck into him. He could feel them penetrate his skin. One pierced his chest, the other was somewhere on his side. Thin wires spiraled from them, leading to the Bob's hands.

The only thing he felt next was his body tensing. He only felt his body fall to the ground like a rigid board. It was like his whole body was pulsing. The pain was like nothing he could ever imagine, pain down to his core. It just wouldn't stop. It went on until everything went black again.

* * *

Roman and Burton watched in horror as Reggie's body fell to the ground.

Burton's fists clenched and his body leaned forward into a sprint. In mid step, Roman tackled his friend to the ground, keeping them in the shadows of the abandoned gas station across the street from the scene. It took all of Roman's strength to hold Burton back.

"I'm going to fuck them up," Burton struggled against him, trying to break free from Roman's embrace. Roman couldn't let another friend get pulled into this mess.

They hadn't expected the night to turn for the worse. When the van was found to be missing from the hotel parking lot, they had suspected Reggie would have gone to the convenience store down the street from the hotel. It was no more than a ten minute walk. A two minute drive.

When he wasn't back after ten minutes, they started to worry. Reggie knew he shouldn't leave the hotel without letting them know. If he did leave to get a snack or something, he had to be back right away.

After thirteen minutes of waiting, they decided to walk to the store. They would catch him on the way back if he was already on the way.

They didn't expect to see him sitting on the curb, two police officers hovering over him. His hands looked bound behind him. There was a fat man in a store uniform talking to them. What could Reggie have possibly done?

It became worse as they watched their friend get tasered and dropped to the ground. Burton was still trying to get free from Roman as the officers picked Reggie up. It looked like Reggie was able to stand on his own, so that was a good sign. He was most likely in a lot of pain and disoriented, but at least he was alive.

The officers took Reggie to their patrol car and threw him into the back. Burton relaxed, knowing it was hopeless to try and get to them at this point.

It was now up to Roman to come up with an idea to free Reggie.

They were going to take him to their jail. This much was clear. The patrol car read Fulton County Police on the side. At least Roman would be able to find him.

"What do we do now?" asked Burton. Roman had never heard him sound so helpless.

"First thing we have to do is grab the van."

The van was parked on the far side of the convenience store, almost hidden from view. Reggie had done that purposely. The police officers and the cashier may not have noticed it. As the patrol car drove away, the fat man went back into the convenience store. The van, with all their equipment and tools for the job sat in the dark. Out of sight.

Once the patrol car disappeared, Roman moved forward, out of the shadows. Burton was right behind him, scanning the area. They left the abandoned gas station pavement and crossed the barren, two-lane road. There were overhead lights that gave off a spherical glow in front of the convenience store. Roman angled their approach to remain in the darkness.

"What the hell did Reggie get caught up in?" whispered Burton as he came closer to the van.

"It doesn't make sense. But it doesn't matter. We need to get him out tonight. What time is it?"

Burton looked at his watch. The light blue glow from the watch's light seemed almost too bright in the darkness they were walking in.

"One, twenty five."

"We have five hours to find him and to get him out. When we get to the van, I'll call Bryce and Hope. Wake them up. We need to do a jailbreak... and we only have a few hours to do it."

Roman walked up to the passenger side and shoved his spare into the keyhole. This was definitely one of those times he was grateful for backup keys and contingency plans. He let Burton in on the driver's side.

Burton started up the engine. They both stared at the front corner of the store. They were out of sight, but there was no telling if the guy running the store would be alert to them.

After a few moments, Burton backed out of the parking spot and then drove to the road. He drove slowly, remaining in the darkness, and kept from revving the engine.

Roman sighed and shook his head, trying to clear it. They needed to run this fast and exact if they were going to make their flight.

It was time to call Bryce.

53

STEEP would have liked a few more hours of sleep. Four hours was not nearly enough, not with the hours he'd been keeping. The DDoS attacks had finally stopped in the early morning. At that point, his team had gathered enough information from the Experfax personnel that staying any longer would have been a waste of time.

After the confrontation with Chester, it actually seemed like all of it was a waste of time anyway. It was obvious to him that Chester and whatever company he belonged to was piggybacking the investigation to justify whatever they were doing behind closed doors. It didn't matter.

Whatever Chester was up to, Steep was sure he couldn't get in the way. He had to let go of the urge to retaliate.

The only ray of hope over the past twenty-four hours had been what Ivan had found. Data records were changing. Or, it looked like they were changing. At first, even Ivan wasn't sure what he was looking at.

There was code being added by the database across all the

records. It seemed innocuous enough, and appeared to be done by database maintenance programs in the Experfax software suites. It wouldn't have bothered Ivan, except for the fact that it was happening to all the records in large, systematic batches.

When Ivan had discussed it with the software engineer, Raj, the one person that should know more about it than anyone, he didn't seem phased. He said it was normal for the software updates from their vendors to upgrade their data from time to time. That was probably what it was.

After asking a few others in the room, Steep realized that even if there was a way to know what the records were showing, there was no failsafe protocol established within this company to stop it.

He decided the only thing he could do was have Ivan look into it further. Maybe he would be able to come up with a solution as well.

And that's where he had left it four hours ago. He had told Ivan to get some rest, but he was too excited and probably didn't.

The local hotel was of the smaller variety, but had enough capacity to block off a section of rooms and a small conference room they could meet in. There was a pool and room service from the Golden Corral restaurant next door.

Steep was rudely awakened by a text from Chester to meet him in the conference room. Steep was already waking up, but decided not to rush down. He took his time to freshen up and made himself a cup of coffee. About thirty minutes after the text, he went to the ground floor to the conference room.

Steep greeted Pickles, who was on shift to guard outside the door. He entered the room and the only person there was Chester perched on the edge of the table along the wall opposite the double door entrance. There were tables lined up in rows throughout the room. Most were covered in laptops.

Chester was on the phone. When Steep caught his eye, he quickly ended his conversation and put his phone away in the inner pocket of his suit. He raised up from the edge of the table and took a step forward as if to greet him. Even though there was no greeting, Steep was surprised the man had even reacted to him entering the room. The gesture was less condescending than usual.

As soon as Steep reached Chester, the man turned and stepped towards the back table. The condescension came back, and Steep hesitantly took the cue and followed next to him to the table.

"Hope the rest was good," Chester said in his characteristically hollow tone.

"Fine. What did you need to meet about?" Steep wasn't in the mood for small talk. Especially with this guy.

Chester took the hint and opened his palm toward the top of the table. Five case-binders were neatly laid next to each other across the tabletop. There were eight and half by eleven inch photos arranged on top of each folder. They looked like crops from surveillance footage from around the Experfax facility.

This must have been from his 'special surveillance access', Steep thought to himself. So special that the head of the technology group didn't even know it existed. There were even a few photos that didn't look like they were taken from inside or around the facility. He pushed his conspiracy thoughts aside for the time being.

Maybe Steep would finally get some answers. "What are all these?"

Chester smirked with satisfaction. "My analysts believe these individuals are part of the crew we are looking for. Possibly even the entire crew."

"How is that possible? How did you get these?"

"Like I mentioned before, my company has many resources. We were able to tap into a data backup we have that Experfax wasn't aware of. This crew was pretty ingenious. Smarter than most. They wiped all the security related servers as well as the company's email servers. There would have been no trace of them being onsite.

Chester continued, "But what they didn't know was that all the servers pipe through the network to the other locations where TRM also has access to. My analysts were able to find every questionable individual present that day. These three were on site. This one," Chester pointed to a shot of a girl, "This one was actually working as a temp at the facility for months."

Steep could do nothing else but listen, slightly flabbergasted. Chester's company was obviously doing something that was borderline illegal, yet evidence was evidence, and Steep was amazed they were finally on the verge of some.

Chester thankfully wasn't done with his presentation. "These two photographs were taken near the power substation just before the power outage. This is just a Seven Eleven down the street. They were getting gas and some snacks, but I'll clarify their ties in a little bit. Your agents went to look at the station, correct?"

Steep nodded, "Summers and Pickles found the transformer that triggered the outage. It was tampered with, but it was hidden very well. It would have passed any scrutiny if it wasn't for us looking so closely."

"Well, that fits my calculation then." Chester walked to the left end of the table to the first photo. "This is Roman Hawker. Occupation unknown. We only have him as 'self-employed.' He came in that day in disguise, but our facial recognition is advanced enough that it found him in our DMV database."

He stepped forward to the next photo. "Bryce Kingston, hedge fund exec. No obvious link in terms of motive, but they were childhood friends. Went to college together. Interesting that he happened to be onsite the day of the attacks to research the company's private holdings. Kingston was in a conference room with the tech personnel."

Chester moved to the next binder. "Hope Warner. Under an alias, she posed as a temp and the last day on her contract was the day of the incident. Again, the links are foggy here, but she is from the same hometown, same grade school. Same as her brother here, Burton Warner. Ex-Marine. Repo man. Probably capable of tampering with the power."

Chester finally came to the last one, "And this one, we think, is your hacker. Reggie Dymond. South African national. A vague link suggests that he was the roommate of Bryce Kingston in college, but records for that are unclear. Computer engineering at NYU. Was at MIT for six months working on a masters. After that, he just fell off the grid. No valid address. Visa expired years ago. Considered undocumented."

Steep stood there and took it all in. He wasn't sure if he should have been impressed or terrified of the display of information he had just witnessed. He stood and waited to see if Chester had anything else.

"Well, that's our crew. We have full jackets on each of every small detail we could find on them. I assure you, it is comprehensive. I assume you will be putting out a bulletin to apprehend them immediately. I still can't figure out what they were trying to do here. That is one thing my analysts couldn't figure out."

Steep suppressed a smile. At least there was one thing his team was better at. He wondered if Ivan had figured anything out yet.

"We have connections with many of the other reporting agencies. We already gave them warnings that this crew could be after them too. They are most likely gathering data to sell on the black market. They are either at one of these other locations, or they could already be back in New York, thinking they got away with another heist. Either way. We need to find them. Now."

Steep and Chester both knew this was more of an order than a request.

54

THE bench was too thin to allow for a comfortable position. The smell from the metal toilet a few feet away was unbearable. The other two prisoners were alternating perching on the bench and pacing around the narrow room. The only window was in the metal door.

For the last two hours, all Reggie had felt was pain. He hunched over, holding his sides as he tried his best to remain seated on the bench without falling.

The pain was more intense now than it had been when he was in the patrol car. His mind was racing then. The shock of everything that was happening to him distracted him from the pain.

The shock had worn off and all he had were his thoughts and loneliness in the small holding room. The throbbing at the site of his taser burn was nothing compared to the pain of knowing that he had ultimately failed. Failed his friends and failed the reason they had been working so hard for the past months.

If only he had stayed in the hotel parking lot, working like he'd been supposed to.

There was no telling what state Jubilee was in at the moment. She could very well be functioning at full capacity. Spreading all over the financial system. But if anything was going wrong, he wasn't there to troubleshoot and repair her.

Even if Jubilee was working flawlessly, there was now a high chance that the third and last company they were going to hit would have enough data to keep debts on people. The third company being infected would have guaranteed all the data would be lost. Now, there would be a chance - a slim one - that data could be recovered.

The feeling of failure only amplified the pain his body was feeling. He had been powerless to being pushed around and abused as he was getting processed. They'd taken his wallet with all the forged IDs and credit cards. They'd taken his picture and his prints, and all of it was now in their system. Eventually, they would realize he wasn't the same person pictured on the California driver's license. That the credit cards were not real. It would take some time, maybe a few days to a week. But eventually, they would find out. And things would become worse.

Roman and the others had no idea where he was. They would be coming down, looking for the van, and have no idea where he had gone. They would have to find the van first. Maybe they would find it at the convenience store. There would be no reason to think that he was in jail. It was inconceivable.

He gently rubbed the small wounds on his chest and side where the probes had punctured his skin. He could feel them through the small holes in his shirt. His entire body shivered at the memory of the electricity pumping through him.

They would have to give up looking for him eventually. Even if they kept looking, it would take them days to realize that he was in jail. They knew how to search public records and police incident reports for his name. But it could be weeks before the name would show up on anything, depending on how slowly the cops filed their reports.

It could even be months.

For the time being, the crew would have to move on without him. There was a backup plan, but it would make the next stage of the heist so much more difficult.

There were exact instructions detailed in a file hidden on a secure cloud server. They each had instructions that Roman had made them create for each of their roles. Contingencies for situations like the one he was in. If Roman followed the steps, it would take him a lot longer, but it would technically work. That was, if he didn't make a single mistake.

If Reggie had a laptop or even a smartphone, he would be able to hack himself out. But he had nothing. It was the middle of the night. The cops told him that he couldn't even make a phone call. Not until morning. His mind was so clogged that he couldn't even remember the emergency phone number.

He leaned back on the bench and stretched his legs out. After trying a few different positions, he was finally able to balance himself enough on the bench where he could get comfortable and relax. He let his eyes close and did his best to ignore the pain in his body. Ignore the regret in his mind. This was an impossible situation. He didn't need to remind himself that he had been through the impossible before.

Just as he was close to sleep, the metal door made the sound of it unlocking. A police officer appeared from behind the door and called, "Reynolds." Reynolds was the name in his wallet. "Follow me."

Reggie stood up from the bench. His body resisted, with a new pain in his lower back appearing. What could they want from him now?

Was he about to be interrogated for something he didn't do? They didn't listen to him at the store. They didn't listen to him in the back of the patrol car. They didn't listen while he pleaded not to be processed. Why would they listen to him now?

He followed the police officer through a common area and narrow hallway. They stopped at a small room with a table and two chairs that were all bolted down to the floor.

"Sit over there," The officer pointed across the table to the chair opposite of the door.

Reggie complied and sat down, trying not to wonder how much worse this situation was going to get. Maybe they already knew his identity was forged. Maybe they had found a faster way to convict him.

Or even worse, maybe they already knew his real identity. Reggie Dymond, undocumented immigrant. They would deport him back to Africa. A place he could no longer call home. Away from his friends, with no hope of return.

"Place your hands on the table in front of you here," commanded the officer, patting in front of shackles that were retained to the table top by a bolted down metal loop. He placed his hands as instructed and the officer snapped the cuffs on his wrists, squeezing both tightly.

Without another word, the officer left him alone in the room with the door closed.

Minutes passed by with no indication of what was going on. All he could think was that he was glad to sit on a normal chair. He laid his forehead down on the table and let his entire body relax. It was the first relaxed moment he'd had all night.

He must had fallen asleep for some time before the door opened. His eyes were still closed when he felt someone sit down in front of him. When he opened his eyes, it took a moment for his sight to clear.

When he saw Roman in front of him, he nearly screamed with joy.

"Hello Mr. Reynolds. Remember me? I'm Brian Jones. Your attorney?" Roman said. He made it clear that Reggie was to follow his lead. Reggie looked up at the corner of the room. A camera recorded the conversation.

"Mr. Jones. I am so glad you found me. This is all a mistake."

"I'm sure it is." Roman glanced over his shoulder at the camera, seeming to determine its exact position. He pulled from a laptop bag what looked like a leather bound writing pad holder. He placed it within reach of Reggie's hands and opened it to reveal a thin tablet PC. It was one of Reggie's from the van.

"I have some paperwork for you to fill in. The officers here have already processed your information into their systems, so I just need some more information from you so that we can start your case."

Roman continued to talk, basically repeating what he'd said already in different ways. It was obviously filler for the benefit of the surveillance camera, because the screen on the pad was open to the notepad app with instructions typed on it.

"Wi-fi is already connected and we are in their intranet. They follow electronic protocol here. Find Judge in Fulton County and send release OR."

Reggie knew exactly what the note meant. A release OR was an order that came from a judge that would allow him to be released on his "Own Recognizance."

Joseph Preacher

It only took a few minutes as Roman kept talking filler. He searched the police station's network and gained access to their court records software. He found a judge that gave eighty percent of the release ORs in the county. He filled in the necessary forms and sent the release order.

He gave a thumbs up to Roman, and Roman smiled with a nod. They waited there together until a police officer came to give them the good news.

55

ROMAN let his tension go as they stepped across the threshold of the police station. The situation could have ended worse, much worse. Still, he couldn't help wonder if fate was starting to resist against what he was trying to do.

He brushed the thoughts aside as they approached the edge of the sidewalk. The white van pulled up to greet them. Hope and Bryce opened the side door to let Reggie in. Hope handed him his laptop before holding him in a long embrace.

Roman jumped up to the front passenger seat and gave Burton, behind the wheel, a nod. They were still on track, minus some rest and trauma that was immeasurable for Reggie.

Roman felt a pang of guilt. He knew it wasn't completely logical, but he couldn't help but blame himself for Reggie's ordeal. What had he been thinking, dragging them across the country, from city to city, facing unknown after unknown, and for what? They were risking their lives for something that had an unknown result. Something that could help the world, just as much as hurt it.

And while this arrest had been a case of mistaken identity, lazy cops, and perhaps even some systemic racism, the next time any of them ended up behind bars could be for crimes they really had committed.

After a few minutes, Reggie seemed to regain his typical countenance. His eyes focused on the screen, typing and studying, as if nothing had happened.

"How are we looking?" Roman asked gently, assessing if Reggie was truly ready to get back in the game. Flashes of Reggie's body stiffening to the ground returned as he noticed scabs and scrapes on the side of his face.

After a brief silence, Reggie looked up from the screen with a smile. An honest smile for his friends to know that he was okay. Roman could feel a sense of relief rush across him. It was fleeting, but it was enough for the moment.

"Jubilee is spreading like it should," Reggie relayed as his eyes scanned the screen. The colored text reflected from his dark eyes.

"We'll be at the airport parking lot in ten. Should be just enough time to get to the flight," Burton said from the driver's seat.

Roman faced forward in his seat but kept an eye on Reggie in the reflection of the wide angle side view mirror. His composure seemed fine, but should it be? The only thing that mattered more to Roman than getting through the rest of his plan was his friends. One small incident had almost cost one of them his freedom. Any more small mistakes could mean the end of them.

They entered the airport's long-term parking lot. They would leave the van there indefinitely. It would eventually be towed and forgotten. There would be no links that could lead back to them.

"We have an hour to get through security and to the gate,"

reminded Bryce.

"I need a vodka. I'm going to sleep the whole way," said Hope.

"We all should. Sleep I mean. Maybe not the vodka. We can rest some more once we arrive. We're almost on the home stretch," Roman added.

Reggie was still working as they unpacked and cleaned the van of their fingerprints and DNA. He sat atop his carry-on luggage off to the side. He was working off cellular data and he had to use every moment he had left to work. Once he was on the plane, he'd be cut off.

"Looks like we're done here. Ready to go, Reggie?" asked Roman.

Reggie's eyes were wide with surprise. He shook his head slowly. There was an uneasiness about him that Roman was familiar with, and didn't like at all.

"What is it?" Roman asked.

The crew maneuvered behind Reggie, all getting a view of his screen.

"We have a problem," Reggie said. "The FBI is on to us."

Once Roman had a good view of his screen, he realized what Reggie was talking about. On the screen there were multiple windows stacked on each other. Each had a DMV photo of each of them. Roman had an idea what they were, but he had to ask.

"What are these, Reggie?"

"They're FBI APB's. With our names on them."

Burton took a step back. "Wait a minute. The Feds? How is that possible?"

"There's no way they could have figured it out from Reggie getting arrested," added Bryce.

Roman placed a hand on Reggie's shoulder. "Let's take it slow. Can we see what this bulletin is about?"

Reggie expanded one of the windows. This one was about Roman.

"These are APBs being sent out on the joint intelligence network. It's saying these individuals are wanted in connection to a cyber-based attack. Locations unknown. Arrest on sight. This is going out nationwide to all authorities down to the local level."

Roman could feel a slight tremor through Reggie's shoulder. He wasn't sure if it was from Reggie or from his own body.

"This isn't good," said Bryce.

"That's an understatement. We're done. We can't show our faces anywhere. It'll take one person to recognize us and we're totally screwed," said Burton.

Roman's mind started spinning. This was a worse case scenario. The moment he always feared in any job they did.

There was always a chance that their identities would get blown, but it was still a shock to actually realize it had just happened. It didn't matter how, or what mistake they had made that had caused their identities to become known. No matter how careful they were, it was done. They were caught.

It only mattered what they did from that moment on.

"What's the time of this bulletin, Reggie?"

"Ten minutes ago."

"Okay, ten minutes ago. That means it's still fresh and isn't fully disseminated. We can probably get past the TSA using our current legends. Bryce, you have your alternate, right?" Roman said, referring to the IDs and other materials that supported Bryce's alter ego.

Roman knew what he wanted to do, but it couldn't only be up to him. He stepped out in front of them at an angle that he could see all of them as he spoke. "This is it. We've been compromised. We've prepared for this, but we have to decide together what to do next. We only have two options. Option one, we cut out, and use our escape plans. We leave each other right now, and escape with our lives and hide. Wait until the heat dies down, before we can even talk to each other, but disappear forever."

They each had in their luggage a well hidden compartment that was camouflaged from looking suspicious in x-ray machines. It contained their emergency legends with passports, local IDs, credit cards and cash. They each had a plan memorized on the itinerary they would follow to get to Morocco. It was a country with no extradition where they could hide indefinitely. It was a place they could access the scores from their previous jobs. Though forced early retirement wasn't ideal, it was the safer option.

"If we take that option, that means that this job is over. That we can't inject Jubilee into target three. That means that everyone's debt will still be valid and the job has failed. But that's okay. We can't win them all. I say we go with option one, and get out of the country before the manhunt for us gets impossible to hide from. The sooner we do it, the safer we are."

There was a long pause as they looked at each other. Reggie wasn't looking at his screen. He was looking at Roman. After a short moment, they all were.

"What's option two?" asked Bryce.

Roman shrugged, as if it hardly mattered. "Option two is that we get on the plane for Chicago. Risk getting caught the entire way.

And we finish the job. By the time we finish, we're not going to be able to use our escape plans. We'll have to figure out a different way to get out of the country."

Burton looked at his sister. "What do you think? I can't risk you going to jail."

Hope glanced at Burton. "I want to finish the job. This is bigger than we are," she said, cutting him off.

Roman swallowed hard. "You really have to think this through. All of you. It's our lives we're talking about. There's a good chance we don't succeed and we still get caught."

"Then we better be careful. I think we should finish the job," added Bryce.

"I want to see Jubilee complete," nodded Reggie, not needing to add anything further.

Burton looked at each of them and then at Roman. "I'm in if you're in."

Roman seemed to be the only one that wasn't sure. This time, he would trust their judgement. If they were adamant about seeing his plan through, his responsibility here was clear.

He would need to concentrate to get them through this. It was going to take the best plan he'd ever come up with.

56

THEY arrived in Chicago around ten forty five. It felt like the longest flight Roman had ever taken. His mind was both exhausted and humming with possibilities, thinking through all the outcomes that came ahead of them.

He rehashed the remainder of the plan and all the contingencies that they had come up with. They had to take down the last of the three big credit reporting agencies. The company had too much data. It would retain the records of debt for most of the population.

This had always been an all-or-nothing game for Roman. Without the third hit succeeding, there was no purpose to any of it. But his friends had looked at him with such trust, he could hardly stand it. Even with the Feds closing in on them, they wanted to stand by him. To see this thing through. He could not fail them now, or ever.

As they left the plane, they separated from each other. They maintained visual contact, but hid amongst the other passengers. The goal was to keep airport security cameras from ever linking them together if one of them were caught for any reason. This was how they always planned to travel, but their vigilance was now more necessary.

Eventually, they all arrived at the long term parking lot. They took separate shuttles and Burton, Hope, and Reggie were already in the large SUV waiting patiently when Roman and Bryce finally arrived.

Roman looked over at his closest confidant, "We're doing the right thing, aren't we?"

Bryce looked up at the late morning sky. The summer air was much cooler than it had been down south. "If we even help a few thousand people, it will be worth it. We have gotten away with so much already. We've done things only for ourselves. This time, the reward will be taking this system down, even if it's just temporary. Even if it only helps a few people. This is the right thing to do."

Roman nodded. It hadn't been so long ago since he had been sitting across from Bryce at their favorite diner, talking him into this whole thing. Roman tried to bring himself back to that moment, when he had been sure this would work.

Roman took shotgun, with Burton already behind the wheel. Burton looked over at him, "Are we going with Alabaster?" He was referring to the original plan.

The third stage of the plan required having multiple set up locations, depending on the situation that waited for them when they landed in Chicago. If there had been no heat at all, they would have been able to carry out a more covert plan that involved many stages across the next few days. They would con their way into the building and sneak around to implant Jubilee. It would have required a lot of finesse and time.

Unfortunately, there was heat. That would require a more direct approach that was more abrupt, but would cause enough chaos that there would be no way to stop what they were going to do.

"No. We're going with Sesame," Roman said. Bryce smiled.

This was a last resort plan that would be much more interesting.

Roman instructed, "Have Greg meet us at the warehouse."

Burton gave a thumbs up. "We're all set."

Hope laughed out loud.

The only one that wasn't excited was Reggie.

57

UNIONTRANS was going to be their toughest nut to crack. Instead of having their own facility, the company opted to use a shared, co-location data warehouse company.

This data warehouse company was called Rise. It was known for rock-solid technology and top-notch facilities. They managed the day-to-day maintenance of the server farms and provided security for multiple clients. Their security wasn't just industry standard, it set the industry standard across the nation.

The crew's target was no exception. Their target was a windowless, three story building that was a part of a two hundred and fifty thousand square feet campus in the middle of a quiet industrial zone. It had less than a hundred employees in this huge area, most of whom were roaming armed security guards.

Everyone knew each other, and anyone that wasn't recognized was scrutinized. The security cameras were on a closed circuit system that had all of its hubs in the same room as the security guards.

There was no way to tap into it from the outside.

There were no floor plans that were published and kept in a government agency. There was no way of figuring out what was behind those windowless walls. There were redundant systems for water, power and air, and the only way they would be able to cut the power would be to take down the main power grid that was less than a kilometer away. There was only one set of double doors on each of the four walls and a single loading bay that was furthest from the public road.

The crew's crash pad was a short drive from the airport. They arrived at a mostly industrial area that was tucked between a green landscaped suburbia and a large railroad yard. They had rented a warehouse that was only used as a haunted house during the Halloween season. The owner was a quiet man who asked no questions when their offer was high enough. There was a lot of space, and it was a only a few miles from Rise's facilities.

Their semi-truck and trailer was already parked at the loading dock. Greeting them at the door was Greg Gonzales.

"How was the drive in?" Burton asked, giving him a bump on the shoulder.

"Good, good. Got here this morning. Got everything that you asked for." Greg had driven the last two days from New York, hauling the trailer that held everything they needed for the last part of the job.

This was the first time Greg had met the rest of the crew. They all knew he was coming on board and already thought highly of him. Greg knew just enough to know that he should respect them.

Burton gave the introductions as they walked into the warehouse.

Roman shook Greg's hand warmly. "Thanks for helping us with

this, Greg. Burton says you do good work."

Greg nodded respectfully and followed them as they walked to the back.

The front half of the building was still decorated from the last Halloween, but the back half was completely bare floor and ready for their use and set up.

Burton opened the loading bay door and opened the large padlocks on the trailer door. The doors swung open to reveal four 750cc Japanese sport bikes and some large cardboard boxes. There were also some large military storage boxes. They were bulky with numerous latches all around. They looked like they contained something sinister.

Burton turned around, beaming at the prospect that all his hard work of gathering these things was about to pay off.

58

THE cluster of buildings was ordinary and looked like nothing more than large warehouses. But looks were deceiving: it was a physical and virtual fortress.

Past the steel fence that covered its perimeter, every square meter was monitored with sensors of every kind and closed-circuit cameras with infrared and night vision. Motion and pressure sensors, seismic for detecting earthquakes. Alarms for smoke, fire, and carbon monoxide.

The facility had a direct link to both the state and local fire and police departments. Any alarm that was triggered would send an immediate dispatch to authorities. It worked twenty four hours a day, all year round.

The facility provided critical technology infrastructure to multiple tenants that included major media companies and financial institutions. Rise was their clients' virtual backbones and they were protected like no other.

The original plan had been to infiltrate the building covertly using stolen credentials off a few of the guards. Take a few days, assemble what they needed, and then enter during the day. Far more security measures were taken during the night, so the crew had planned to simply avoid that time of day.

That was the original plan. To follow their modus operandi, to remain hidden. To make it so that no one would even realize they were there.

Technically, it was inconceivable that taking down all three companies was possible.

And now they only had one left.

And it would not be simple.

The situation was suddenly accelerated.

At any time, the authorities could be on top of them. There was no way for Reggie to know where they were in their investigation; he had tried. There was no time to dig deeper. They would have to go with the contingency and hope for the best.

The contingency wasn't going to be quiet. It was going to be very loud.

59

THEY were ready. Roman was sure of it. He revved the motorcycle's engine. Reggie, Bryce, and Hope revved their own engines next to him.

All four of them were clad in leather motorcycle race suits. They were about to ride aggressively and needed all the protection possible. Roman flexed his hands, testing the fit of his gloves. There was one minute on the clock display attached to his bike's instrument cluster. Sixty seconds until the plan was in effect.

They had practiced this plan only a dozen times over the last few months. It was only supposed to be a contingency, after all.

They would have to be exact in the execution. They would only have one chance at it.

Twenty seconds. Roman leaned forward on the bike, bringing up the kickstand.

"Everyone. Ready?" he spoke into the helmet mic.

"Ag, man, I don't know about this..." Reggie said.

"You'll be alright," Roman replied.

"Ready," the others said in unison.

The timer beeped at zero and went into stop-clock mode, counting the milliseconds. Roman revved his engine again and released the brake, bringing up his feet. The motorcycle rocketed forward. The tires squealed under him and the wind against his helmet made it impossible to hear the others behind him. But he knew they were there.

They raced through the suburban streets, passing a few cars here and there, but the area was rarely congested. They remained in a straight line formation, about a car's length apart. It was important to remain tight and coordinated. They only changed lanes to weave around the occasional car.

The stop-clock on Roman's dash read two minutes and thirty seconds. They were exactly on time as they approached the front gate of the Rise facility.

The front gate looked more like it was protecting a military compound than server farms. There was a large entry barrier that folded down to the ground once vehicles were allowed to pass by. The guard booth was manned by two uniformed armed guards. There would have been two guards there if it wasn't the time that the guards changed shifts for the entire facility. They did the change over at exactly two PM daily, without fail.

That was the exact time the two sport bikes sped past the entry barrier. The barrier kept normal vehicles out, but there was just enough room to allow bikes past without obstruction.

60

A few miles away, Burton and Greg were sitting in position in a black tinted SUV, hidden beneath an underpass with a municipal surveillance camera that no longer worked. Burton was in the driver's seat with Greg riding shotgun. Greg was monitoring little dots on a map that represented the crew. They were utilizing specialized GPS trackers that only Greg's computer had access to.

"They're at the gate," Greg relayed to Burton.

Burton had his own laptop open in front of him. On his screen was a single dialog menu; Reggie had been kind enough to make Burton's job as simple as possible. The dialog read, 'Open CCTV program' with an 'OK' button and a 'Cancel' button. According to the open text document with instructions, it was not yet time to do anything.

The anticipation was still making him sweat.

"So don't press the 'OK' yet?" Burton asked Greg for confirmation.

"No boss, just hang tight."

Burton smiled and spoke into his mic, "You know, Dungeon Master. I don't get why you think this is so hard."

61

ROMAN and Bryce raced past the entry barrier at full speed. The two end-of-shift guards were already completely out of the guard house, awaiting the two oncoming guards walking up to the guard booth. They were dumbfounded as they watched the first two bikes pass.

They didn't even register the two motorcycles behind them, with Hope and Reggie coming to a full sideways and screeching stop.

Roman and Bryce also came to a drifting stop fifty yards ahead, just short of the two oncoming guards. They were just as surprised and jerked back, afraid that they were coming into a head on collision.

It was close. Roman and Bryce lifted their tasers in unison. As soon as the red flashing lasers were center mass of their targets, wires and prongs made contact on both guards. Both fell instantly; the bodies became rigid, only moving from spasming muscles.

Hope took care of both of the guards that were next to the booth herself, wielding a taser in each of her hands. She hit both of them in their backs. They fell forward from the sudden shock. The guards had rifles aimed at Roman and Bryce, but they didn't get a chance to let off a shot before they were stunned.

While she held onto the trigger, the five thousand volts kept pumping into them until they were obviously incapacitated. Reggie looked away, not wanting to remember his own ordeal.

Reggie unslung his own weapon. It was a paintball gun that was set up to hit a target as accurately as a bullet from fifty yards away. He aimed it at the security camera dome attached to the roof of the guard booth. White balls splattered against the black glass dome, blocking any possible view the camera beneath it had. Another splatter hit the camera attached to the top of a pole across the entranceway. In the seconds that passed during the second wave of the attack, Roman and Bryce went to work binding the limbs of the disabled guards tightly with large plastic zip ties.

Hope started towards the incapacitated guards as Reggie let down his kickstand and dismounted his motorcycle. He kept the engine running as he walked to the guard booth.

Inside, he raised his visor, but kept his helmet and gloves on. He scanned the booth to figure out what was where. There was just enough room for two people, with a built in desk that housed two computers and a metal control panel with a few large buttons on it. It looked like there were buttons for different lights and the motorized barrier. There was also a panic button, which the guards would have hit if the crew had come a few seconds too soon.

Reggie hit the switch for the barrier and looked out the booth window to see that it was coming down. As soon as he confirmed it, he pulled a small computer out of his backpack. It was about the size of a shoebox. He had spent only a few days building it, but it was precisely configured for their needs.

He searched the back of one of the computers for the network cable. He found the right one, disconnected it from the computer and connected it to the one on his shoebox computer. He did the same with the monitor and keyboard. The unit was already running on its own built in battery, so there was no need to wait for it to start up.

Reggie opened up a terminal window and ran the script program to connect to the facility's security system. After it was done, he confirmed that they were able to control whatever they wanted. He set the camera feeds from the paint balled cameras to loop a video of a two minute video segment recorded earlier in the day.

"How are we doing in there?" Roman's voice came over his helmet speaker. He looked out to see Roman dragging the body of one of the unconscious guards behind the bushes that lined the driveway. Bryce was already next to the booth, helping Hope bind the last guard. Those two would soon be dragged into the booth.

"We are all set. Lookout should now have control of the Rise systems. Lookout, confirm." Reggie said, referring to Burton and Greg.

After a brief silence, Burton responded, "We are in." The small computer also had a high-speed cellular data connection.

A minute later, all four guards were hidden away, the barricade was left open and they were back on their bikes.

With the entrance open, Roman estimated that they had about ten minutes before the vulnerable guard outpost attracted suspicion.

They would need every moment.

All four sped into the facility.

62

BURTON stared at the screen, trying his best to remember everything Reggie had taught him. Teaching was not Reggie's strong suit. And learning wasn't Burton's.

Why would Roman want him to play this part? Hope, or even Bryce, would have made more sense. No, he knew why, but dammit, he hated computers. He looked over at Greg, who was busy monitoring the others' progress.

"Are you ready, Lookout?" Roman's voice asked in Burton's ear.

Burton tried to hide his nervousness. "I'm all over it."

"We're coming up to stop two. Fifteen seconds."

"No pressure there," Burton said as he looked at the text document of Reggie's instructions on the screen. He scanned what he needed to do and went to the window displaying the access controls for the entire compound. He found the correct door, and moved his mouse using the trackpad. He right clicked and selected 'open'.

Greg was scanning the video array and relayed, "Door is opening. You'll be clear in three… two… one".

Burton let out a sigh of relief. He looked at the next step on the instructions and readied his mouse pointer.

* * *

Roman could see what Burton and Greg were relaying. The loading dock door was opening on their target building just 2 meters ahead. The others were right behind him.

He started to decelerate.

His mind refocused to the point that time seemed to slow down. He watched the clock on his dash. It was six minutes since they passed the gate. Everything was still on track.

The loading dock was two trailers wide with a ramp that led up to the high loading platform and two rolling steel doors. Greg had opened the one on the right. The loading dock was used to allow trucks with full size trailers to back into it. The building was made to accommodate any configuration, allowing for large specialized equipment to be moved in and installed easily. This made it future proof - and easier to upgrade and keep efficient. That meant larger corridors, larger doors throughout. And easier for motorcycles to get from one side of the fifty thousand square foot building to the other, where they needed to be.

Roman sped at thirty mph up the ramp on the side. He made a sharp turn when he reached the loading level and, without braking, entered the building. He could hear the echo of the others' engines as they entered the space behind him.

The space was wide open like a large warehouse. The ceiling vaulted up to the roof line, showing the steel rafters. All ducting and wiring was visible, but well-organized and routed in a way that made it easy to follow and manage. The only divisions of the space were freestanding structures that acted as small rooms. Some of these housed sections of server racks and not much else.

There were no offices here. No personnel. It was nothing but a warehouse of technology that required only occasional maintenance. Otherwise, it was all managed remotely.

Even though UnionTrans was the smallest of the three companies, their security measures were the most advanced. Multiple layers of encryption and protocols triggered at any sign of intrusion. If they had tried to access the network remotely, there was too much of a chance that they would be detected and shut out.

If Reggie had more time, he would have found a safe way into the network and they would have been fine. But with the Feds on their asses, there was no time. They had to inject Jubilee immediately.

They had to do this the hard way. It would have to be about speed. It would have to be done before anyone realized they were even there.

Since hacking in remotely was out of the question, they had to get Reggie right next to the machine this time. There was no way Reggie could remotely plug in. He would have to actually type on the system keyboard physically.

"Reggie, which one is it?" Roman said as he slowed to a cruise. He realized he had just said Reggie's real name, but didn't have time to worry about it. They only had four minutes before they had to make their way out of the compound.

"We need to find the central hub, where everything is connected." Reggie was behind him stopping. Roman and the rest stopped with him.

UnionTrans was also the most advanced in crypting their

documentation. Reggie was able to find pieces of information on how their network was configured, but there was little documentation when it came to this facility. And they didn't have time to find it. It wasn't how Roman normally liked to work, but it was the only thing they could do, and Reggie would have to figure it out.

Roman watched as Reggie looked across the ceiling, his helmet moving as he scanned the ducting and wiring.

"I think I found it." Reggie said.

"I'll follow you." He looked over at Hope and Bryce. "You two know what to do?"

Both of them nodded. They maneuvered their bikes in different directions and sped off down two separate pathways.

Reggie pointed his bike and went towards the east side of the warehouse. Roman followed.

Reggie took a high-speed turn to the right and then to the left. He went so fast that Roman nearly missed the second turn.

They stopped in front of a large white drywalled structure. If Roman was to guess, it was about two meters, perfectly cubed. It was close to being a central location in the building and it did look like all the cabling from the other structures were leading to the top of this main structure.

"Are you sure it's this one?" Roman asked.

"I'm sure." Reggie looked determined. "Let's do this."

63

ROMAN looked down at the stop-clock. Three and a half minutes. They were cutting it close. Reggie wouldn't have much time. They planted their kickstands, leaving the engines running. They walked up to the door of the hub. It was glass, but looked like it was shatterproof thick. There was a keypad and biometric sensor on the side of the door.

Reggie walked up to it and typed in a combination of asterisks, zeros, nines and pound signs. It was the sequence to get into admin mode for the locking system. Most electronic locking systems were equipped with an admin system set with a default passcode. At some level, most companies never thought to change the admin passcode, especially when there were multiple layers of security on top of it.

Reggie had memorized every admin code for every technology locking model made in the last ten years. As expected, a buzz sounded and a green indicator lit above the keypad. They were in.

"Keep your helmet on," Roman reminded. Even though Burton and Greg were in control of the security system, there was always the possibility someone could appear that could identify them, or that there were other cameras on a subsystem or could make recordings off the system.

Reggie nodded and only lifted his visor so he could better see. Roman scanned the area even though he was pretty sure no one would appear. If someone did, it would be too late. He entered the room behind Reggie.

Reggie could have done this part on his own, but Roman knew that he didn't like to be this close to the action. If Reggie made even one mistake, the job would be over, and they would have to risk Jubilee not having a permanent effect. So if Roman being there made Reggie more confident and less likely to make a mistake, it was worth it.

Reggie scanned the racks of servers. He speed walked down the center aisle, turning his head from left to right as fast as he could. Roman followed behind and scanned down the aisle at a slower pace, helping Reggie look for a workstation terminal. A simple keyboard and monitor that made it possible to access the servers.

Reggie ran down the last aisle and came up to a server rack at the end. There was a screen mounted flush to the rack. Reggie pulled on a handle below it to reveal a drawer holding a keyboard and small trackball.

Reggie tapped a key and the monitor came to life with text.

Roman looked at his watch. "Can you do it in two minutes?" he asked Reggie.

"I can do it ninety seconds," Reggie responded.

Roman watched as Reggie unzipped a pocket on his motorcycle jacket and pulled out a USB. He plugged it into an exposed port above the monitor.

Reggie focused and got to work. Roman walked to the door to

keep a lookout.

64

THROUGH the glass door, Roman caught a glimpse of movement around their motorcycles. He ducked down low and rushed towards the door, trying his best to keep himself hidden behind the wall around the doorway.

He hated having to keep the helmet on, because it was too large to peek around. He didn't have time to think. There was no time for caution. He took a deep breath and moved forward, opening the door. He scanned the entire area. There was only one man there. The man was looking at the motorcycles curiously. He looked like a security guard, most likely roaming the area. Roman rushed forward, assessing the situation as fast as he could while trying not to make a sound.

The man had his back to Roman. It looked like he was reaching for something on his belt. It was a radio. The man suddenly jerked around. He could hear Roman coming. The man was fast and reached up to grab Roman as they impacted. Roman lead with a punch to the guard's face. It made contact, but not as hard as Roman would have liked. He felt a punch to his gut, but he threw the rest of his body at the guard, leading with his helmet. The helmet made better contact with the guard's face, making him fall backwards with Roman on top of him.

The man grabbed Roman's helmet under the chin and started to pull, nearly jerking the helmet off. Roman threw another punch, and this time, it was hard enough to make the guard release his helmet. Roman threw himself off and attempted to get up.

The guard tackled him, wrapping his torso with his arms. Roman felt himself get pushed back. He realized that the man's head was under his right arm. It took him two tries, but Roman was able to put his forearm under the man's chin and used his left hand to assist. He tightened his arm, his muscles aching from the strain.

He could feel his body tilt left slightly as the man tried to free himself. Roman gritted his teeth. He mustered his will, challenging himself to squeeze harder. The man bucked again, and slowly weakened. Roman could feel his body go limp. He held his choke hold for a few more breaths.

When he was sure the man was truly knocked unconscious, he released his grip. He could feel his muscles numb from the relief. The man's body slumped to the floor.

As Roman stood up, Reggie came up behind him. "It's done."

Roman caught his breath. "Jubilee is planted. Are the charges set?" He was directing the question to Bryce and Hope.

They were on opposite corners of the building where they had set up home made bombs with cellular detonators. These would cause small explosions that were just big enough to set off smoke and fire alarms in the building.

"Number one set," Bryce responded.

"Number two set," Hope followed.

Roman breathed with relief as he jumped on his motorcycle.

Reggie was already on his, kicking up his stand.

"Meet at the rally point," Roman commanded.

Their tires wailed against the polished concrete as they raced back the way they came.

As they approached the still open garage door, Roman could see the tail lights of Bryce and Hope exiting. They had made it. There was no stopping Jubilee.

As they exited the building and went down the ramp, Roman tapped the send button on the burner cell phone he had taped to the fuel tank of the bike. It would group text a specific code to both detonators. Two seconds later, he heard the explosions behind him. There were only two, and the sounds they made were much more powerful than the destruction they would cause. The man he'd left unconscious would wake up to nothing more than a fire alarm and foam from the chemical suppression system.

The explosives were there to trigger a chain reaction. The UnionTrans servers in that building were not unique to the company. It was only a part of a larger network of duplicate server farms. These server farms were located all over the world and acted as redundant systems for each other.

When there was a natural disaster or fire or any other unforeseen event that threatened the data in a particular location, the system would instantly synchronize all its data and software to all the other locations. For speed, it would bypass any security barriers to assure that it would transfer all the data.

Jubilee had just taken a one-way express trip into UnionsTran's entire secure network.

65

STEEP was tired of flying. As soon as the APB was issued, the team closed shop in McKinney. They were now on a plane that Chester had arranged, and it was much more luxurious than the Air Force G-V. They were heading to New York, hoping that the crew would come back to their home. Maybe they wouldn't know there was an APB out on them. Maybe they were already there. It was their only lead.

He had been studying the suspects' files for hours. There was no conceivable way that Chester could have legally come up with the evidence and links to them.

But they made sense. Roman Hawker must had been the leader, if they ran that way. It was either him or the other guy, Bryce Kingston. But Roman seemed more of anti-establishment type. The kind with an IQ high enough to cause a lot of trouble.

On paper, they all seemed to be non-threatening, law abiding citizens. All living within their means. All with normal or explainable gaps of employment. Credit records seemed normal.

Their records were very clean.

The only red flag about it was that they were all near the Experfax incident. If it wasn't for Chester and his team finding obscure links between them, it would have been an excusable oversight.

In the files were the photos from the ATM job. Nothing but motorcycle outfits and helmets. But he could make the connection. There were random photos from their social media accounts. Nothing interesting there. If they were a crew, they were one of the most disciplined crews Steep had ever seen.

Steep kept fingering through the files while sitting next to Ivan. He was getting to know the crew as Ivan was trying to understand what their hidden malware was doing. Ivan's only explanation was that he knew there must be some exploit happening even though he couldn't see the exploit happening. There were no obvious rogue programs. There were no visible alterations that were common with rootkits.

Ivan tried to sync a backup that was made before the attack, and its data was corrupted within seconds. They tried doing the same on a clean install system, and that only took a moment for the old backup data to be corrupted. But it wasn't clear what the corruption was, and Ivan still wasn't sure what the extra data in each record did.

They could have been simple hashes that were common with databases. There were a number of other fields that contained hashes.

All he knew was that every time he removed it, it added itself back. There was underlying machine language that was compiled and working, but it was like Ivan couldn't find the translator.

Ivan explained it as something like a dormant monster. Hidden, sleeping, waiting for the moment to act. But they didn't know what the monster was up to, and there was no stopping it. The only other option would be to delete the record altogether.

Steep had faith in Ivan. If anyone could figure it out, he could. Steep wondered if Chester had the same caliber of people on his hidden team of analysts. He tapped his fingers on the record binders in front of him. There was no doubt he did. He probably had many of them, all working together, using techniques that would be against the law for Steep to use.

Steep's phone received a text message. It was Pistone. "Attack on UnionTrans in Chicago. Possible bombing. Undetermined damage. Continue setup in NYC."

Steep responded with a confirmation, not knowing what else to add. If his order was to continue to NY, then he had to continue to NY. He would get more details when he landed.

He looked ahead at the partition that separated the cabin his team was in from where Chester was. He took a deep breath and rose up from his seat. He didn't want to talk to the guy any more than he had to, but this was probably important to share.

As he walked up to the curtain that separated the two sections, he could hear Chester speaking, even over the low hum of the jet engines. Steep thought that he must be on the phone since he knew he was in that section alone.

His voice was loud and agitated. "Wasn't there a team there? How did they not realize they took down security?" There was a long pause. "If you think they are still in the facility, have the team find them. Launch the helicopter. Activate team bravo and charlie. Can you handle that?"

Steep considered barging in, but waited to see if he could get any more morsels of information.

"No, I'm continuing to New York. If you screw up, I'll have to be ready for them there. So don't screw up." There was nothing for long moments after that.

Steep assumed the call ended. He pulled aside the curtain and stuck his head and shoulder past it. "I have some news. Chicago..."

"I know," Chester said as he looked back at Steep coolly.

"Shouldn't we go there?"

"No, I have a team on the ground there. And Pistone already sent the locals. Our resources are better spent in New York."

"Very well," said Steep as he backed away from the curtain. There was no point in adding anything.

As he walked back to his seat, the short walk allowed his thoughts to wander. Maybe it was his blood pressure or just standing up pushing more blood to his brain, but it made him come up with a realization.

He sat back down next to Ivan. "So if you delete the records, nothing really happens, right? It's not like the record comes back. Could it be that these records are being marked for deletion?"

Ivan rubbed his chin, thinking as he always did. He nodded, "This is not an impossibility."

66

IT was done. Roman couldn't believe that they were actually done. They'd been able to inject all three targets and now there was no stopping Jubilee.

At the designated time in a few days, any sign of electronic debt would disappear.

They had done it. That's all he was thinking as they raced the way they came towards the front gate. He could see Hope and Bryce about a hundred meters ahead. There was a sense of relief that washed over him.

Their identities were lost, and they could never go back home. They would be on the run the rest of their lives. But at least they had accomplished this one thing. At least in a way it seemed worth it. They could change their identities. They knew how to remain hidden.

The winners and losers of the debt system would soon switch places.

He started to slow down as he approached the gate. The barrier was still down and he could see where they had hidden the guards behind the bushes. Hope and Bryce had slowed down as well, and their distance apart was shrinking. Just as he passed the gate, he noticed lights and sirens coming from his far right. It could only mean one thing. The authorities were onto them, and they were coming in fast.

"We have heat! My three. We have heat!" Roman yelled into his helmet.

Hope and Bryce took the hint without hesitation and accelerated, remaining in the direction they were going.

"Reggie, stay tight," Roman called, his mind racing, ignoring call signs and protocol.

They both accelerated, wide open, their engines screaming to their limits. He focused on the road in front of him, but could see that there were four black unmarked Mustangs flashing red and blue lights from their windshields and front grills. They were about a quarter of a mile away, but coming at them fast. As he watched Hope and Bryce ahead, he could see a helicopter coming in their direction. It must have come from the airport nearby.

"Do you see the helicopter? What do we do?" said Hope. It was still far enough away, but they were about to run out of road.

"We need to split up. Hide in the neighborhoods. Burton, you're going to have to find us." Just as Roman finished his statement, Reggie took a sharp turn behind him and raced down the road. He could see that Hope and Bryce had also split up. The distance between the Mustangs and him grew, and he took the next right turn he could make.

Roman would have to trust that they all knew what to do. They raced into the suburban neighborhoods that surrounded the area. They would park their bikes in the first cover they could find and throw on the gray bike covers they all had with them. They would go on foot and hide in the first shelter they could find, and wait for Burton and Greg to come and get them.

It was the only plan they had. As long as they were hidden before the helicopter hovered above them, they could easily disappear.

Roman would have to use the distraction. They were being hunted, and all the radio scanners and communications were focused on them. Without slowing down, Roman tapped the speed dial number on the burner phone and hit send.

The number sequence would initiate the detonators Burton and Greg had set on the fiber optic lines days before. Those specific fiber lines provided high-speed connectivity between the Chicago and New York exchanges. They were designed to be redundant and if one fiber line went down, there would be no loss in connection. That was, unless Burton and Greg set the thermite devices on all the connections.

At that very second, all fiber connections between Chicago and New York markets were cut. There were other backup connections that they would turn on, and the markets would only lose a few hours at most. But it would be just enough of a catastrophe that the authorities would need to split their resources or at least be confused as to what was going on. There would be smoke and fire coming from the manholes. There would be mass hysteria about the loss of the connections that investors depended on.

Hopefully it would be just enough for him and his crew to disappear.

* * *

An hour went by.

Roman found a small shopping center he was able to walk to after he stripped off his motorcycle suit and helmet. He looked like a normal guy in shorts and a t-shirt, complete with sunglasses. He found a local coffee shop and sat at one of the stools at the window table. He browsed his phone while he sipped his coffee as if he had nowhere to go.

From the window, he could see the helicopter from time to time, scanning the area. He didn't see the unmarked Mustangs, but was sure they were driving through the neighborhoods. He had parked his bike inside an open garage and left the keys inside. Maybe the homeowner would get the hint and just enjoy it.

He hoped that the rest of the crew were hidden as well. Burton would search out their GPS signals and pick each of them up.

He saw the black SUV pull into the parking lot. When he walked up close enough, he was relieved to see that everyone else was already picked up.

Everyone seemed equally relieved and concerned. After brief hugs, they rode quietly back to the staging warehouse.

"So what do we do now?" asked Burton once they were inside.

"We can't take a plane from O'Hare now," said Bryce.

"We can drive to St. Louis and take a couple connecting flights to Morocco," Roman replied.

"Wait... We're not going to stop back at the apartment?" Hope asked. A sudden panic rose in her voice as she seemed to remember something important. "I have to go back!"

"There's no way we can go back. Especially to the apartment. They're looking for us. They're probably sitting on the apartment, waiting for us to show up," said Roman. He added gently, "Hope, you knew this."

Hope's face reddened. "I know... I did. I should have..." She shook her head, flustered. "But I just have to go. I can go on my own."

Burton stared at Hope. "Don't be ridiculous."

"I can! I can figure out a way to sneak in by myself. They won't suspect a thing."

"Do you know how insane you sound?! We're already going to have a hard time getting out of the country. There's no way we're going, let alone you going by yourself," Burton added.

"You don't understand. I can go! I'll be okay..." Tears of frustration started to well in her eyes. Hope seemed to be grieving some great loss that the others couldn't fathom.

Roman looked away, not wanting Hope's emotion to affect his reasoning. They couldn't go back. That was all there was to it. A quiet fell over the group as Hope struggled to contain her tears.

"There's a problem," Reggie said behind them. He had been sitting at the table, working on his computer, not saying a word for some time.

Roman groaned. "What is it?"

"Jubilee won't be able to initiate."

"What?! Why not? I thought you had it all set up?" Roman snapped, suddenly frantic.

"It was all set up... but I'm missing the initiating code that I have to enter to start the sequence." Reggie shrugged. "I lost it when they searched me. When I was arrested."

Roman could feel everyone's eyes on him, gauging his reaction. They would take their cues from him. He closed his eyes, reaching for calm. "Go on."

"All I had to do was enter it once we were done, initiating all three locations, and Jubilee would do the rest. But now I don't have the code." Reggie sounded sheepish. That one incident kept coming back to haunt him.

Roman sighed. "Okay. Can you figure out what the code is? Did you have another copy?"

Reggie raised his eyebrows as if afraid to answer. "It's… I think there's a copy in my room. At the apartment."

"You have got to be kidding me! Reggie, why? Why would you have left it at the apartment?"

"I thought I had it. Maybe I thought we were going to go back?" Reggie put his palms out, helplessly.

"You were supposed to leave New York as if we would never come back. You knew that." Roman felt like he was losing his breath. "We all knew that." They were so close. Even though he was upset, he couldn't really let himself get angry. All of them had risked their lives for him. They had abandoned their former identities. All for a vision. His vision.

He couldn't get angry. Not even at this mistake.

He took a second to think. He was built for situations like this.

He shrugged, sighing once more. "Okay. If we have to go back, that's what we'll do."

67

IT was the Fourth of July, and instead of being at home in D.C. and preparing for neighborhood BBQs and fireworks, Steep's people were sitting around their makeshift work stations at the Javits Federal Building. They had been there for days and there had been no sign of the crew since the incident in Chicago.

Chester was in a far section that was partitioned off and much more private than Steep was comfortable with. There was no sign that he was going to give up the search for the crew anytime soon. Their causing the market to panic that day had made Chester more zealous. Steep had a feeling whomever Chester worked for was the cause of his pressure.

At that moment, the only lead they had was the apartment. The apartment that was under the name of Bryce Kingston was only blocks away. Steep could run there in twelve minutes flat from where he stood, even in his current flagging physical condition.

If the crew was planning to come back to New York, which Steep doubted, both the FBI and the NYPD would be on top of them in moments. Being this close to the new World Trade Center meant the area was crawling with every governmental law enforcement division in existence. And the images of the crew's faces were now canvassed across the city, being shared at every briefing as a high priority.

Steep walked over to where Ivan had made his temporary home. Steep had no idea where he had found a plush leather armchair, but he didn't care. He was glad his best man was comfortable, with his feet propped on a milk crate as usual.

"Find anything new?" Steep asked as he took a seat on a less comfortable conference room chair next to him.

"All the data samples from all three companies have the same type of hashes," Ivan replied.

He had given Steep a lesson on how hashes worked, but Steep still didn't completely understand it. Since UnionTrans had also been hit, Steep and Chester had opened the investigation at Equirian as well. There was also a breach there, but there was no indication of how it had happened.

Ivan spoke as he continued his chats on the screen. "And I've tested ways to remove them. They return as quickly as they are removed. I have run this through all my contractors and all three companies' programmers. Same result. No solution. We have tried everything. Clean installs, air-gapped systems, loading old backup data. The extra hashes still appear."

"How do you know these hashes shouldn't be there?"

"If I wasn't looking for them, I would think they were supposed to be there. But I checked all the documentation and these shouldn't. We still cannot isolate which software or system is creating them. The only thing I can imagine is that the hash contains a hash function in itself."

"What about new data records?" Steep was just grasping now.

"We have tried recreating the records manually. Same thing. Even changing what each record says. Even if there is only minimal fields for the record, that extra hash adds itself."

"What's the minimal number of fields?"

"Every record must have an identifier, at minimum. It's what connects the record to other records in the database. And it's only useful if there's at least one more field. Like a name, address, anything."

"So what happens if you don't add the identifier? If there's only a name?"

"The hash won't appear. But then, the record is useless."

"So they're not stealing the data." Steep was baffled. "They either want to delete the data... or render it useless?"

"That is the only conclusion I can come up with."

"And there's no way to stop it?"

"If there is, it will take years for researchers to figure out. This code is years ahead of current hacking theories."

Steep shook his head. This was unbelievable. If they were interpreting what Ivan found correctly, all of the data in all three companies were marked to be deleted. Every single record.

But what would be the gain of just deleting the information? There was no monetary value in that. Stealing the data for sale on the black market would have made sense, but it was obvious to him that wasn't the crew's goal. And if it was obvious to him, it would be obvious to Chester.

Chester's attitude had grown even more intense since he had

learned that the crew had disappeared in Chicago. Steep was in touch with the field station there, and it seemed that even they were annoyed with the tactical team from TRM. They were being treated like local beat cops, and refused respect over their jurisdiction.

The crew's photos were on a media blast in the entire region. The same was being done in New York and the surrounding cities. If any member of the group even attempted to enter the area, there would be no way they could escape.

The media didn't say anything more than that they were suspects in a cyber attack at Experfax. That people's identities were at risk, and that the suspects were on the FBI's most wanted list. The major media networks said they would run the story through the Fourth of July.

After the holiday weekend, the only thing active would be the APBs, but the strength of the search would die down to the point that it would no longer be effective.

So Roman Hawker and his crew were deleting people's records of debt. Illegal, yes. Very illegal. It fell within the realm of cyber terrorism. Steep should have had some zeal towards catching them, but he had to admit, this hypothetical motive made him see the whole thing differently. This crew weren't run of the mill criminals that were doing something just for themselves. They were after something different.

For the moment, he wouldn't share what Ivan had discovered. Chester and his shadow world probably already knew about it, anyway. There would be no point in bringing it up to him.

68

IT started with only a trickle at first. Only one person entered the park in the late afternoon. Then another. They knew they were there for the same reason from the masks they wore.

The unmistakable long white face with rosy cheeks. The upturned ends of the mustache and skinny goatee. The pointy nose, and perfectly raised eyebrows. They both wore the same mask that depicted Guy Fawkes. The same mask that symbolized the well-known network of activists and hacktivists, Anonymous. The two were joined by more, slowly at first. The tourists that were sitting idly around the space started to notice. The group started out small, but as it grew larger, the tourists became wary and started to step away.

Zuccotti Park was three thousand one hundred square meters of pavement, symmetrically furnished with granite benches and tables. Perfectly manicured trees with tall, skinny trunks and thick, green tops were spaced out perfectly amongst the various seating areas. It was the site of the first Occupy Wall Street movement in 2011 that had run through to 2012. Protests that focused on social and economic inequality. The ninety-nine percent oppressed fighting for their lives against the rich and powerful one percent. It had since been emptied and smaller subsequent protests had gained little traction.

The security guards posted at the site watched on as more and more masked individuals started coming into the park from all directions. Signs that read, 'How much debt do you have?' and 'You are not a loan!' started to speckle the growing group.

As the protesters became a crowd of about one hundred, the number of guards also increased. They brought out the barricades. News vans started to line the sidewalk as the police presence increased.

Hundreds became a thousand as the sun started to descend and the rectangular white lights set in the pavement of the park were turned on.

The crowd of masks became two thousand plus and the signs and chanting became loud and in unison.

That was about the time when Steep and Chester started watching the crowd next to the Red Cube, a twenty eight foot tall sculpture that stood defiantly on one of its corners. They were safer there, across the street from the madness. Some of Steep's agents were patrolling the crowd, fruitlessly looking for members of the crew. Steep sensed that Chester had some of his people doing the same, either in uniform or dressed in plain clothes. Even after asking, Steep wasn't offered any courtesy of knowing who they were.

Ivan and the other analysts remained at the office to monitor surveillance cameras in the area. Ivan had also been keeping an eye on the data at Experfax. Over the last few days, he had found evidence that the same was happening at Equirian and UnionTrans. Still no explanation as to how. Still no explanation as to when.

If Roman was as clever as Steep thought he was, today would have been the choice day for something like that to happen.

Independence Day. The day that America, as a country, declared its independence from the oppression of the British Empire.

He watched the signs across the street, reflecting what the crew might have been trying to do. Was it something that had grown as a grassroots movement on its own, or was it instigated by the crew for cover? Was this protest a slap in the face?

He listened to his earpiece as his agents relayed that their positions were clear.

He keyed his mic and said, "Just keep at a distance and focus on who we're looking for. Do not, I repeat, do not get involved in the actual protest or anything related. Let the locals handle anything that's not our subs."

Everyone returned a copy. Chester was a few feet away from him, but could tell that he was managing his team the same way.

The crowd of Guy Fawkes faces started to overflow the barricades containing the park. The image was surreal. He felt that the chanting had become louder. Around him, the crowd of spectators was also growing. What was normally a steady flow of pedestrians was now at a standstill.

Before Steep realized it, the crowd across the street started to move, and the volume of the chanting kept getting louder.

He keyed his mic, "What's going on? Why are they letting them out of the barricades?"

After a few seconds, Summers responded, "There's an approved protest march scheduled. Permits state they are going to walk down Liberty Street, around the Fed and back up Maiden Lane."

"What the hell are they thinking?" He watched as police officers stopped traffic, allowing the protesters to flow down the emptied street. The officers yelled only when there were strays that veered from the crowd, but it seemed orderly.

It couldn't have been more perfect. Liberty Street would pass right in front of Bryce Kingston's apartment building. He could tell Chester may have been thinking the same thing, but only just realized it. He was speaking into his mic in what looked like panic. The spectator crowd had become so congested that Steep could no longer maneuver around.

"I need eyes on the marchers. Does someone have eyes on the apartment?" He waited for a response, but the protesters chants were so loud where he was, he couldn't imagine what it was like in the thick of the mass of people. "I repeat. Do we have eyes on the apartment?"

"Negative. We'll make our way there, but it's going to take us a while."

69

ROMAN couldn't see them any more as he followed the flow of the legion of masks. Burton and Bryce were somewhere in the front of the pack, leading the protesters at an even pace down Liberty Street. His left hand was holding a sign that simply stated DEBT with a red solidus on top of it. His right hand was firmly gripping the top handle of Hope's backpack. Reggie was somewhere behind him. With their masks on, they looked no different than everyone around them.

Truly anonymous.

It was a ploy that he'd thought up a few years ago, but never thought he would have to actually use. He hadn't even been sure if the Anonymous community was still active enough to stage a large-scale protest such as this.

As they'd ridden in the back of the semi truck together from Chicago, Reggie had logged onto the darknet and blasted all the boards to incite the protest. He'd even gone through mainstream social media channels to assure the greatest number of people possible would show up. He had forged the right permits, backdating the original request as necessary.

The city was going to be already crowded, with people from all over the world making their way to the rivers to watch the fireworks. The streets would be lock jammed with cars and taxis. Every train in the subway and PATH would be full. If it was hard for regular citizens to get around, it would be even more difficult for authorities to pick them from the masses. And this ad hoc protest was icing on the cake.

As they approached the apartment lobby entrance, he took a quick look around. Back at the park, he spotted all the FBI and similar agents in plain clothes. It was obvious to him that they weren't there to guard the protest.

As the march started, they fell behind, and it looked like they would have a hard time to catch up to where he was. When they reached the door, Roman lightly pulled on Hope's backpack handle to signal that is was okay to go. The march's edge went right up against the building, crowding the sidewalk as well, and when the three of them broke from the crowd and entered the lobby, there was no way anyone could have noticed.

"Hey, you can't be in here," Roman heard the doorman say.

It was Joe. And Roman had been afraid that it was going to be his shift. He liked the guy.

"Hey, Joe. It's us," Roman said as he lifted his mask. Joe was only a foot away, and his first reaction was a happiness to see him. It was immediately followed by a somber expression. That he was going to have to do something he didn't want to. Like he was already told to contact a number if he saw any of them show up.

Roman didn't hesitate and stepped forward, wrapping his arm around Joe's neck and coming around him. They were instantly facing the same direction, with Roman behind him, his forearm and bicep squeezing Joe's trachea, cutting off air and circulation. Roman stepped back, pulling Joe backwards and down as he squeezed. Joe's doorman hat fell off as he swung his arms, trying to pull at Roman's, but losing the struggle. Moments passed until Joe's body went limp and Roman was sure he was unconscious.

Reggie helped him pull the doorman behind the long desk.

When they made it to their floor, they approached the door cautiously. There was a large notice taped to the door notifying that no unauthorized access was allowed. The locks would have been changed, and there were probably alarms set to go off when the door opened.

Roman grabbed the crowbar from Hope's backpack and set it where the deadbolt was. In one motion, he levered towards the door, and he heard the wood break as the doorway gave. He looked down and saw that an alarm was tripped.

"We have three. Make it fast."

70

"THERE'S an alarm coming from the apartment," Ivan's voice said.

Steep was still stuck, trying to make his way to the protestors. "Can anyone get up to the apartment?"

"We're a minute away from the lobby," said Pickles.

"We'll head straight up," added Summers, out of breath.

Would they go up to the apartment if they thought they'd be trapped? Not at all. They had to have a getaway plan. He looked ahead and saw that Chester was past the crowd of spectators but only watching as the legion of masks passed by.

Steep imagined the city block in his mind. Summers said that the march's path would come back around Maiden Lane. That was on the opposite side of the block as the apartment, but it could be easier for Steep to get to.

If he was Roman, he would have always had an escape plan out of the apartment. The building lobby couldn't be the only exit. He

Joseph Preacher

turned around and hoped he was heading in the right direction.

71

HOPE ran to the room that Burton and she used when they stayed at the apartment. It was more than a guest room, but a second home. She felt Reggie behind her, but assumed he was going to his room to look for the code. It looked like some things had been moved around. Maybe the Feds looking for evidence. She prayed they didn't take the thing she came for.

Hope went straight for the closet and found what she was looking for. She let out a sigh of relief and let herself catch her breath as she stuffed it into her backpack. She looked up to see Reggie at the doorway as she turned around.

"You got what you came for?" asked Reggie.

She nodded, "Did you find the code?"

"There was no code. Jubilee is autonomous." Reggie's smile broke through under his robotic tone. "But I knew this was the only way to get you back to the apartment. I had a feeling what you were coming back for. I was right." Reggie said with a simple smile.

"Reggie," Hope was close to speechless, patting his shoulder. But she'd never be able to thank him enough. "Let's get out of here. Roman's waiting."

They ran to the back of the apartment where Roman had moved aside a shelf that hid a passageway.

"Got it?" asked Roman.

They both responded with a nod as they passed by him into the passageway. At the end of the short hall, there was a steel spiral staircase that only went up. It was such a tight spiral that Hope felt her head grow dizzy as they ran up. They exited through a skylight onto the roof of the building.

As soon as all three exited, they made their way across the roof towards the Maiden Lane side of the block. The building rooftops were all connected and they only needed to lower themselves to another roof. They ran to the roof access door, unlocking it with a bump key. This stairwell would lead them to the street.

72

STEEP was getting anxious as he looked up and down the street, looking for anyone leaving from the Maiden Lane side of the building.

It was a gamble that they would be coming out this side. They could have had exits setup on any of the four streets around the block. But his gut said that this was where they would reappear. His team and Chester's would have the Liberty side covered and the march had to have been a part of their escape plan. It had Hawker, Kingston, Dymond and the Warner siblings written all over it.

Steep could see the front of the march turn the corner. As the legion of masks came closer and closer, he started to give up hope.

The first of the protesters started passing him, escorted by the police detail. Maybe he was wrong. Maybe there was another exit.

Just when he was about to turn around and head back to Zuccotti Park, he saw two masked bodies exit the fire escape door just five meters away. They entered the crowd and instantly disappeared into the masses.

He ran towards the door at full speed, hoping there was at least still one of them left. He was at the door as it opened. Without looking, he grabbed at the person by the arm, released his cuffs from its case on his right side and secured it to the person's wrist and then his own.

His capture was completely surprised and struggled to get away until he realized it was a handcuff that held him.

"What the fuck," he heard the man say, muffled from behind the mask.

Steep adjusted his cuffed hand's hold and wrestled the man until his chest was pressed up against the wall. Steep used the entire weight of his body to restrain the guy, holding his cuffed arm in an elbow lock. He looked to his left and right, hoping the others wouldn't return, trying to save him.

He was about to key his mic, but paused. He looked around him again. The protesters didn't seem to even notice them as they passed by with their signs and chants.

He pulled the man's mask up to reveal Roman Hawker's face. Roman said nothing, but glanced down at the patch on Steep's chest that read 'FBI.' Steep registered his brief look of disgust.

Time to call it in.

Come on, Steep. Call it in.

His face lingered on Roman. Proud, defiant even. Captured, but not defeated. Steep's mind raced as he thought about what was going to happen to him next. Chester would question him, and it wouldn't be pleasant. Somehow or another they would get all his friends through him. Most likely through some horrible, soul-deadening, borderline Geneva conference violating way.

"Tell me something," Steep said between his teeth, inches away from Roman's ear so he could hear.

Roman flinched at the warmth of Steep's breath on his ear. "What?"

"What you and your crew did. Why did you do it?"

Roman hesitated. Steep pushed harder. "Is it going to eliminate everyone's debt?"

After another moment, he relaxed, as if knowing why Steep was asking. Even though Steep himself didn't know why. "Yes. It's going to erase everyone's debt. Everyone. Every record of it."

"How sure is it going to work?"

"Guaranteed."

"Is there any way to stop it?"

"Impossible."

Steep didn't care how it worked, but if there was no way to stop it...

There was only one reason to arrest Hawker. To punish him. To make him pay for what he'd done. And, if he understood Chester correctly, Roman and his crew would pay dearly.

"Who is paying you to do this?"

"Pay? No one is paying me. There's no money in it."

Steep only had one question left, "Then why?"

Steep relieved the pressure enough for Roman to turn his face towards him. He looked into Steep's eyes and said, "It needed to be done."

Steep stepped away from the wall. He looked up and down the street. There was still no sign of his agents. Still no sign of Chester and his team. The masked protesters were still moving past them, like the flow of a river.

He took out his handcuff keys and unbound Roman. Without another word, Steep stepped back.

Roman seemed to not understand for a second, but soon showed relief on his face. He stepped backwards into the crowd as it passed by. He lowered his mask and disappeared among the passing crowd without another word.

73

ROMAN looked out over the water as they approached the designated area. There were already a number of other boats in a holding pattern in front of Liberty Island, readying themselves as the sun began to set behind the New York City skyline. He looked at his friends, finally relaxing in the seating area.

Burton was at the helm of the PJ Niniette 63. The yacht had been parked at the North Cove Harbor as an escape plan for years, but he'd never thought they would actually need it.

He wasn't sure why the Fed agent had let him go. Maybe he had a lot of debt, too? Whatever the reason, he wouldn't have escaped otherwise. Roman felt oddly grateful toward the man, whoever he was.

Bryce and Burton had been able to lead the protesters past the permitted area, continuing on towards the Hudson River. The protest passed the Memorial Pools that marked the Twin Towers where thousands died on September 11, 2001. Towering above the site was the new glass and steel structure that unofficially symbolized

Freedom in the western hemisphere.

Once they had reached the river, they would let the other self-designated guides lead the march back to Zuccotti Park. The five of them had broken off and, leaving their masks behind, jumped down to the North Cove Yacht Harbor, where Greg had met them in the boat with the engines running.

With no APBs released with his identifiers, Greg was safe to stay in the City. After handing the helm over to Burton, Greg stepped off back onto the pavement and into the gathering crowd. For as long as it was safe, he would remain as their link back home.

They would take the boat up to Canada, where they would ditch it and charter a plane. They would bounce around from location to location until they were certain they were not being tracked. Then they would eventually end up in Morocco, their final destination.

They would be away for a long time. Years, definitely. Maybe even decades.

"I can't get a signal out here," Reggie complained.

"Enjoy the real world for once. Look at her. You can't see that on a little screen." Burton pointed out over the water to the reason they came this way.

"Wait, did you set up the initiation code?" Roman leaned forward, suddenly serious.

"Everything is good, baas." Reggie smiled, mostly at Hope.

Roman sat back, letting himself relax again.

They had a perfect view of the Statue of Liberty. The bright spotlights were already shining on her from around the stone pedestal. Roman stared, lost in awe. Living so close, he had never given the symbol much thought. It was just a statue that he'd learned about in grade school. Welcoming immigrants, in search of a better life. In the past, but not so much in the present.

He could just barely see the broken chains at her feet.

He imagined what it was like for those that had journeyed to America this way. Their first image of it was the Statue of Liberty, representing their hopes that they would be able to live the American Dream.

People lined all along the Hudson River waterfront walkway along the Jersey side. Even as far away as they were, Roman could see them all waiting with eagerness. They had no idea that after tonight, they would have a new kind of independence. A rebirth of the American dream.

As soon as the fireworks show was complete, all their debts would disappear. Reggie had set up Jubilee to trigger at that specific time.

From the time they had implanted the first instance of Jubilee in the first server, she had spontaneously spread to every system she could come in contact with. She had propagated until she found every reference to every person's debt. When she found her target, she remained dormant, waiting for the right moment.

The right moment... ten PM, eastern standard time. There was no stopping her. Reggie no longer needed to monitor Jubilee, because there was no controlling her.

The ones that had come so close to catching the crew wouldn't be able to stop her. Even if Jubilee was discovered, she was on too many systems to try and eliminate her. There would be no time to even understand what she was about to do.

This singular event was about to give hundreds of millions of people their true independence. Independence from the debt collectors that plagued them. From the records that defined them and limited their futures. Independence from holding jobs they didn't want, only to try to pay off debts they could never afford.

Tonight their world would change. The world of those that created debt would also change. Their greed would fail them ultimately. There would be no bailouts for them. There would be no retribution. Maybe they would learn their lesson. Maybe they would use their energy and drive to create a better world. Or maybe they would try to determine the next way to screw people over.

Bryce passed around some plastic cups half full of champagne. Even Reggie took a cup.

As he was still lost in thought, Roman sensed Hope walk over to him. She sat down next to him, leaving no space between their bodies. She handed him a box.

"What is this?" Roman asked, surprised.

"Open it."

Roman slowly opened it, revealing photos filed neatly with care. He fingered through them, realizing they were the photos that had been on the wall of his childhood home.

He pulled out a photo that he had never realized he loved so much. It was a simple one where his father was much younger, standing with his arm around his beautiful mother. Roman stood in between them, a child of only three or four, but just old enough to recognize himself. They looked so happy in that carefree time. Before the cancer and medical bills. Before the debt and deaths that they couldn't endure.

Roman could feel tears slowly trail along his cheek. He felt he could finally put their memory to rest. Their family tragedy had forced a better outcome for millions of people. A peace he had not expected began to envelop him as he looked up at Hope.

"Thank you for this." He instinctively wrapped his arm around her. He looked up to see Burton looking over at them. He tipped his head at Roman and raised his cup in approval.

There was no way Roman could keep hiding how he felt. How much he truly wanted to be with her. Hope looked deep into his eyes, reading his thoughts. She laid her head on his shoulder, and entwined his fingers with hers.

For once, he was not going to have a plan.

74

SENATOR Rich Manning was disoriented as he stepped off the helicopter. He still had no idea where he was. His only instruction had been to follow this silent Secret Service agent he didn't even know. He was told nothing else.

It was infuriating.

The rotor wash intensified as it took off as soon as he left the helipad area. He could see that another helicopter was already coming in for a landing approach. He wondered who it would be. The agent didn't allow him to wait, and led him down a stone path through a dense, well-manicured garden.

From the green grass, palm trees, and the tropical air on his skin, he deduced he was somewhere in the Caribbean. Turks and Caicos possibly. That would make sense from the amount of time he was in the air.

He did have a small idea what was going on. The news that morning wouldn't stop talking about what had happened. Banks and credit card companies all over the world were reporting that their networks had been hacked overnight. No one was sure what the exact effects were, but there was a lot of data that had been corrupted or lost. Other than that, the anchors seemed confused about what was going on. Market exchanges were closed worldwide until further notice. The Independence Day long weekend was given an extension.

He had been just about to leave for the office when this agent had appeared at his door. The agent had the appropriate paperwork, instructions for the Senator's immediate cooperation and attendance. Attendance to what, it did not disclose.

As they turned the corner, the grand facade of what looked like a resort came into view. It gave the impression of a castle from the stonework and architecture. As he approached the entranceway, he could now see that the property was along a beach shoreline. He could hear the ocean somewhere close in the background. It should have still been early evening, but the sun was hiding behind thick dark clouds. It looked like a storm was coming in.

As they entered the lobby, a feeling of dread came over him at the sight of Chester Smith.

"Senator," was all Chester said, without as much as a handshake.

"Chester. What's the meaning of all this?"

"All in due time. You'll be given an itinerary shortly."

"Screw that! And I want to know now!" Manning's anger grew as he spoke. He couldn't hold his bottled up thoughts any longer. "I have been flying for hours, without any details. Show me some respect. I deserve to know where the hell I am and what I am doing here!"

He was being treated like a child and he was not about to take it from this hired help.

Chester looked back at him with his steely eyes. Manning realized he had never really looked the man directly in his face. Moments passed as Manning tried to hold onto his anger. As time went by, the anger turned into another feeling. One he refused to admit to.

"Senator. There are many issues being handled right now. There are meetings already underway. I suggest you prepare yourself for a long stay. All your personal needs will be accommodated by the staff."

Manning just realized that Chester's hands were gloved in black leather. Even though he held his hands together in front of him casually, it gave his whole posture a more ominous stance.

"I do not have time to answer all your questions," Chester continued. "There are far more important people I need to be concerned about here. For the time being, do as you're told. You are not to leave the compound for any reason. You are not to make any phone calls. You are here to work. Once decisions are made, you are to be a part of the solution."

Manning looked down at Chester's chest, completely deflated.

"This is why you are part of the Joint Economic Committee. You know this, Senator. Now I suggest you go up to your room. Await your itinerary. The staff is ready to provide food, drink, change of clothes. Whatever you need to make your stay more comfortable."

Chester nodded to an open elevator where the Secret Service agent was already waiting. Manning contemplated on a retort, but had nothing to say.

This was why he was here. To be a part of a solution. He gave Chester a silent nod and walked sheepishly to the elevator. Here, he wasn't the man in power. Here, he was to do as he was told. His only purpose right now was to be a part of the solution.

Joseph Preacher

THE END

Stay connected to me:

Www.josephpreacher.com

Contact@josephpreacher.com

More to come.

*

Joseph Preacher is a tech, economics and politics junkie that is endlessly fascinated by the way the world could be. A former Marine and corporate finance guy, Joseph writes to exercise his curiosity and investigate possibilities. While this is his first published work, Joseph is a lifelong creative that has long explored the world and the people in it through the lens of fiction. Having lived in Texas, Hawaii, New York City and Bangladesh, he is currently exploring Japan.

Joseph Preacher is a tech, economics and politics junkie that is endlessly fascinated by the way the world could be. A former Marine and corporate finance guy, Joseph writes to exercise his curiosity and investigate possibilities. While this is his first published work, Joseph is a lifelong creative that has long explored the world and the people in it through the lens of fiction. Having lived in Texas, Hawaii, New York City and Bangladesh, he is currently exploring Japan.

www.ingramcontent.com/pod-product-compliance
Lightning Source LLC
Chambersburg PA
CBHW061513020726
47502CB00006B/2057